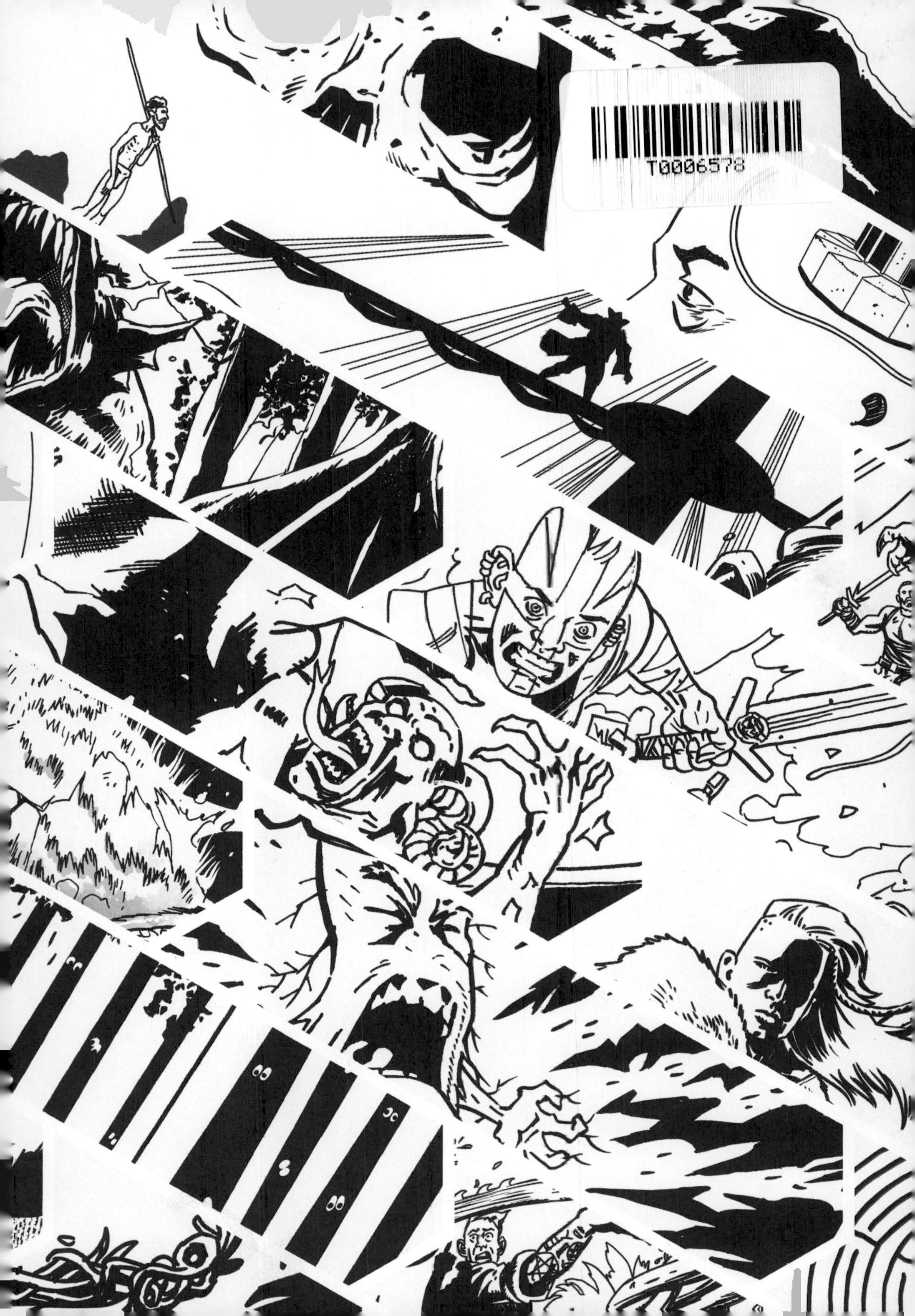

FASCINATING FOLKLORE

◆ A COMPENDIUM OF COMICS AND ESSAYS ◆

First published in 2023 by Liminal 11

Words copyright © 2023 John Reppion
Images copyright © 2023 PJ Holden

Graphic Designers: Jing Lau and Tori Jones
Editor: Eleanor Tremeer
Editorial Director: Darren Shill
Artistic Director: Kay Medaglia

Printed in China
ISBN 978-1-912634-72-9

10 9 8 7 6 5 4 3 2 1

www.liminal11.com

WHEN JOHN AND PJ FIRST CAME TO US WITH THEIR IDEA TO draw a weekly comic using our Twitter hashtag #FolkloreThursday, I expected much from a collaboration between two of the comic world's most prolific figures. They certainly did not disappoint! Willow and I are both honored and amazed to see the seeds of the #FolkloreThursday themes take root and grow into such a uniquely creative work. In short, this cleverly curated collection mixes the ancient and arcane with a refreshingly contemporary twist. Yet, it deserves so much more than a twee summation. It has achieved something no other offering I've come across before has managed: it preserves diverse cultural heritage in an entirely new way.

Traditional folklore essays are often dry and academic, while illustrated folklore books are usually over-simplified or presented as tales for children. We see single tales — or motifs and characters — retold and reinterpreted in the few graphic novels that touch on folk wisdom and its stories. Here, John doesn't shy away from complex and little-known lore from old tomes. Instead, he digs deep into folkloric fact while keeping his ever-engaging contemporary style. What we find is a quirky journey through a diverse parade of lore — and the weight of history behind it.

PJ's comics are a perfectly curated collection of folklore-like artifacts in themselves. His unique ability to delve beneath the tales and unearth the true human — or monster — experience adds extra depth to the lore that we don't often see so clearly. We can now empathize with the Devil and his backside more than ever before, and feel in our bones the shriek of every mandrake dragged from the soil.

This collection of tales and traditions is an immersive experience that deserves to be read again and again to unearth the layers it contains. The myths and meaning that inspired each piece were garnered over centuries. Yet, in the pairings themselves, we are seeing the result of months of collaborative storytelling unfolding in front of us. Each tale truly keeps the folklore alive by breaking down barriers of past and present in an act of pure creativity. John and PJ have managed to make our wealth of cultural heritage even more relevant and accessible to today's 'folk' — young and old — and for future generations to come. The old gods would be proud.

~ Dee Dee Chainey, #FolkloreThursday co-founder

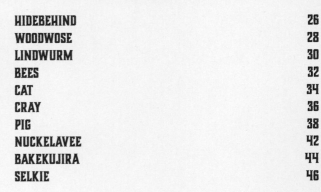

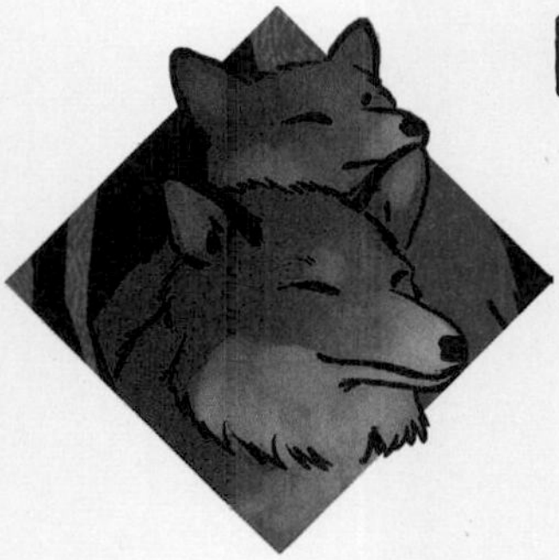

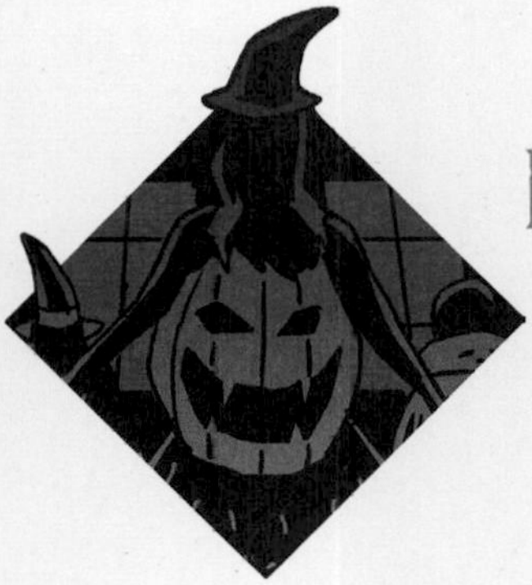

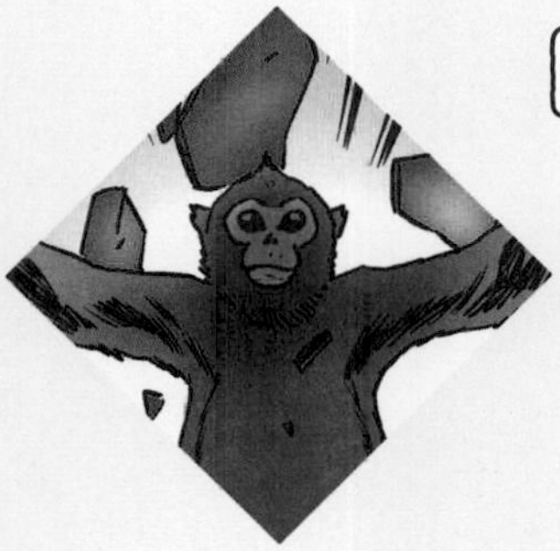

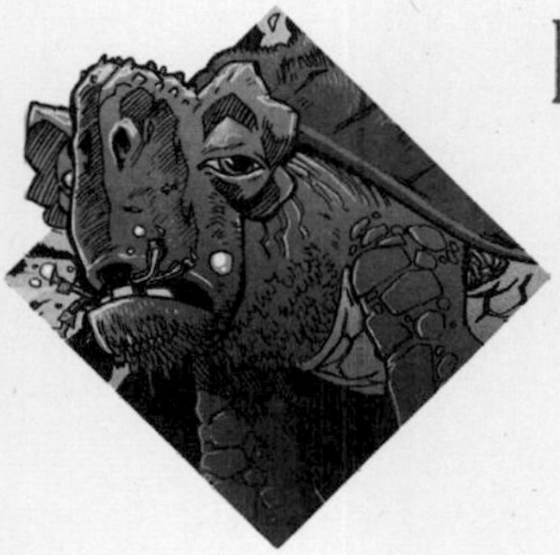

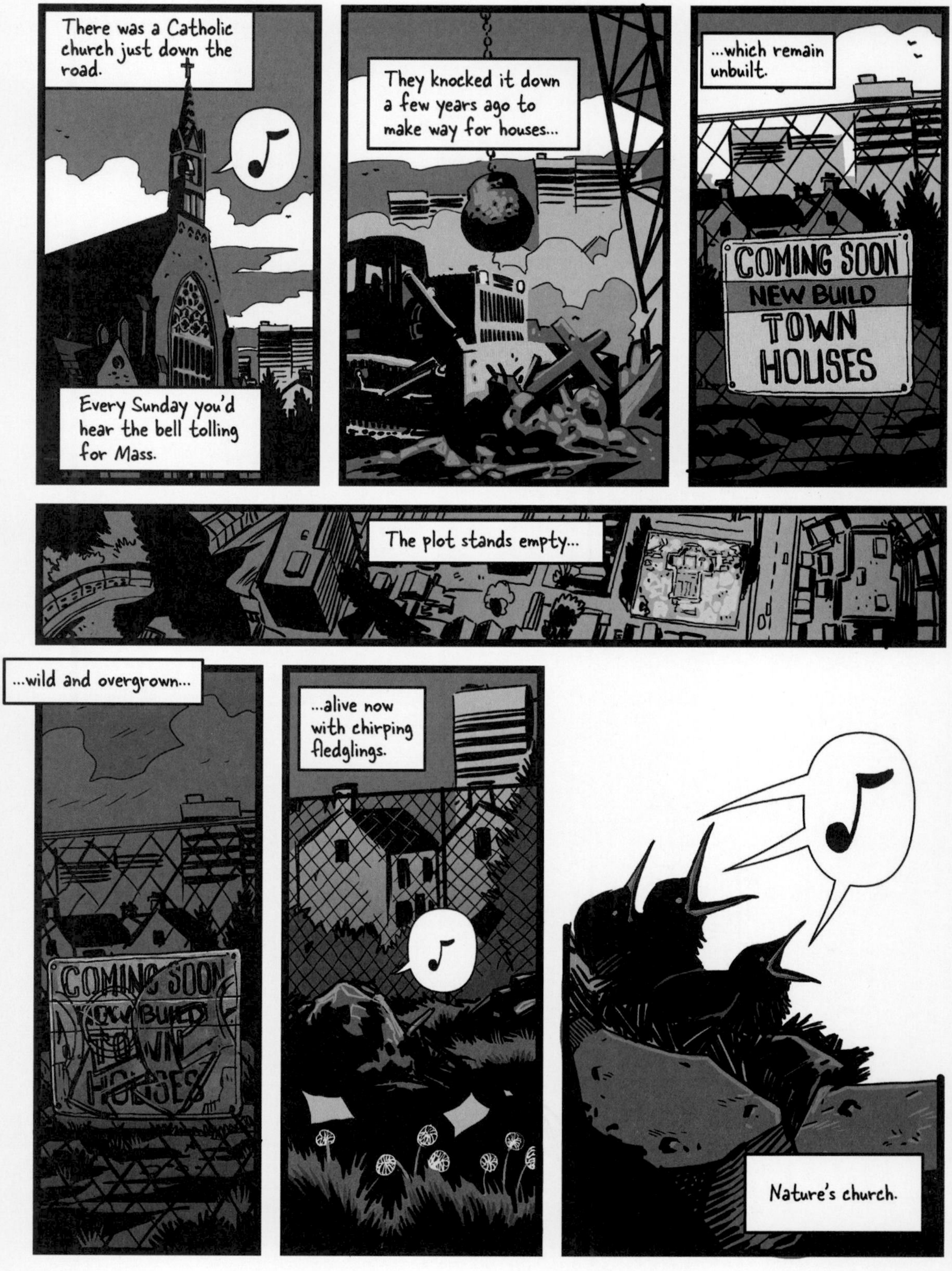
There was a Catholic church just down the road.
♪
Every Sunday you'd hear the bell tolling for Mass.
They knocked it down a few years ago to make way for houses...
...which remain unbuilt.
COMING SOON
NEW BUILD
TOWN
HOUSES
The plot stands empty...
...wild and overgrown...
...alive now with chirping fledglings.
♪
♪
Nature's church.

INTRODUCTION

THE VOLUME YOU HOLD IN YOUR HANDS GREW FROM A SEED PLANTED ACCIDENTALLY IN 2019. On the 3rd of July that year, John posted a tweet:

> There was a Catholic Church just down the road. Every week you'd hear the Sunday Service bell tolling. They knocked it down a few years ago to make way for houses which remain unbuilt. The plot stands empty, wild and overgrown, alive now with chirping fledglings. Nature's Church."

Inspired, PJ created a seven-panel, one-page comic, dividing the tweet's text up into captions. "I hope you don't mind," he tweeted at John, and John replied that he definitely did not. The comic, titled 'Nature's Church', was posted to Twitter, and people really seemed to like it. PJ and John decided that maybe they should do more of these little Twitter comics. Maybe they could manage one a week. What would they be about, though?

The "Folklore Thursday" hashtag trended weekly on Twitter with a brand-new topic relating to the date or season. John, who had been fascinated with folklore, Forteana, weird history, myths and legends from an early age, thought that the Folklore Thursday hashtag would be a good source of prompts for PJ's and his weekly Twitter comics. PJ loved drawing monsters, so why not? Dee Dee Chainey and Willow Winsham, the founders of Folklore Thursday, were kind enough to share their top-secret list of upcoming themes with John and PJ. This would give the pair a chance to have their tweets and comics done and ready for posting every Thursday. All of this seemed like a simple and fun enough little plan and, on the 25th of July, 'Blackberries' – the first of these weekly instalments – was shared on Twitter by PJ and John.

Somewhere along the way, the idea of writing some short essays to go with each comic came up – just a little extra to add a bit of background to the 140-character-limited mini-explorations of each week's topic. Again, people really seemed to like the essays, so John wrote more of them.

The final of PJ and John's weekly Twitter comics, 'Return', was posted on the 23rd of July 2020. The pair found that they had accidentally amassed a folklore-themed body of work which neither of them really had any idea what to do with. Maybe they could be collected into a book...?

This, dear readers, is that very book.

PJ's comics are reproduced here with minimal tweaks, but they appear more or less as they were when he first created them in 2019–20. John's essays have been thoroughly revised and generally knocked into shape with the invaluable help of editor Eleanor Tremeer. Many of the essays which appear in this volume have been newly written in 2022–23 and have never before appeared online or in print. What began life as a fun little weekly creative exercise has ultimately borne fruit of a strange and unexpected kind.

Welcome, then, to PJ Holden and John Reppion's *Fascinating Folklore: A Compendium of Comics and Essays*.

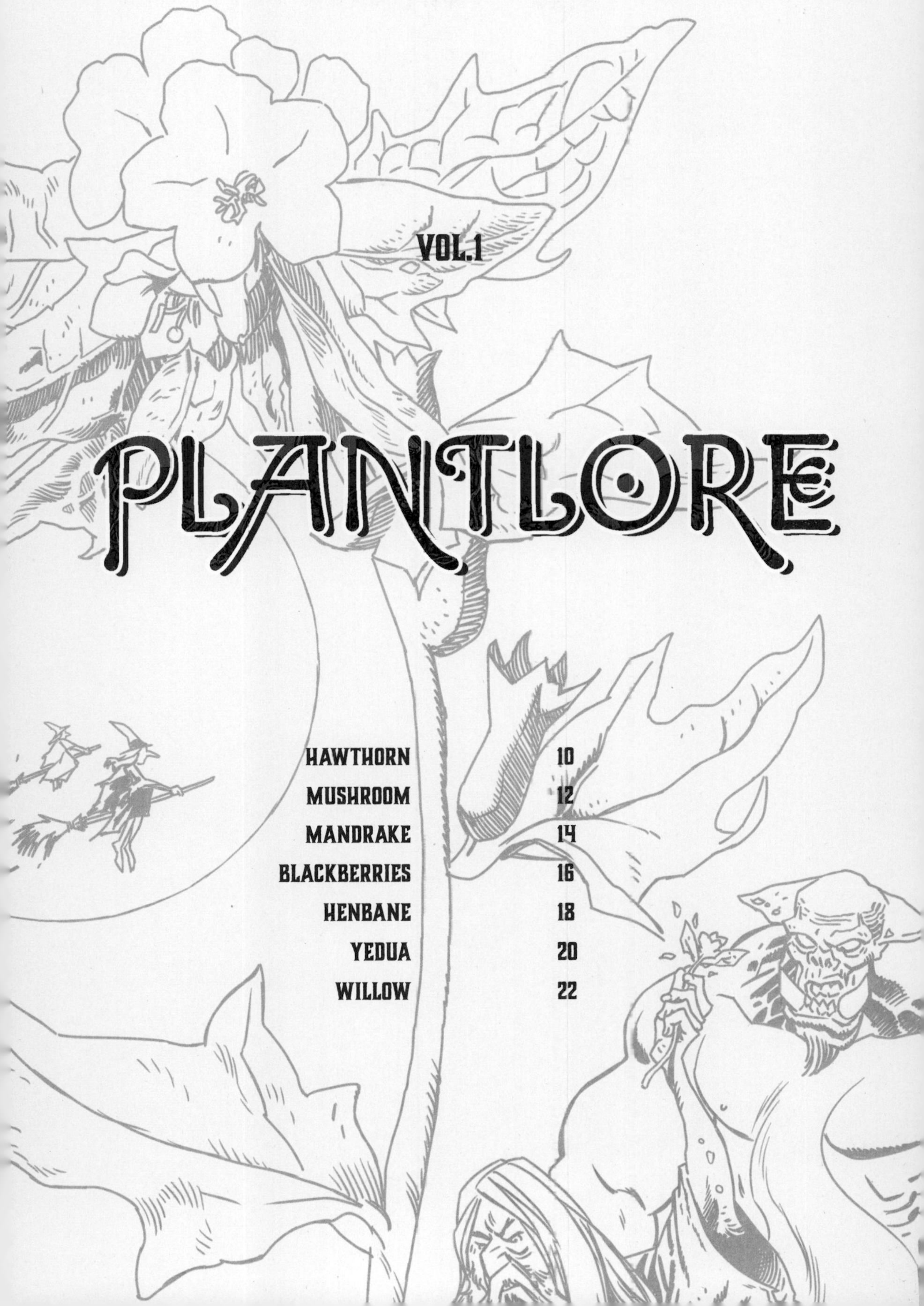

VOL.1

PLANTLORE

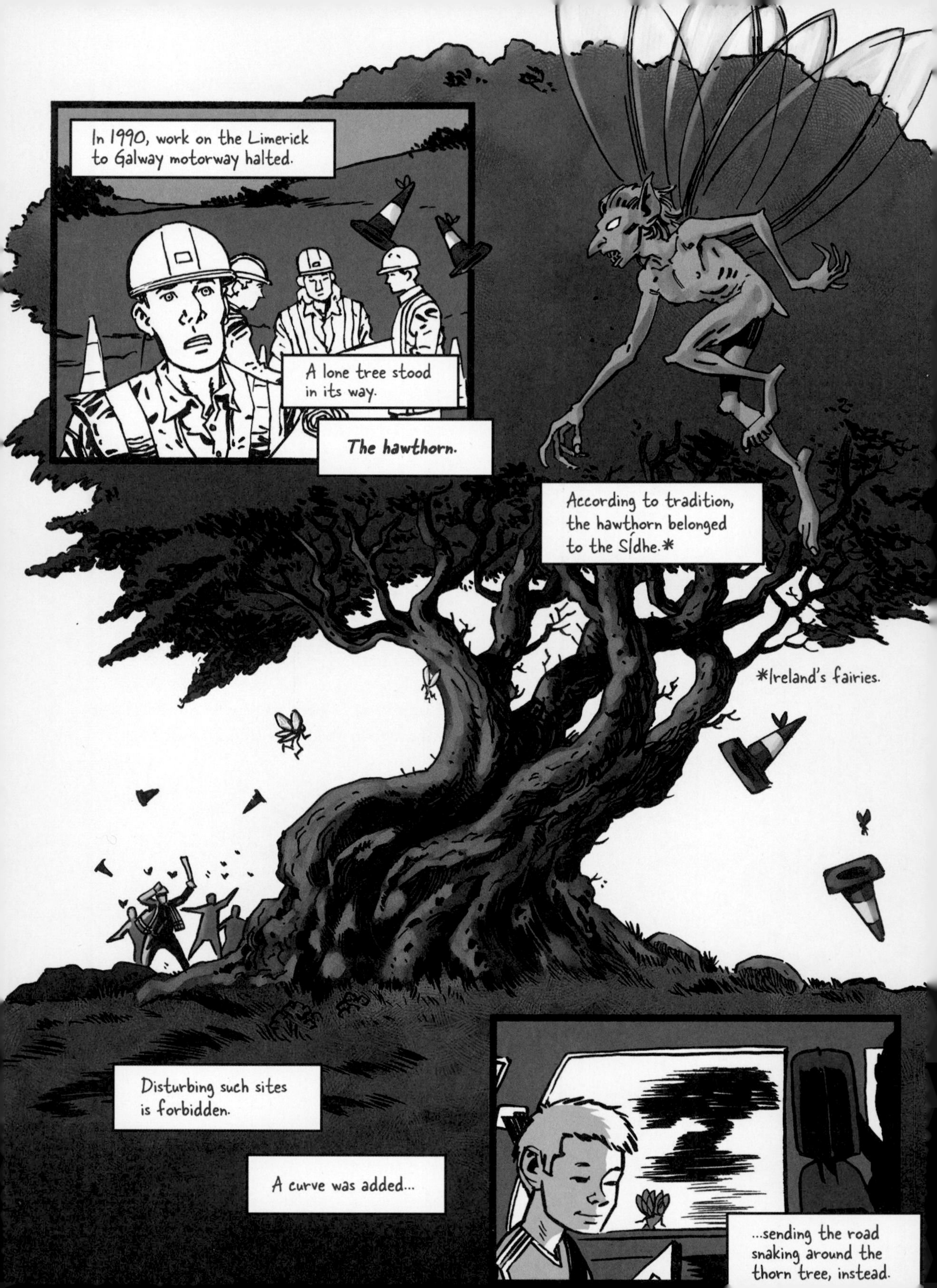
In 1990, work on the Limerick to Galway motorway halted.
A lone tree stood in its way.
The hawthorn.
According to tradition, the hawthorn belonged to the Sídhe.*
*Ireland's fairies.
Disturbing such sites is forbidden.
A curve was added...
...sending the road snaking around the thorn tree, instead.

HAWTHORN

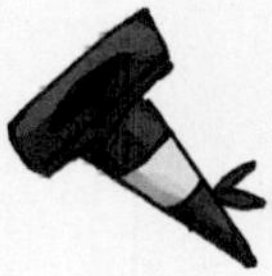

In Irish folklore, "fairy-thorns" are lone trees, most often hawthorn, which are believed to belong to the fae[1]. These trees must not be touched lest the fair folk become displeased with those who have disturbed them.

Eddie Lenihan is often referred to as "Ireland's greatest living storyteller"; he is a folklorist, an historian, and an expert on traditional Irish fairy lore. In 1999, Eddie made headlines across the world. Earlier that year, an article appeared in the *New York Times* in which he was interviewed. Pointing to a white-blossomed hawthorn bush standing alone in a field in Latoon, he issued a warning, saying that if the bush was bulldozed to make way for the planned highway bypass, the fairies would come. The road would be cursed; brakes would fail, and cars would crash. This, Eddie asserted, was the kind of mischief which fairies could easily cause if they were angered. And, he stated, they were easy to anger.

The fairy-thorn (*sceach* in Gaelic) at Latoon was, according to Eddie, an important marker on an ancient fairy path. Specifically, it was believed to serve as the meeting place for the fairies of Munster whenever they prepared to ride against the fairies of Connacht. Eddie was informed by a local farmer that he had seen white fairy blood at the spot, proving that the hawthorn was still in use by the fair folk.

Eddie weaponized his storytelling skills as a form of nonviolent protest and activism. Repeating the old tales as loudly and widely as he could, he drew the interest of first the national, and then the international, press. And it worked. The route of the much-delayed motorway, originally begun in 1990, was ever-so-slightly altered, to skirt around the sacred tree.

In a letter published in the *Irish Times* shortly after work was completed, Clare County engineer Tom Carey, who oversaw the project, claimed that there was no influence of the fair folk, however. It was simply easier to go around the tree. That had always been the plan, he insisted. Nothing to do with fairies at all. Still, there are those who were, and who remain, rather skeptical of this official back-pedaling. We all know that people are often ashamed to admit that they believe in fairies these days, but that doesn't mean they don't fear the consequences of upsetting them.

1 For more on the fae, see 'Mushroom' (pg. 12), 'Cat' (pg.34) and 'Cray' (pg. 36).

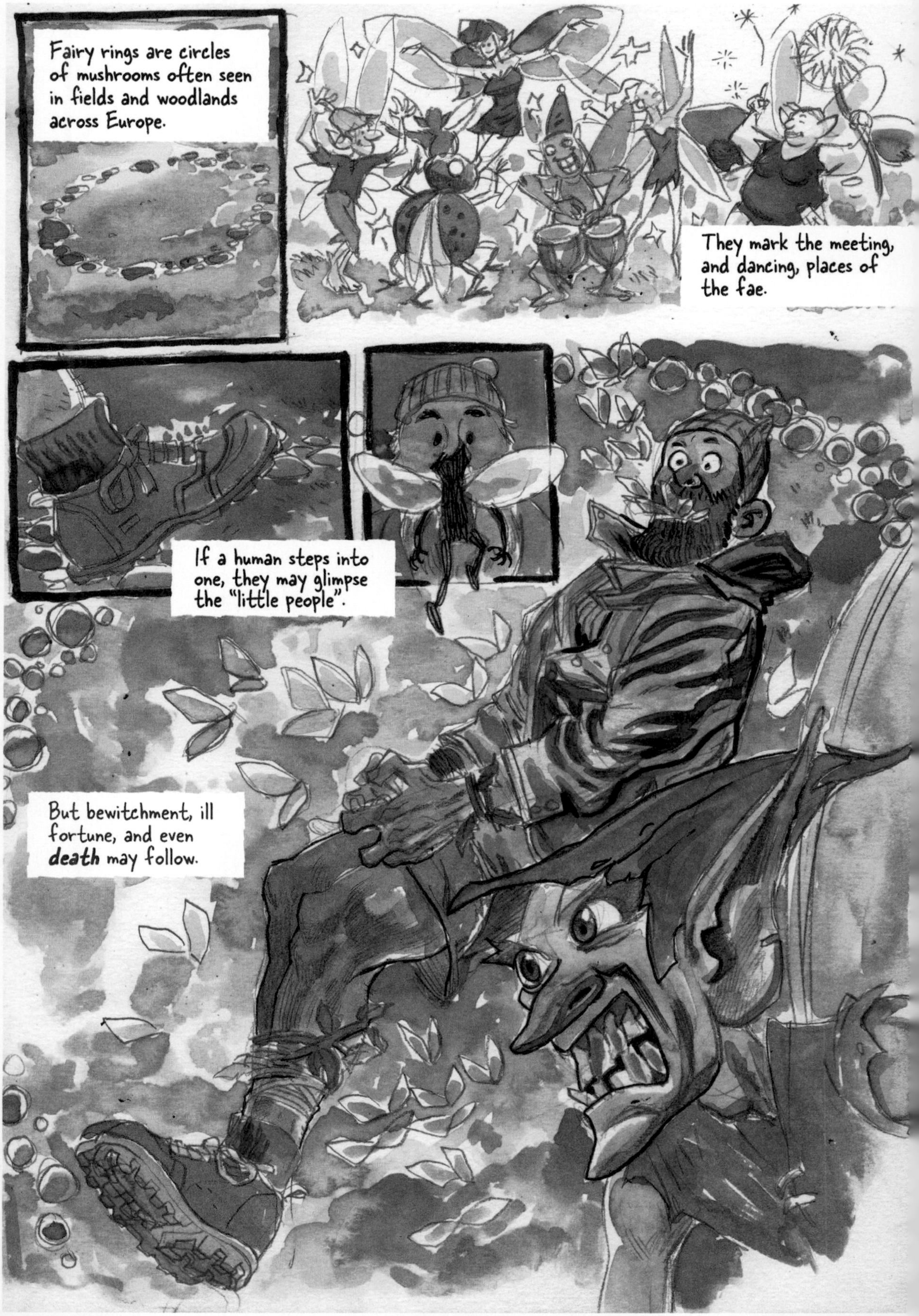
Fairy rings are circles of mushrooms often seen in fields and woodlands across Europe.
They mark the meeting, and dancing, places of the fae.
If a human steps into one, they may glimpse the "little people".
But bewitchment, ill fortune, and even **death** may follow.

MUSHROOM

In British and Irish folklore, it has long been recorded that fairy rings mark the spot where the fae dance around and around in a circle, often by moonlight, and especially on May Eve and Halloween.

Fairy rings are, of course, real things: they are naturally occurring circles of mushrooms. More than sixty species of mushroom are known to grow in a circular, or semi-circular, fairy-ring pattern, including that champion champignon of fairy tale and lore: *amanita muscaria* a.k.a. fly agaric. In France, fairy rings are known as *ronds de sorcières*, and in Germany as *hexenringe*, both of which translate as "witches' rings."

Willfully destroying or breaking a fairy ring is thought to bring bad luck[1], which may plague the vandal until their dying day. In his book *The Popular Rhymes of Scotland* (1826), Robert Chambers recorded the following old Scottish verse:

"He wha tills the fairies' green
Nae luck again shall hae:
And he wha spills the fairies' ring
Betide him want and wae.
For weirdless days and weary nights
Are his till his deein' day.
But he wha gaes by the fairy ring,
Nae dule nor pine shall see,
And he wha cleans the fairy ring
An easy death shall dee."

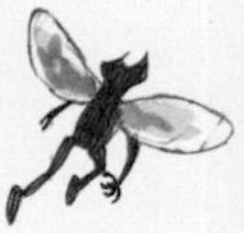

Someone stepping into a fairy ring of mushrooms might be magically forced to dance with the fae, which may result in exhaustion, madness, or even death. A transgressor may be rendered invisible to those outside the fairy ring and forced to remain within until rescued. A year and a day is the common span of time reported in many folkloric tales which must elapse before someone can be freed from within a circle. Fairy rings may act as literal gateways to Faerie – the realm of the fae – where people can become trapped or lost. Time passes differently in Faerie, meaning that those who do find their way back to our own realm after feeling they have been away for hours may in fact have been absent for years.

In folklore, seeing fairies when they have not voluntarily chosen to be seen often comes at a hefty price. Being "away with the fairies" has come to mean being adrift from reality in one way or another. On the whole, it seems that, should one come across a fairy ring of mushrooms, the best course of action would be to leave it well alone.

1 The idea that misfortune would follow the destruction of plantlife associated with an otherworldly creature appears in multiple cultures. See also 'Hawthorn' (pg. 10) and Kodama (pg. 90).

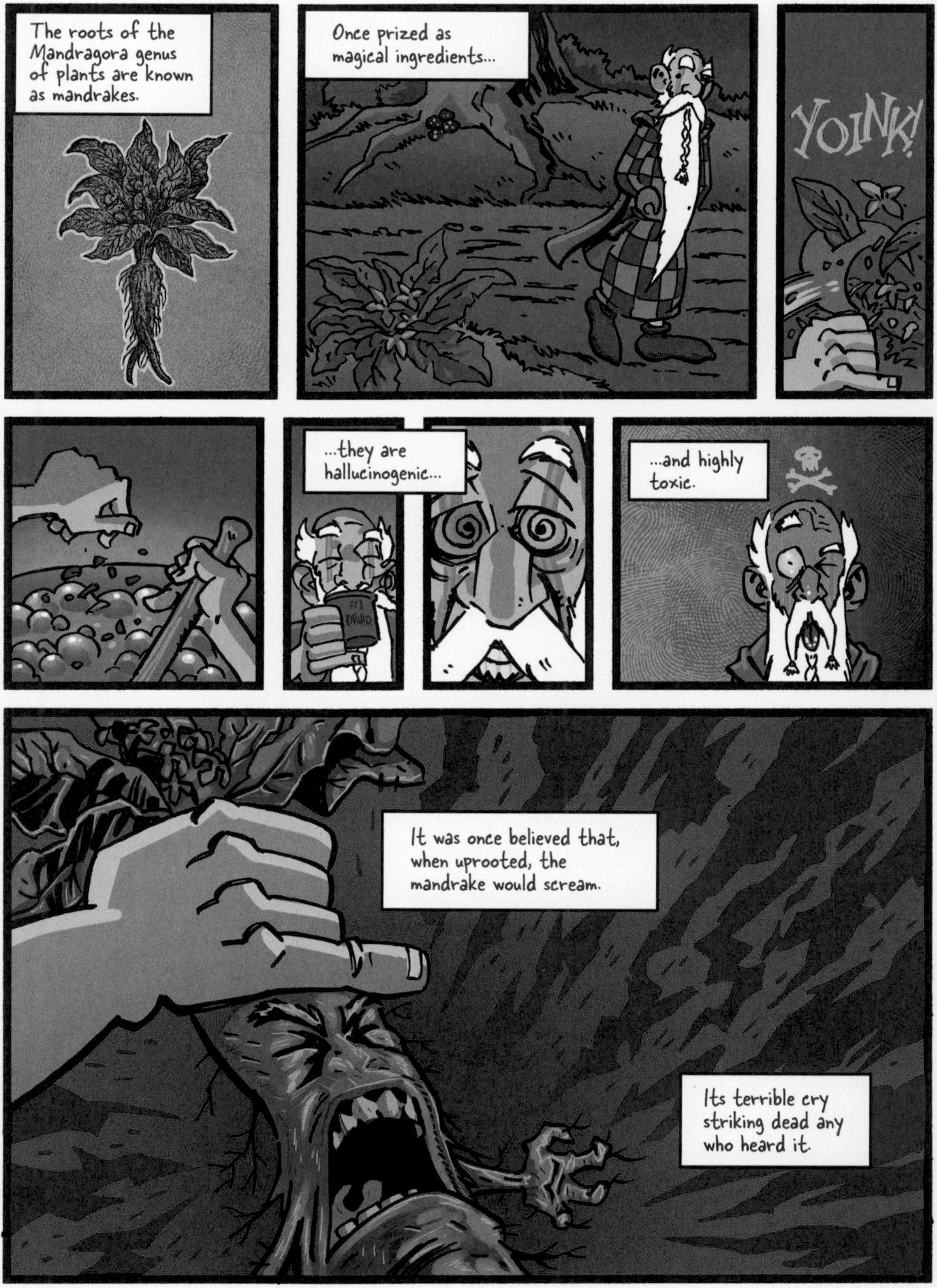
The roots of the Mandragora genus of plants are known as mandrakes.
Once prized as magical ingredients...
YOINK!
...they are hallucinogenic...
#1 DRUID
...and highly toxic.
It was once believed that, when uprooted, the mandrake would scream.
Its terrible cry striking dead any who heard it.

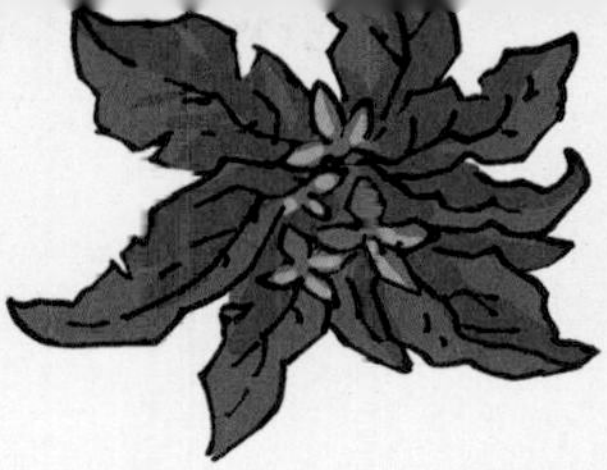

MANDRAKE

The most enduring myth surrounding the mandrake is that this strange, quasi-human plant refuses to be uprooted. The scream emitted by a mandrake root when prised from the soil is said to be so ear-splitting and so terrible that it may kill anyone who hears it, or else render them forever insane. One ancient solution to this was, apparently, to tether a dog to the leaves and stem of the plant. The dog would then be called to its master, and the mandrake subsequently uprooted remotely. Sadly, some sources record that the root's terrible cry was, nevertheless, fatal to any dog thus employed. Exactly why a longer leash was not used, or why the mandrake harvester didn't simply uproot the plant from a safe distance themselves using a sufficient length of rope, remains unclear (to me, at least).

In his work *The Secret Teachings of All Ages* (1928), Manly P. Hall recorded the following:

> "The *Mandragora officinarum*, or mandrake, is accredited with possessing the most remarkable magical powers. Its narcotic properties were recognized by the Greeks, who employed it to deaden pain during surgical operations, and it has been identified also with *baaras*, the mystic herb used by the Jews for casting out demons. In the *Jewish Wars*, Josephus describes the method of securing the baaras, which he declares emits flashes of lightning and destroys all who seek to touch it, unless they proceed according to certain rules supposedly formulated by King Solomon himself."

For centuries, mandrake has been reputed to have been one of the key components in witches' flying ointment[1] (a hallucinogenic compound used for ritual purposes) and other magical brews. It was revered as an aphrodisiac by the ancient Greeks, and the Bible records that the plant aided Rachel in conceiving Jacob. In the Middle Ages, dried mandrakes were carried as charms, a lucrative market in carved counterfeits inevitably springing up in the wake of this fad.

Undoubtedly, mandrake's strangely humanoid appearance has always been a key component in its otherworldly mythology, but the plant does have genuine medical properties and uses. Indeed, the drug etoposide – derived from mandrake – is used today in first-line treatment for certain cancers. To paraphrase Arthur C. Clarke, any sufficiently advanced pharmacology is indistinguishable from magic.

1 See also 'Henbane' (pg. 18).

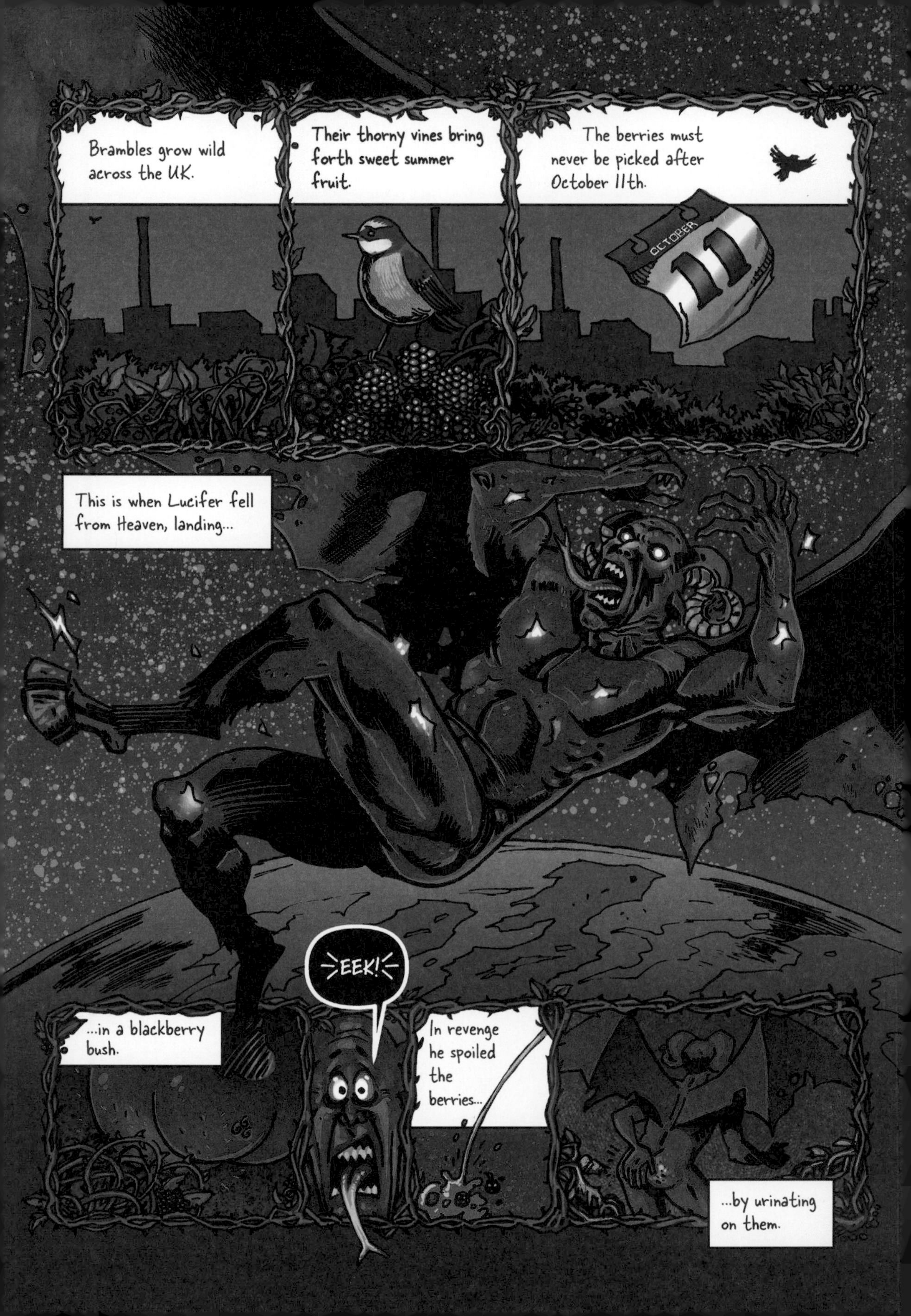

Brambles grow wild across the UK.
Their thorny vines bring forth sweet summer fruit.
The berries must never be picked after October 11th.
OCTOBER
11
This is when Lucifer fell from Heaven, landing...
...in a blackberry bush.
EEK!
In revenge he spoiled the berries...
...by urinating on them.

BLACK BERRIES

IN DIFFERENT REGIONS OF THE UK, LOCAL FOLKLORE SAYS THAT THE DEVIL STAMPS, SPITS, vomits, or even urinates on blackberries all along the hedgerows, rendering them inedible after Michaelmas.

William Brockie's *Legends & Superstitions of the County of Durham* (1886) records the following:

> The fruit of the blackberry bramble (*rubus timbroms* or *fruiticosus*) is vulgarly known in this district by the name of bumblekite, from its being supposed to cause flatulency when eaten in too great a quantity. No knowledgeable boy will eat these berries after Michaelmas Day, because the arch-fiend is believed to ride along the hedges on the eve of that great festival and pollute everything that grows in them, except the sloes, by touching them with his club foot. The same notion prevails further north, where the bramble-berries are called lady's garter berries.

This blackberry folklore has been around for so long, however, that the date of Michaelmas Day itself has changed. Where once it fell on the 11th of October (still sometimes referred to as "Old Michaelmas Day"), today it is celebrated on the 29th of September. Why should the Devil take it upon himself to spoil the blackberries though?

Saint Michael (he whom Michaelmas celebrates), aka the archangel Michael, was a warrior. Revelation, the final book in the Christian New Testament, describes a literal war in Heaven between one group of angels under archangel Michael's command and another band of rebel angels, led by the Dragon, a.k.a. Lucifer. The war in Heaven was eventually won by Michael and his angelic troops, resulting in the expulsion of Satan from the realm above into this, the lowly mortal plane. The Devil descended to Earth and, apparently, his fall was broken by a bramble bush. Quite understandably, Satan was not best pleased with this. So, as the folklore goes, each year on the anniversary of his prickly landing, Old Scratch makes sure to ruin the blackberries.

In the UK, blackberries are best picked between August and late September or early October. After that time, they tend to have become overripe and inedible. This fact was certainly known long before Christianity came to these islands, and passed down through generations via word of mouth. "But why do the blackberries taste so bad after that time?" someone asks. "Well," someone else answers, "there's a story..."

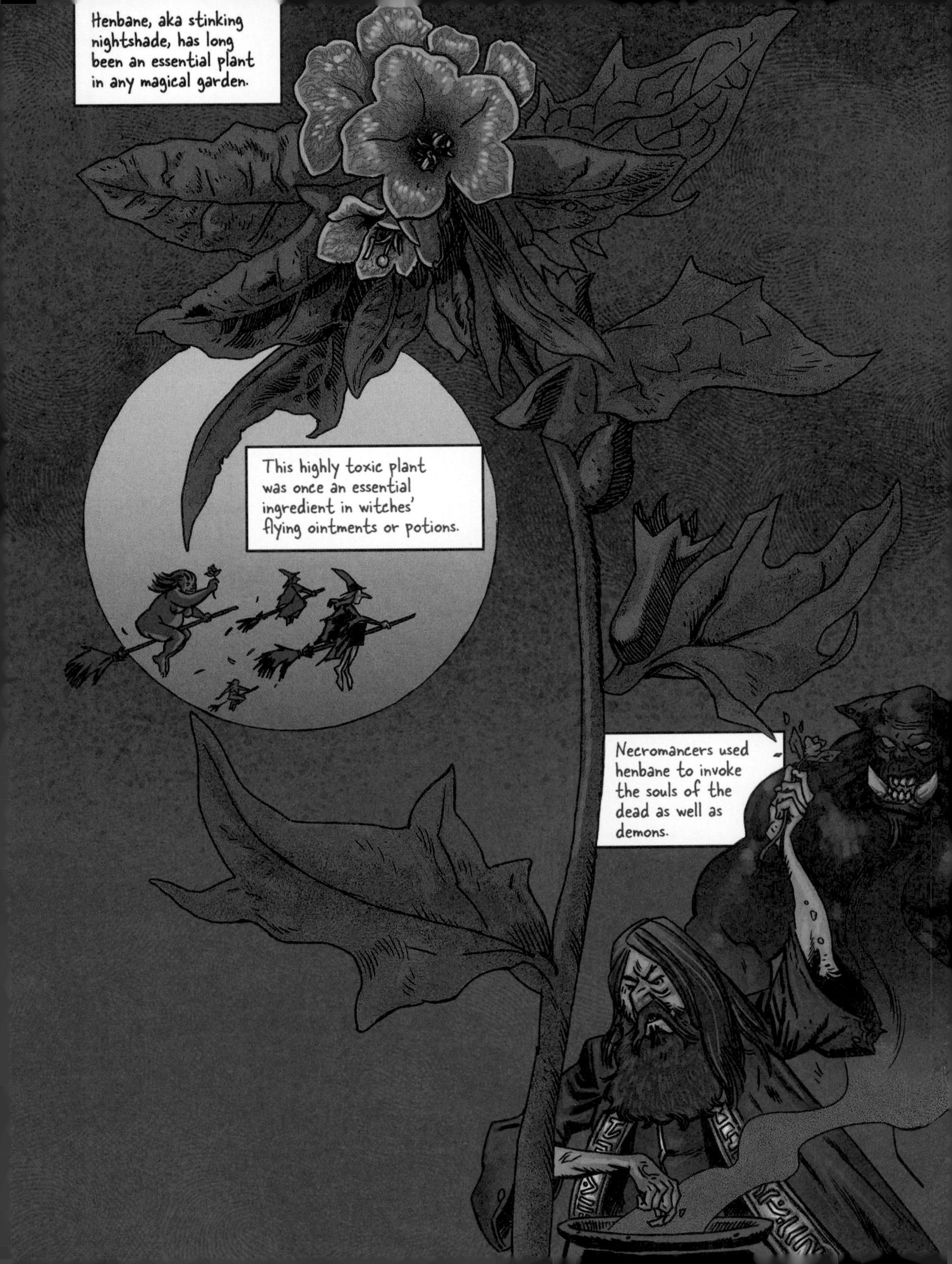
Henbane, aka stinking nightshade, has long been an essential plant in any magical garden.
This highly toxic plant was once an essential ingredient in witches' flying ointments or potions.
Necromancers used henbane to invoke the souls of the dead as well as demons.

HENBANE

HYOSCYAMUS NIGER IS MORE COMMONLY KNOWN AS STINKING nightshade, black henbane, or simply, henbane. The nickname "henbane" has several possible explanations, the simplest of which is that if a farmer were to allow their chickens to eat the plant, it would surely kill them.

Henbane contains hyoscyamine, scopolamine, and other tropane alkaloids, all of which are psychoactive – producing hallucinations and an altered state of consciousness if ingested. High doses can cause paralysis, unconsciousness, and even death. Pliny the Elder wrote that henbane was "of the nature of wine and therefore offensive to the understanding." Henbane seeds found at a Viking gravesite in Fyrkat, Denmark, in the 1970s led to speculation that the plant may have been responsible for the battle madness of the much-feared Norse berserker warriors.

During the witch panic of the early modern era, henbane, like mandrake[1], was regarded as one of the key ingredients in many magical potions and ointments, including witches' flying ointment. Magical use of the plant was already well documented by this point; Albertus Magnus reported that necromancers used henbane to invoke demons and spirits of the dead in his 1250 work *De Vegetalibus*. Writing in 1864, the English herbalist John Gerald recorded that the juice of the plant could cause a sleep so deep that the person who drank it may never wake.

Nevertheless, henbane has been an important ingredient in many medicines since antiquity. Used in the treatment of rheumatism, toothache, asthma, coughs, nervous diseases, and stomach pain, it is also a powerful analgesic and sedative. Indeed, the Greek physician Pedanius Dioscorides recorded its effectiveness as such, writing in the 1st century. When applied externally as a solution or ointment, rather than ingested, henbane's toxic effects are significantly lessened. *Hyoscyamus niger* is still cultivated and used in both folk medicines and commercial pharmaceuticals to this day.

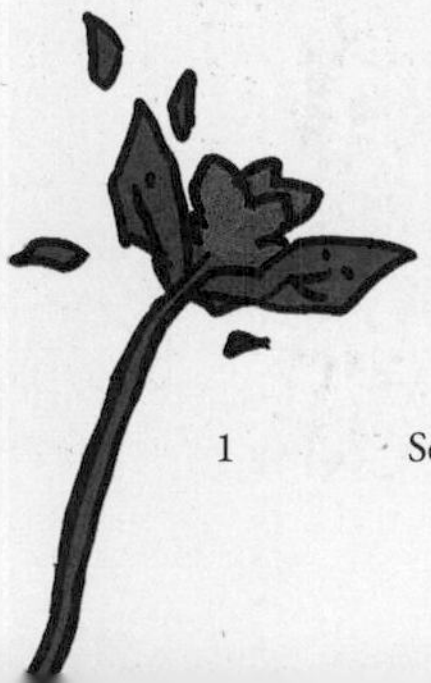

1 See 'Mandrake' (pg. 14).

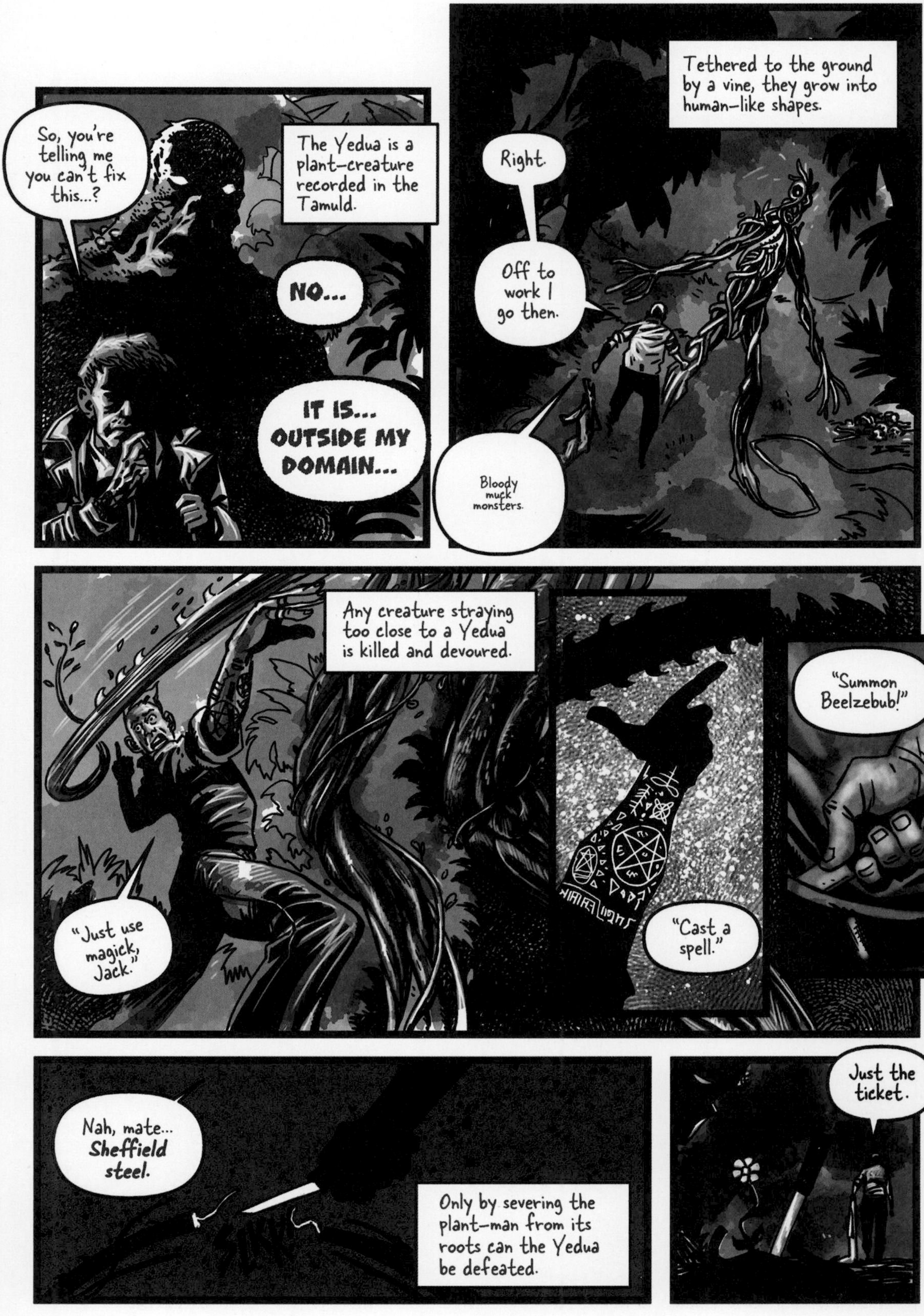
So, you're telling me you can't fix this...?
The Yedua is a plant-creature recorded in the Tamuld.
NO...
IT IS... OUTSIDE MY DOMAIN...
Tethered to the ground by a vine, they grow into human-like shapes.
Right.
Off to work I go then.
Bloody muck monsters.
Any creature straying too close to a Yedua is killed and devoured.
"Just use magick, Jack."
"Cast a spell."
"Summon Beelzebub!"
Nah, mate... **Sheffield steel.**
Only by severing the plant-man from its roots can the Yedua be defeated.
Just the ticket.

Y E D U A

ZOOPHYTE (LITERALLY "ANIMAL-PLANT") IS A NOW-OBSOLETE TERM USED UP UNTIL THE 19th century. The Yedua (variously also spelled Yadu'a, Jeduah, Fedua, Jidra and otherwise) are part of this strange subcategory of plant-lore in which the line between flora and fauna has become blurred.

In the Mishna Kilaim (vin, 5), a portion of the Talmud, we find a brief passage which reads: "Creatures called *adne sadeh* ('lords of the field') are regarded as beasts." The 13th-century Rabbi Simeon commented upon this as follows:

> It is asserted in the Jerusalem Talmud that this creature is the "man of the mountain." It draws its food out of the soil by means of the umbilical cord: if its navel be cut, it cannot live.

Rabbi Meir, the son of Kallonymos of Speyer, added the following remarks:

> There is an animal styled Yedua with the bones of which witchcraft is practiced. It issues from the earth like the stem of a plant, just as a gourd. In all respects, the Yedua has human form in face, body, hands, and feet. No creature can approach within the tether of the stem, for it seizes and kills all. As far as the stem (or umbilical cord) stretches, it devours the herbage all around. Whoever is intent on capturing this animal must not approach it, but tear at the cord until it is ruptured, whereupon the animal soon dies.

This quotation appeared in a 1915 article taken from *The Journal of American Folklore*, written by Berthold Laufer. Willy Ley's 1959 work *Exotic Zoology* repeated much the same information on the creature, which he called the Jidra, citing the 1858 German work *Zoologie des Talmuds* by Dr. L. Lewysohn as its source.

Why would anyone wish to kill the Yedua? Well, apart from the fact that these creatures seemed to want to murder anyone who came too close to them, it is reported that the bones of the Yedua were thought to be useful in magic. If held in the mouth of a sorcerer, these bones (exactly what form these zoophyte bones would take is not recorded) were supposed to grant the ability to foretell the future.

The Vegetable Lamb of Tartary is another strange example of a creature which was supposed to be neither wholly flora nor fauna. Widely believed now to have come from the first reports of the cotton plant with its wool-like yield, the Vegetable Lamb seems to have undergone a significant number of evolutions as accounts were passed from person to person. Some stories tell of a large gourd, inside of which, when ripe, could be found a lamb-like creature. Others tell of a living, moving, grazing lamb-like fruit, tethered to the plant from which it grew by means of an umbilical vine. It is this latter version of the Vegetable Lamb that bears a noticeable resemblance to the 13th-century Rabbis' descriptions of the Yedua.

Many scholars now argue that these brief records of the human-like "man of the mountains" actually represent second-hand accounts of encounters with apes or monkeys. The umbilical vine of the Yedua, therefore, was possibly a misinterpretation of the (trapped?) tail of such a simian.

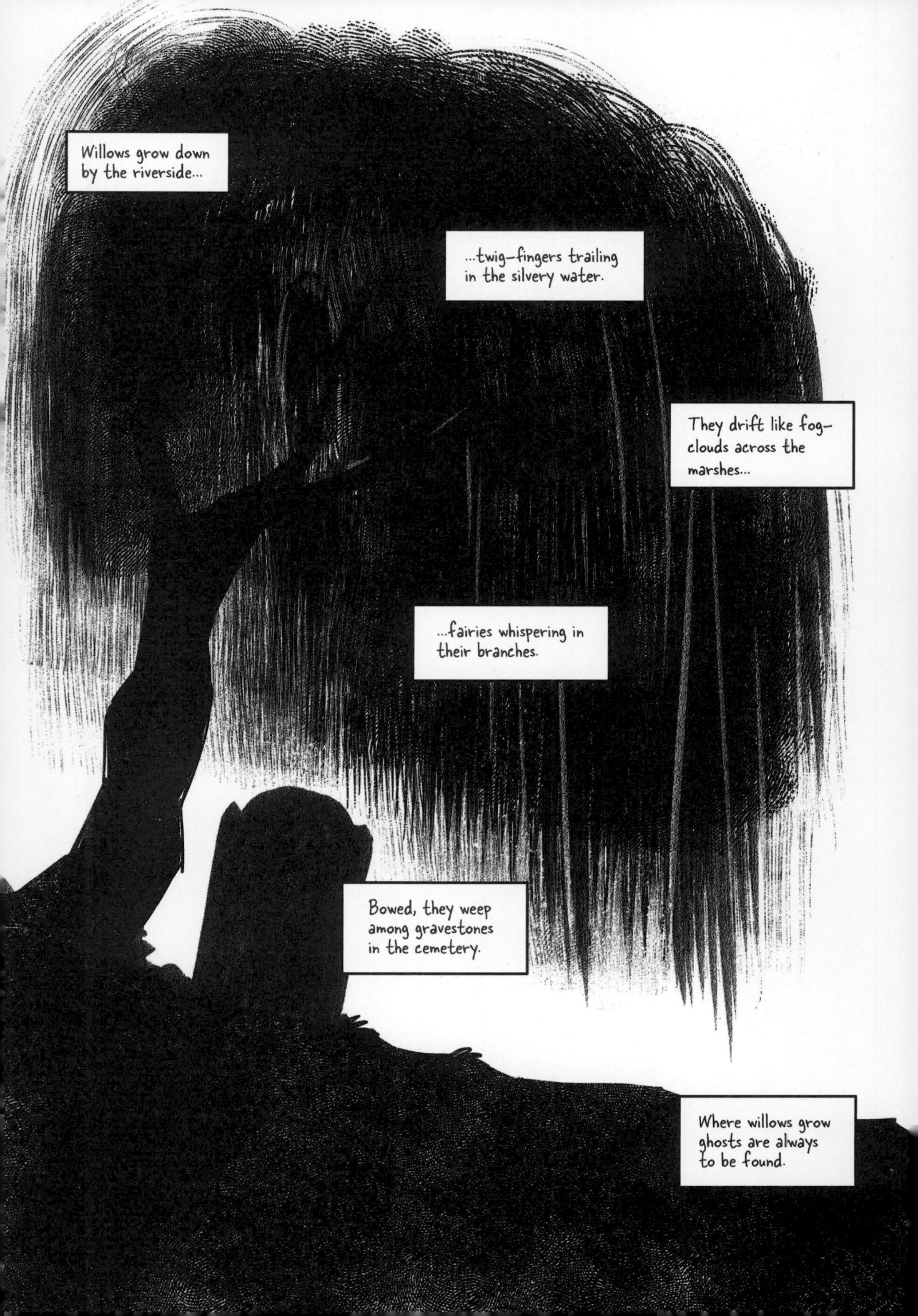
Willows grow down by the riverside...
...twig-fingers trailing in the silvery water.
They drift like fog-clouds across the marshes...
...fairies whispering in their branches.
Bowed, they weep among gravestones in the cemetery.
Where willows grow ghosts are always to be found.

WILLOW

THERE ARE OVER 400 SPECIES OF WILLOW – ALSO KNOWN as sallow and osier – ranging from mighty trees to low-growing, creeping shrubs. Willows grow in the tropics, in the Arctic, and almost everywhere in between.

Perhaps the most familiar species is the weeping willow – a tree native to northern China but which, thanks to millennia of trade between East and West, is now found across the world. With its long, slender branches, drooping with cascades of small, green leaves, the weeping willow appears to "hang its head" in grief.

The weeping willow's scientific name, *salix babylonica*, was given in 1736 by the Swedish botanist Carolus Linnaeus. The name is a reference not to the origin of the tree, but to Psalm 137 in the book of Psalms:

> "By the rivers of Babylon we sat down and wept
> when we remembered Zion.
> There on the willow trees
> we hung up our harps."

It should be noted, however, that there were no weeping willows in Babylon, and that the trees mentioned in the psalm are believed to have been poplars (also a member of the willow family).

Because these trees were traditionally used as grave-markers, their association with the dead, with death, and with Yin, has become deeply ingrained over thousands of years. In folklore then, willows have become a kind of magnet for Yin, and for ghosts themselves.

The Qingming Festival (more commonly known as Chinese Memorial Day or Ancestor's Day in English) is a traditional Chinese festival observed by the Han Chinese people of Mainland China, Taiwan, Hong Kong, Macau, Singapore, Indonesia, and Thailand, and by the Chitty people of Malaysia. During the festival (which takes place on the 15th day following the spring equinox[1]), families visit the graves of their ancestors where they pray and leave offerings[2]. Willow branches are traditionally used to sweep the gravesites and tombs, but willow is also fixed above doors and gates during Qingming in the belief that it will prevent other spirits, wandering abroad, from entering where they are not wanted. It's interesting to note that in English folklore, fixing willow leaves or branches above a doorway was believed to act as a protection against witches.

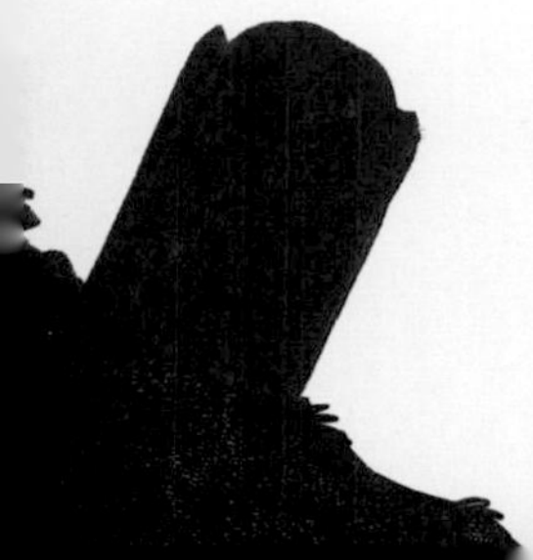

1 For more on equinoxes and solstices, see 'Celestial' (pg. 94).

2 For similar practices, see Dia de los Muertos in 'Hallowe'en' (pg. 100).

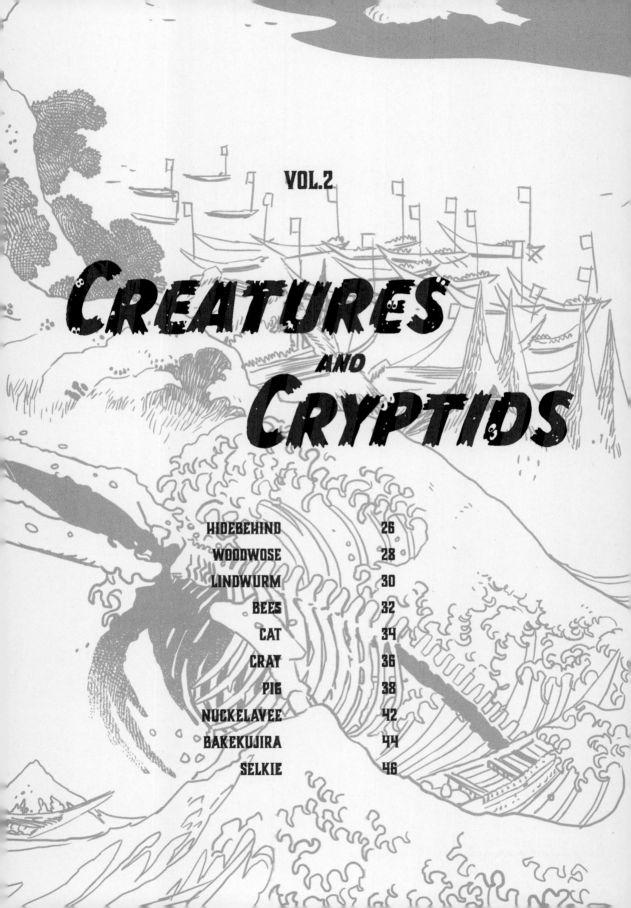

VOL.2

CREATURES AND CRYPTIDS

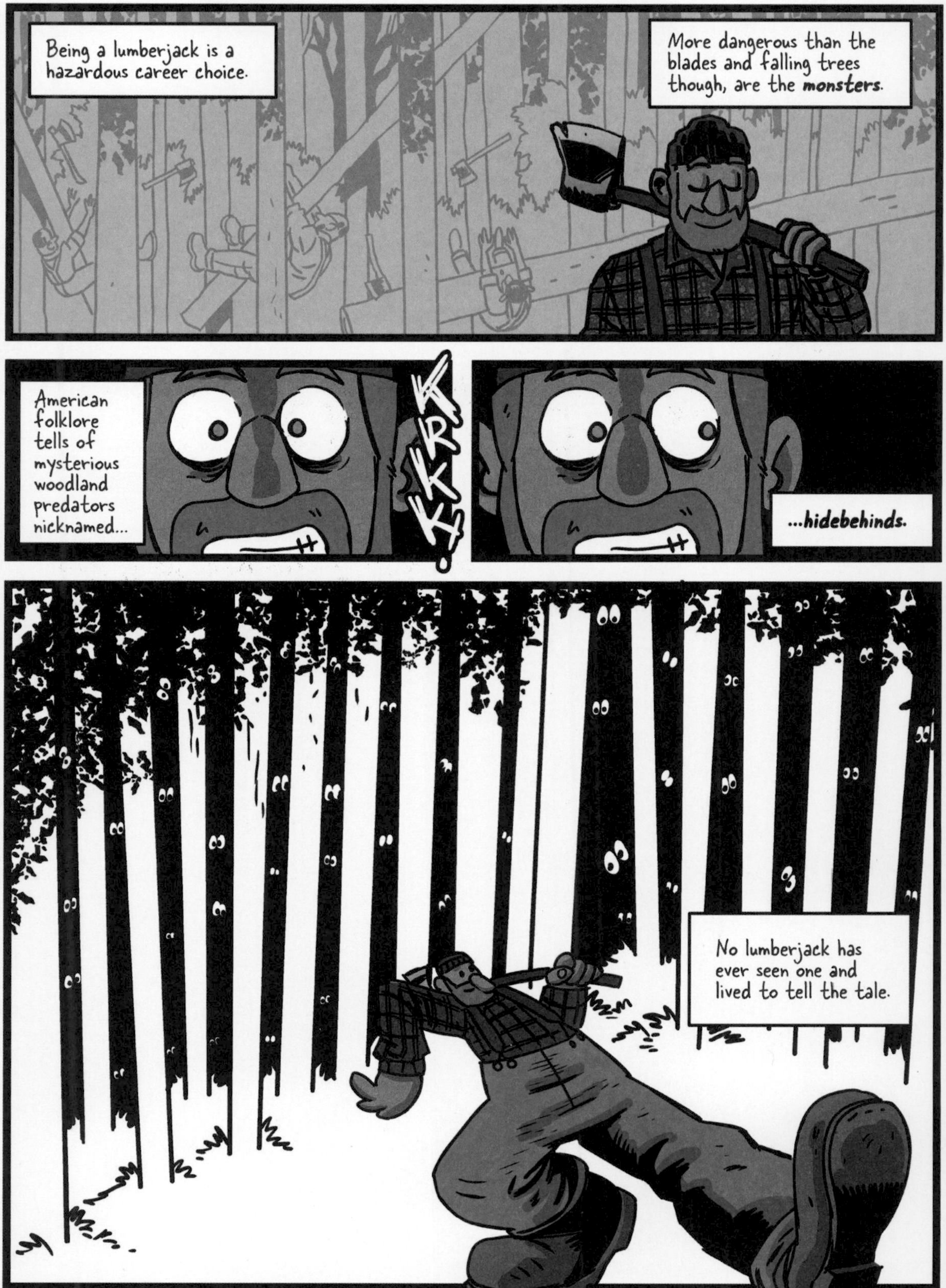
Being a lumberjack is a hazardous career choice.
More dangerous than the blades and falling trees though, are the **monsters**.
American folklore tells of mysterious woodland predators nicknamed...
KRKKK!
...hidebehinds.
No lumberjack has ever seen one and lived to tell the tale.

HIDE

BEHIND

IN THE TIMBERLANDS OF LATE 19TH- AND EARLY 20TH-CENTURY AMERICA, LUMBERJACKS LIVED A migratory lifestyle. Moving from camp to camp, down from the Northeast of the country, into the Upper Midwest, and eventually into the Pacific Northwest, the loggers kept themselves entertained during non-working hours by swapping campfire tales. These stories took on a life of their own as they were passed from lumberjack to lumberjack, and camp to camp, becoming the folklore of the woodcutters.

Many of these stories dealt with what came to be known as "fearsome critters"– strange, otherwise unknown or undocumented creatures which roamed the forests. Many of these stories originated as a means of scaring or pranking newcomers to an area (very much like the infamous "drop bear," which tourists are warned about in parts of Australia), with several storytellers in on the joke warning about the particular hazards which might be faced in that region. That said, some seem rather more sinister, and less overtly comical than others.

One such creature, often blamed for the mysterious disappearance of any logger who left the camp that morning but who was not back by the fireside that night, was the "hidebehind." Described in *Fearsome Critters*, 1939 – a (suitably tongue-in-cheek) field guide to the creatures of North American forest folklore, written by Henry H. Tryon – we are told that the hidebehind has never been, and will never be, seen in the open. These carnivorous creatures conceal themselves behind tree-trunks, always staying to the rear of the unfortunates they hunt. As a result, their appearance remains a mystery to all but those who have been dragged back to the shadowy creatures' lairs to be devoured. Their favorite meal, apparently, being the intestines of loggers.

Fear not though, because Tryon recorded that hidebehinds hated the smell and taste of alcohol and tobacco: a good enough excuse for any lumberjack to always make sure he had a pouch of tobacco and a hipflask with him.

While Tryon described the hidebehind comedically, the creature's always-hidden-until-escape-is-impossible nature taps into a fundamental human fear. Scopaesthesia – the ability to detect that one is being observed without being able to see the observer – has never been scientifically proven, and yet most of us feel we have experienced something like it. We know when someone, or something, is watching us; perhaps hiding in the shadow of a tree trunk in an otherwise silent forest...

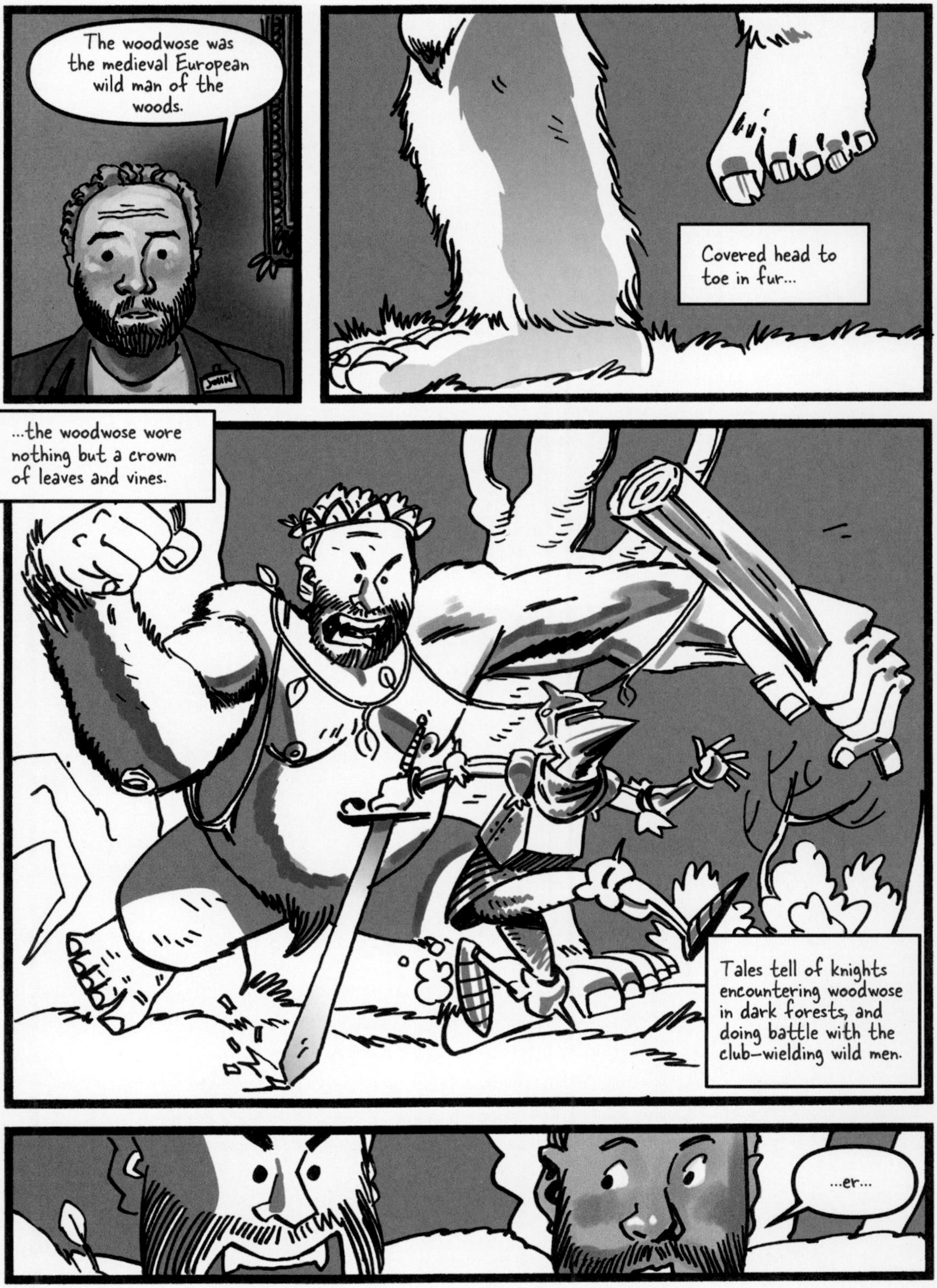
The woodwose was the medieval European wild man of the woods.
JOHN
Covered head to toe in fur...
...the woodwose wore nothing but a crown of leaves and vines.
Tales tell of knights encountering woodwose in dark forests, and doing battle with the club-wielding wild men.
...er...

WOODWOSE

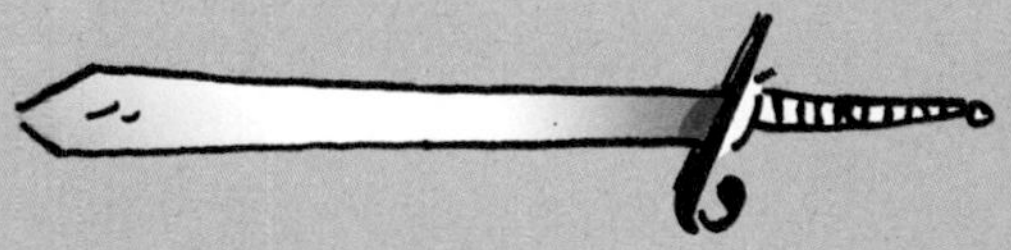

Woodwose (or wodewose) are a hairy species of wild man recorded, under various different names, in European mythology. These wild men are sometimes interpreted as the European cousins of America's Sasquatch or Bigfoot. Many medieval tales of the woodwose, however, seem to hint at the idea that, rather than being a distinct species, they may have been humans who had abandoned civilization, becoming feral and animalistic.

Woodwose are typically depicted as strong, large, bearded men – sometimes twice the size of a human – their bodies covered in hair, though their hands, feet, and upper face remain un-furred. Often, they wield a crude staff or club, while leaves and vines tangled in their hair give the appearance of a crown. Female woodwose, who are depicted less often, are just as hairy as the male woodwose, but lack hair or fur on their breasts, making them similar to late medieval images of Mary Magdalene, who is said to have grown a "hair suit" whilst wandering in the desert.

The earliest recorded use of the term "woodwose" dates from the 1340s, when it was used in the description of a tapestry owned by Edward III. Woodwose became popular in art and literature in medieval Europe, and depictions of them survive today within heraldic imagery created during that time. Alongside the Green Man[1], woodwose were a favorite subject of carved decoration in churches in medieval England. Examples of carved woodwose survive in Norwich Cathedral, Canterbury Cathedral, and in many smaller English churches and chapels.

In the 13th-century Middle High German poem *Sigenot*, the legendary hero Dietrich von Bern does battle with a huge, hairy wild man deep in the forest. Dietrich's mighty sword cannot penetrate the creature's matted fur, which acts like armor, and despite his heroic strength, he cannot strangle his opponent either. Only through use of a magic spell does Dietrich von Bern eventually best the woodwose. These wild men are also mentioned (as "wodwos") in the 14th-century Middle English Arthurian Romance *Sir Gawain and the Green Knight*, in which they are said to dwell in the forests of Northwest England.

As with Bigfoot and other large, ape-like hominids said to haunt forests around the globe, it is possible that tales of woodwose may be folk-memory relics of the long-ago when Homo sapiens and Neanderthals shared territories. The truth is that hairy wild men did indeed once dwell in these places, and that we are their descendants.

1 For customs associated with the Green Man, see 'Jack in the Green' (pg. 98).

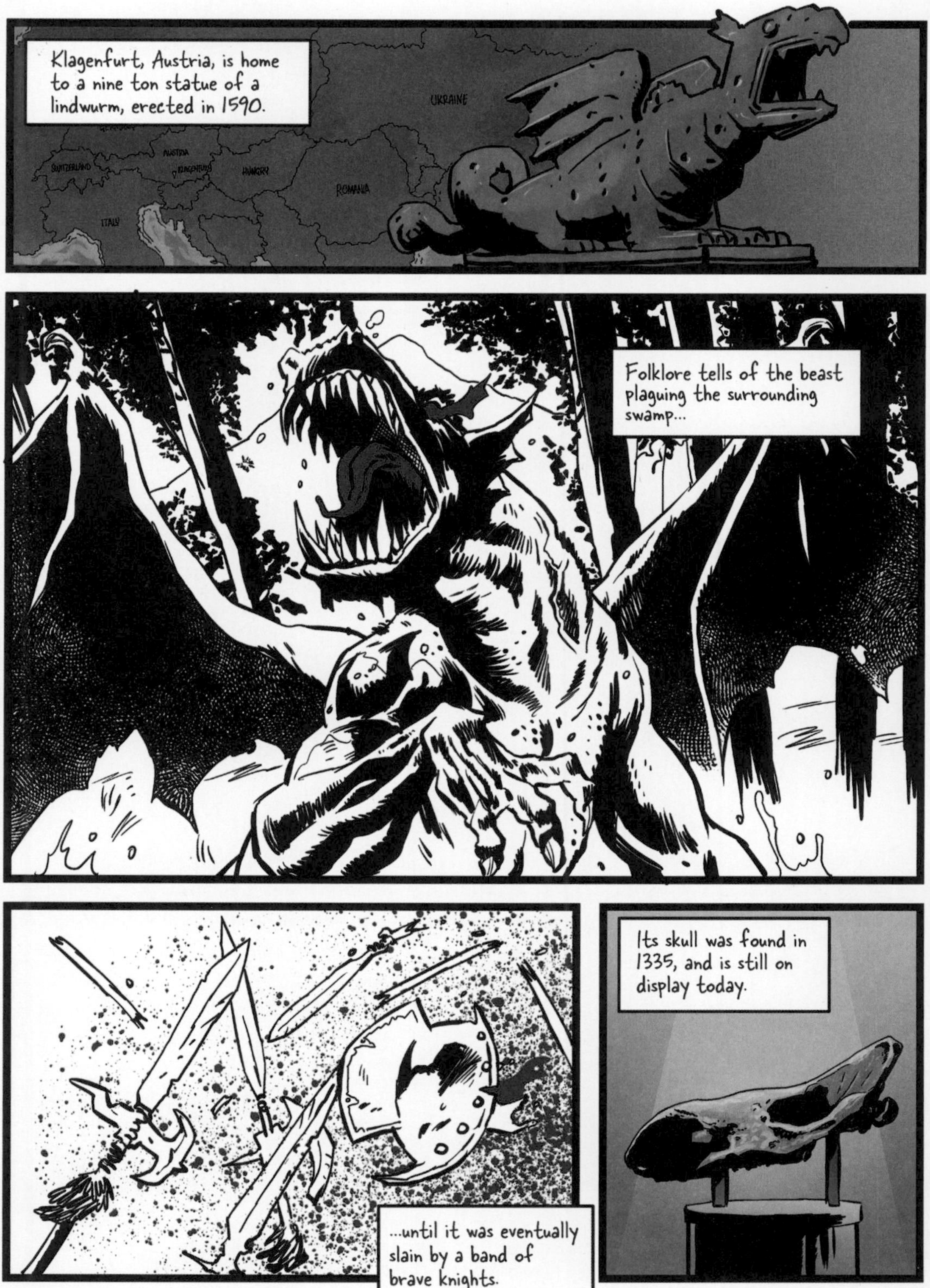
Klagenfurt, Austria, is home to a nine ton statue of a lindwurm, erected in 1590.
UKRAINE
SWITZERLAND
AUSTRIA
KLAGENFURT
HUNGARY
ROMANIA
ITALY
Folklore tells of the beast plaguing the surrounding swamp...
...until it was eventually slain by a band of brave knights.
Its skull was found in 1335, and is still on display today.

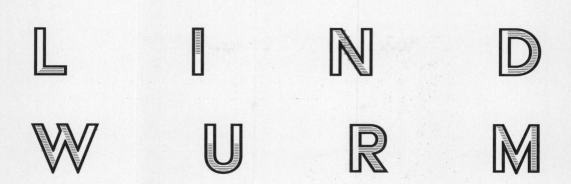

LINDWURM

THE LINDWURM, OR LINDWORM, IS USUALLY DEPICTED AS A TWO-LEGGED, WINGLESS, serpentine dragon. Lindwurms appear in the imagery on many 11th-century Swedish runestones and seem to be analogous with the monsters which feature in the English tales of the Lambton Worm and the Sockburn Worm.

Belief in lindorms – a somewhat smaller, wholly limbless subspecies of lindwurm – persisted in Sweden into the 19th century, and folklorist Gunnar Olof Hyltén-Cavallius collected many contemporary eyewitness accounts of the creatures. In 1884, convinced of their reality, Hyltén-Cavallius offered a cash reward to anyone who could successfully capture a lindorm. The reward was, sadly, never claimed.

Klagenfurt is the capital of the state of Carinthia in Austria, and its coat of arms features an image of a winged lindwurm integral to the city's foundation myth. Legend has it that the moors where Klagenfurt now stands were once the domain of a fearsome lindwurm which fed freely upon travelers and livestock alike. After a reward for the beast's destruction was offered, a special platform was constructed out in the mire. There, a chained bull was used to bait the lindwurm; a custom-made, hooked harness on the beast's back designed to catch in the monster's throat like a gargantuan fishhook. This plan proved successful, and the lindwurm was captured and decapitated, its head cast in triumph into the swamp. Legend has it that Klagenfurt was founded on the spot where the lindwurm was slain.

In 1335, a monstrous skull believed to be that of the long-ago vanquished lindwurm was recovered from a quarry in Klagenfurt. The skull was put on display in the town hall in Carinthia and, in 1593, it served as the model for a statue constructed under the supervision of one Ulrich Vogelsang. Carved from a single, huge block of chlorite slate, the statue was four-legged and resembled a traditional European dragon more than the strange, winged lindworm depicted on Klagenfurt's coat of arms. In 1624, this dragon statue was installed as a fountain, with water pouring from its open mouth, in Klagenfurt's central Alter Platz (Old Square), where it still stands.

Today, the skull which served as the model for the dragon fountain is on display at the Landesmuseum für Kärnten (State Museum of Carinthia). It is now labeled correctly as that of a *Coelodonta antiquitatis*, or "wooly rhinoceros."

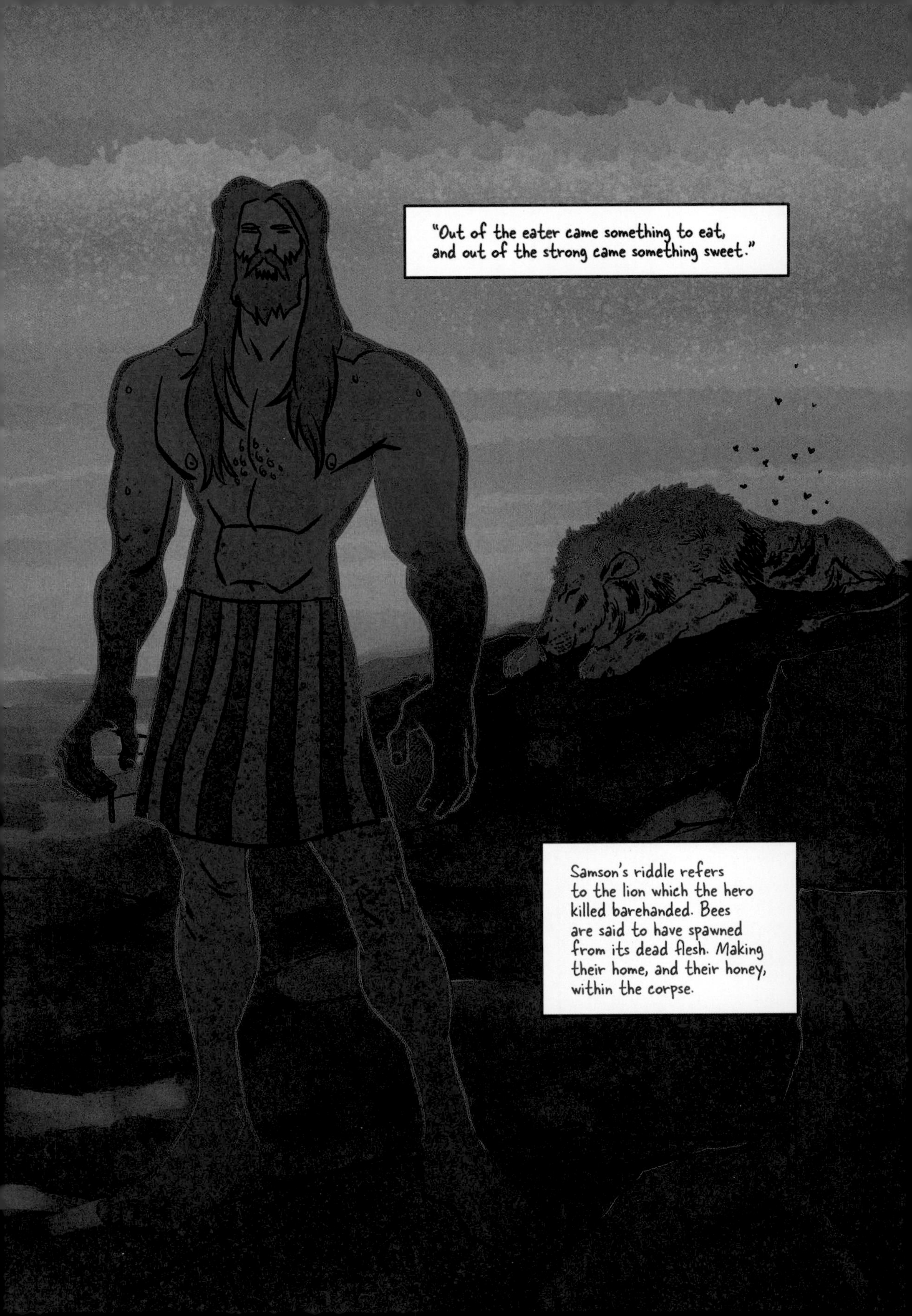
"Out of the eater came something to eat, and out of the strong came something sweet."
Samson's riddle refers to the lion which the hero killed barehanded. Bees are said to have spawned from its dead flesh. Making their home, and their honey, within the corpse.

B E E S

Tate & Lyle is a British food ingredient manufacturer. It was formed in 1921 when two rival sugar refiners, Henry Tate & Sons and Abram Lyle & Sons, merged into a single company. Tate & Lyle's Golden Syrup has been one of the company's most recognizable products since its release in 1885. Still sold today in tins which, to modern eyes, look more like paint pots than food containers, Tate & Lyle's Golden Syrup has an image of a dead lion on its front, with the words "out of the strong came forth sweetness" printed beneath. Bees buzz around the maned beast's corpse, seeming to issue from within.

The strange image and motto have their origins in an Old Testament text: Chapter 14 of the book of Judges. In the verse, Samson – he of the infamous betrayal by Delilah – offers a riddle: "out of the eater came forth meat, and out of the strong came forth sweetness." None could solve his riddle, so Samson explained that he had killed a lion and later saw that bees had made a hive in its corpse.

In ancient times, some believed that different species of winged insect were spontaneously generated from the flesh of dead animals. Bees were (usually) thought to originate from the bodies of cows, while wasps came from the corpses of horses. In ancient Egypt, oxen were sometimes deliberately buried with only their horns left exposed above the earth in the belief that this would spawn a hive of honeybees.

Many species of wasp will eat carrion and will also feed on many of the smaller insects which feed and breed on or around a corpse. There are three species of South American stingless bees known collectively as vulture bees, which do feed on meat. Entering the corpse via the eye-sockets, forager bees devour the flesh and, returning to their hive, regurgitate it for workers to process into a salty, smokey, honey-like substance.

Even in Britain and Ireland, bees and wasps do sometimes make their nests in the skulls and bones of the dead, the corpses' cavities offering the same protection as other naturally occurring structures. In 2016, in a strange echo of Samson's tale, a hive of rare, native Irish honeybees took up residence within a hollow statue of a maned lion in Mote Park, County Roscommon, Northern Ireland.

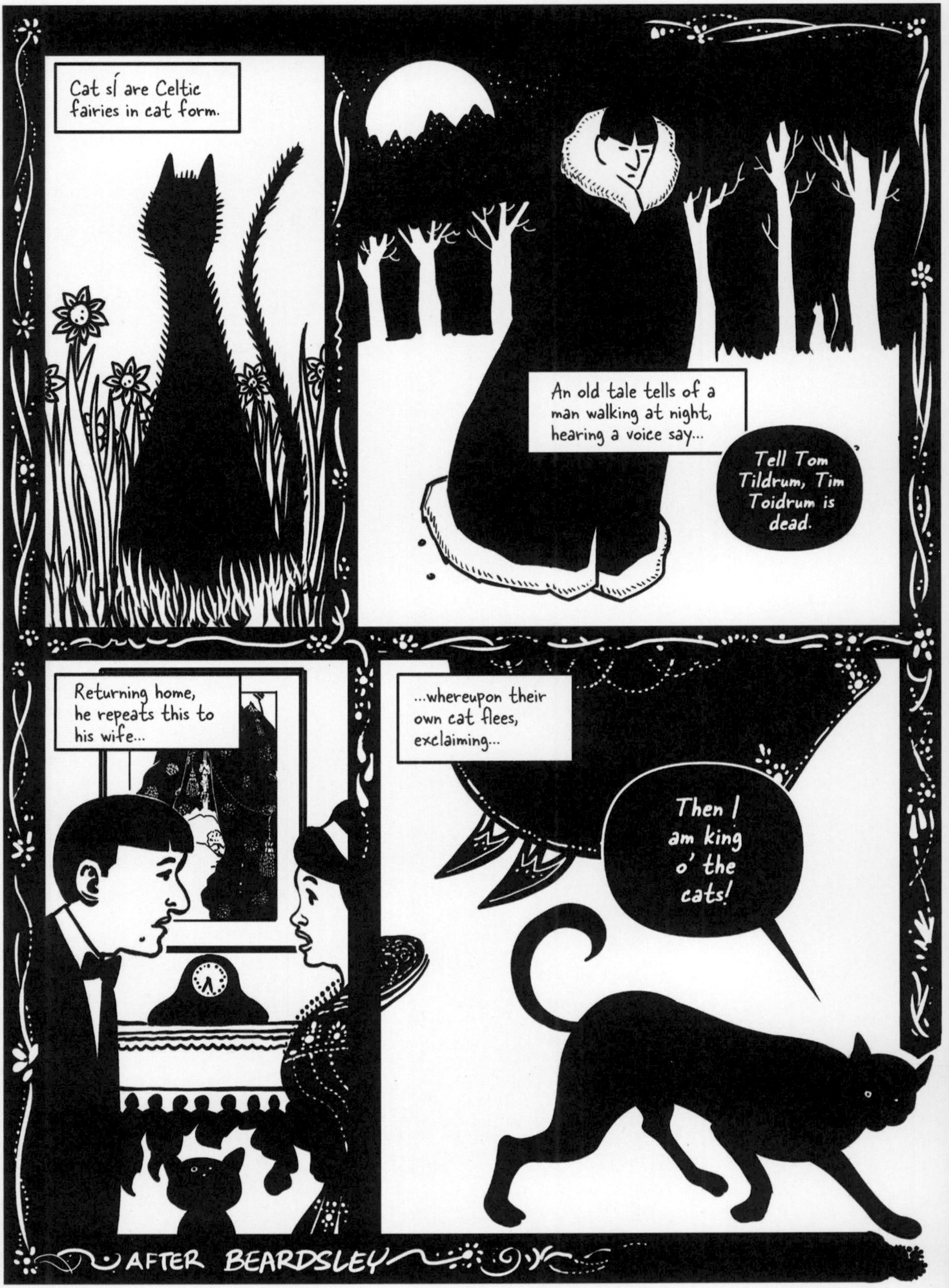

Cat sí are Celtic fairies in cat form.
An old tale tells of a man walking at night, hearing a voice say...
Tell Tom Tildrum, Tim Toidrum is dead.
Returning home, he repeats this to his wife...
...whereupon their own cat flees, exclaiming...
Then I am king o' the cats!
AFTER BEARDSLEY

 CAT

IN CELTIC FOLKLORE, *CAT SÍ* (IRISH LANGUAGE) OR *CAT-SÌTH* (Scottish Gaelic) are fairy creatures said to resemble large, black cats, often with a single spot of white fur on their chests.

In his 1531 work *Beware the Cat*, the English author and poet William Baldwin mentions a folktale entitled *The King o' the Cats*, which has been told and retold in print countless times since. Joseph Jacobs recorded his own version of the tale in his 1894 collection *More English Fairy Tales*.

In Jacobs' telling, a church sexton returns home from his evening's work to be greeted warmly by his wife as her large black cat, Old Tom, sits by the fireside. The sexton, in a state of great excitement, asks his wife, "Who is Tommy Tildrum?" She does not know the name and asks him whatever the matter is. The sexton explains that he fell asleep down in a grave he was digging for a burial the next day and was awakened by the miaou of a cat. Here, Old Tom gives a miaou, as if in answer. Peering over the edge of the grave, the sexton tells his wife he saw nine black cats "all like our friend Tom here, all with a white spot on their chestesses." Eight of these cats were carrying a cat-sized coffin "with a black velvet pall, and on the pall was a small coronet all of gold." The ninth cat walked ahead, leading the procession. Every third step, the sexton says, these cats let out a solemn miaou, and here again Old Tom miaous, as if partaking in the conversation. The cats halted at the edge of the grave in which the sexton stood, and their leader approached the man. With its eerily shining green eyes fixed upon his own, the sexton heard the cat say, "Tell Tom Tildrum that Tim Toidrum's dead." That, he explains to his amazed wife, is why he asked who Tommy Tildrum is.

> "Look at Old Tom, look at Old Tom!" screamed his wife.
>
> And well he might look, for Tom was swelling and Tom was staring, and at last Tom shrieked out, "What – old Tim dead! Then I'm the king o' the cats!" and rushed up the chimney and was nevermore seen.

An Irish variant of the tale tells of a little neighborhood in which everyone leaves a nightly saucer of milk out for the cat sí by way of an offering. One night, a skeptical man, seeking to end the superstition, leaves a poisoned dish of milk outside his own home. The next day, a black cat with a white breast lies dead on his doorstep. In the local pub, the man describes the deceased feline and asks if anyone knows to whom it belonged. Hearing his words, the pub's own large black cat springs up from the fireside and declares, "Well then, that makes me King of the Cats!" As in Jacobs' version, this cat makes a speedy exit, never to be seen again, but not before savagely scratching the poisoner.

Tales of the cat sì are most prevalent in Scottish folklore, and it has been suggested that these stories may relate to Kellas cats. The Scottish wildcat is the only surviving wildcat population in the UK, and Kellas cats are melanistic hybrids of these indigenous felines and the domestic cats brought into the country by Roman invaders. As recently as the late 20th century, tales of these large and elusive black wildcats were dismissed by many as mere folktales, or else hoaxes. Then, in 1983, a gamekeeper shot and killed a large, black, male cat beside the River Lossie in Kellas, Morayshire, thus giving the Kellas cat its name. A stuffed and mounted specimen on display at the University of Aberdeen's Zoology Museum is wholly black aside from its fine white guard hairs and a small patch of white on its chest. The cat's (glass) eyes are a striking emerald green.

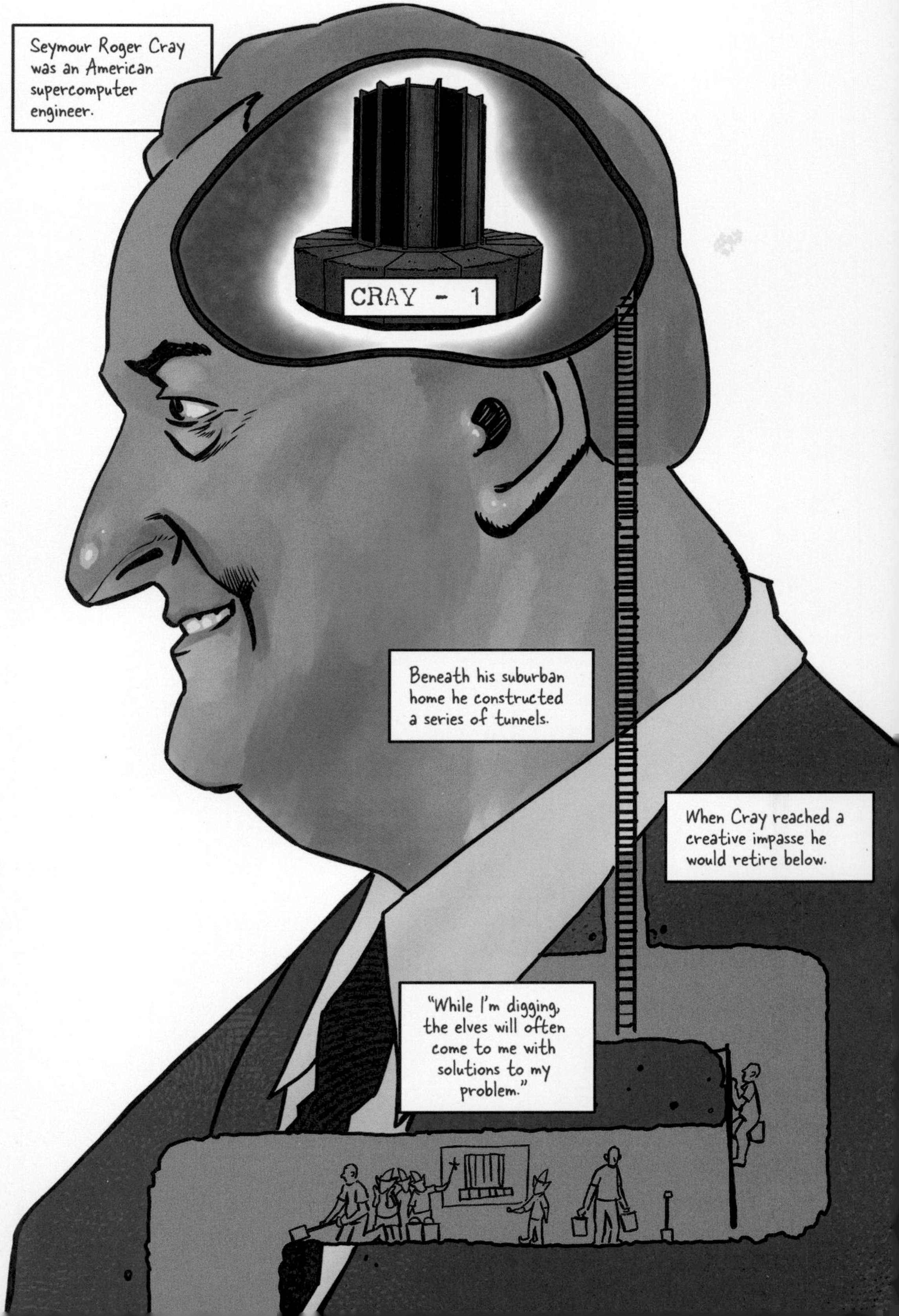
Seymour Roger Cray was an American supercomputer engineer.
CRAY - 1
Beneath his suburban home he constructed a series of tunnels.
When Cray reached a creative impasse he would retire below.
"While I'm digging, the elves will often come to me with solutions to my problem."

CRAY

FOLKLORIC CREATURES, OR EVEN DEMI-DEITIES, WHO HELP humans with their work can be found across many cultures. In Slavic paganism, the Domovoy ("house lord") is usually represented as an old, gray-haired man with bright eyes. He (and sometimes his female counterpart, Domania, being more rare) shows himself in the form of a visiting animal or in the shape of a departed ancestor, occasionally with the addition of a tail and small horns. Offerings of leftover food, slices of salted bread, and prayers were (and are) made to the Domovoy in order that he keep the home and its occupants safe.

The house brownies of Scotland and the hobs of England were once left similar offerings, sometimes in exchange for minor domestic chores such as sweeping up, but mostly in an effort to stop them causing mischief such as hiding keys and other small objects. Perhaps the most famous instance of the "other folk" helping humans with their work is recorded in the fairy tale *The Elves and the Shoemaker*. More modern, and surprising, stories do exist however, with the fae offering their expertise in very modern ways.

Arthur Edward Stilwell was the founder of Kansas City Southern Railway and of Port Arthur, Texas. After his retirement in 1912, Arthur wrote several books detailing his life and works. Something which attracted particular attention in these memoirs was Stilwell's admission that "brownies" had assisted him throughout his life and career. These creatures visited Stilwell at night and advised him, even supposedly telling him which railways and bridges he should undertake to build next.

Stilwell was not the only engineer who took advice from fae folk. Seymour Roger Cray was an American electrical engineer who designed a series of computers which were, for a long time, the fastest in the world. In 1997 – the year after Cray's death – an article published in *Personal Computer World* revealed some interesting mythology surrounding the man and his methods. It was reported that a former colleague of his, John Rollwagen, told the story of a French scientist who visited Cray in his home. Asked what the secret of his success was, Cray showed his guest a tunnel which he had dug out beneath the building. When he was stuck, Cray told the astonished Frenchman, he would come down to the tunnel and the elves who lived there would help him find a solution. Whether Cray's elves were literal "other folk", or a kind of metaphorical muse, is left up to the reader.

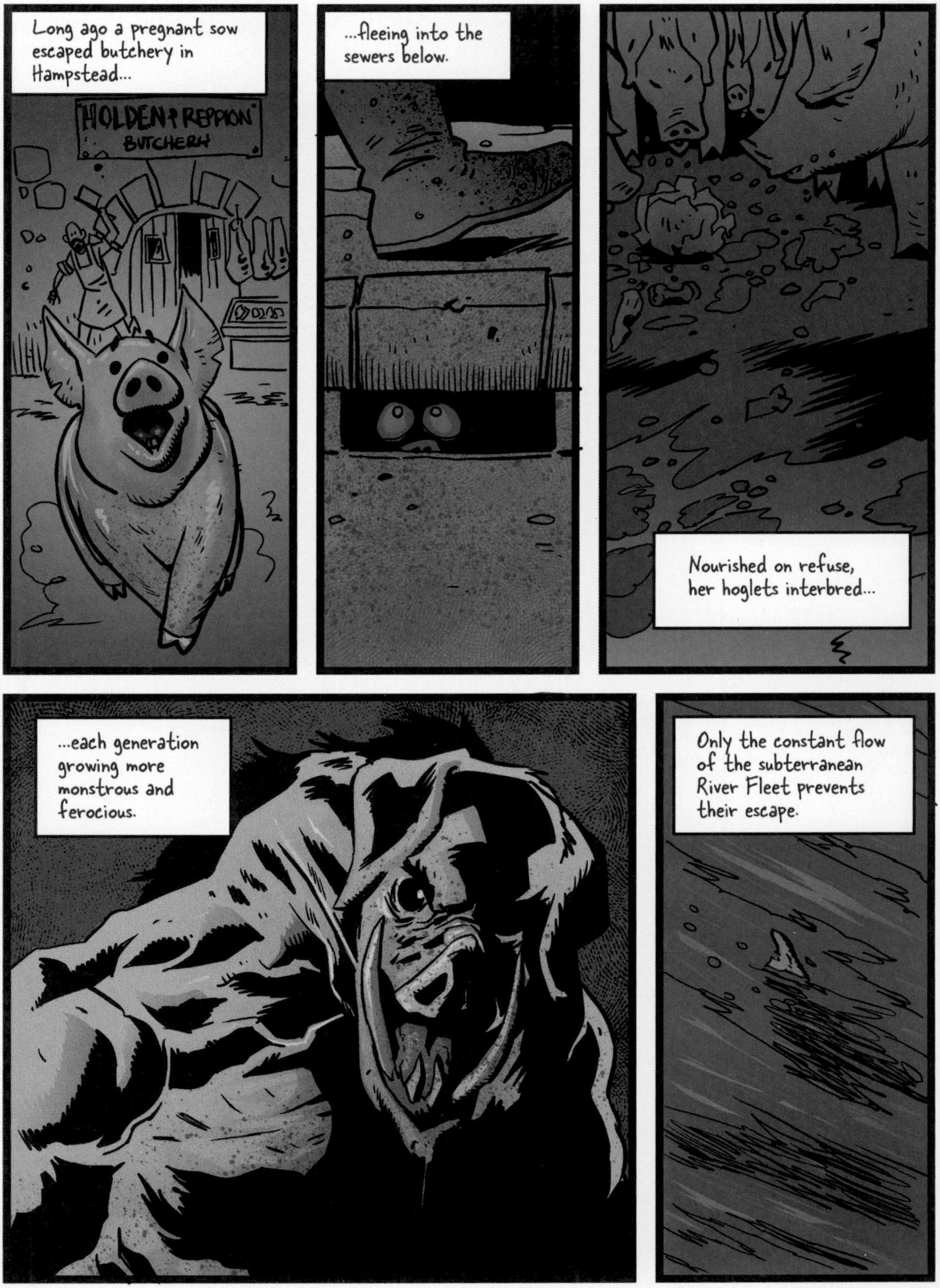
Long ago a pregnant sow escaped butchery in Hampstead...
HOLDEN & REPPION BUTCHERY
...fleeing into the sewers below.
Nourished on refuse, her hoglets interbred...
...each generation growing more monstrous and ferocious.
Only the constant flow of the subterranean River Fleet prevents their escape.

Every day, city-dwellers the world over go about their overground existence, oblivious to the hidden realm beneath their feet and their streets. A labyrinth of sewers and service tunnels – a city under the city – lie below. Exactly who, or what, might make its home down there in that dark domain has long been a fertile area of speculation in folklore and urban legend alike.

In volume two of Henry Mayhew's *London Labour and the London Poor*, published in 1851, the author recorded a very odd, and at the time, current, piece of London legend:

> The story runs, that a sow in young, by some accident got down the sewer through an opening, and reared her offspring in the drain, feeding on the offal and garbage washed into it continually. Here, it is alleged, the breed multiplied exceedingly, and have become almost so ferocious as they are numerous.
>
> This story, apocryphal as it seems, has nevertheless its believers, and it is ingeniously argued that the reason why none of the subterranean animals have been able to make their way to the light of day is that they could only do so by reaching the mouth of the sewer at the river-side, while, in order to arrive at that point, they must necessarily encounter the Fleet ditch, which runs towards the river with great rapidity, and as it is the obstinate nature of a pig to swim against the stream, the wild hogs of the sewers invariably work their way back to their original quarters, and are thus never to be seen.
>
> What seems strange in the matter is, that the inhabitants of Hampstead never have been known to see any of these animals pass beneath the gratings, nor to have been disturbed by their gruntings. The reader of course can believe as much of the story as he pleases, and it is right to inform him that the sewer-hunters themselves have never yet encountered any of the fabulous monsters of the Hampstead sewers.

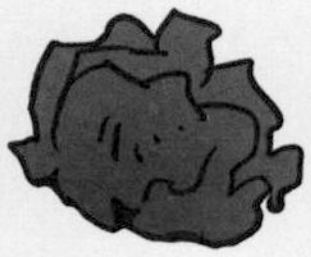

Charles Dickens himself (briefly) mentioned these subterranean monster pigs in a piece published in his own periodical *Household Words*, in 1852:

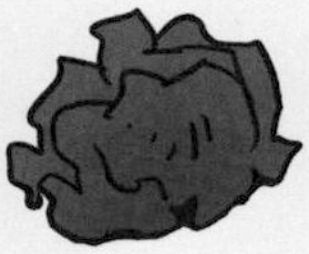

> "We have traditions and superstitions about almost everything in life, from the hogs in Hampstead sewers to the ghosts in a shut-up house."

An article published in the *Daily Telegraph*, on the 10th of October 1859, also mentioned the legend:

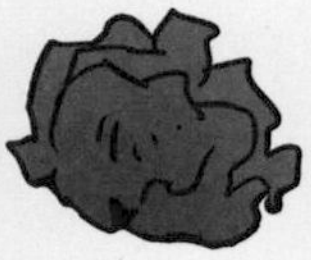

> "It has been said that beasts of chase still roam the verdant fastness of Grosvenor Square, that there are undiscovered patches of primeval forest in Hyde Park, and that Hampstead sewers shelter a monstrous breed of black swine, which has propagated and run wild against the slimy feculence, and whose ferocious snouts will one day up-root Highgate archway, while they make Holloway intolerable with their grunting."

19th-century tales of Hampstead's sewer hogs seem to be the British predecessor of the 20th-century American urban legends of alligators living and breeding in the sewers. Robert Daley's 1959 book *The World Beneath the City* included an interview with a man claiming to have been a New York City sewer commissioner during the 1930s. Under his supervision, this man claimed, a population of sewer gators was discovered and methodically eradicated. Purchased as pets when they were small enough to swim in a fishbowl, the story goes that growing gators were flushed down toilets, surviving to live and breed in the sewers below. It is worth noting, however, that the interviewee in question was later proven to have never been a sewer commissioner – and that the New York City Department of Environmental Protection (who maintain the city's sewers) deny any and all claims of such events.

All of that said, in March 1984, a living Nile crocodile was pulled out of a sewer in Paris. As well as being a romantic tourist destination, Paris has an impressive and elaborate sewer network, parts of which date back to the 14th century. The crocodile, now named Elenore, currently lives at the Aquarium in Vannes. Perhaps then, there is a chance that the descendants of the Hampstead swine are still down there somewhere beneath London's streets, running wild against the "slimy feculence."

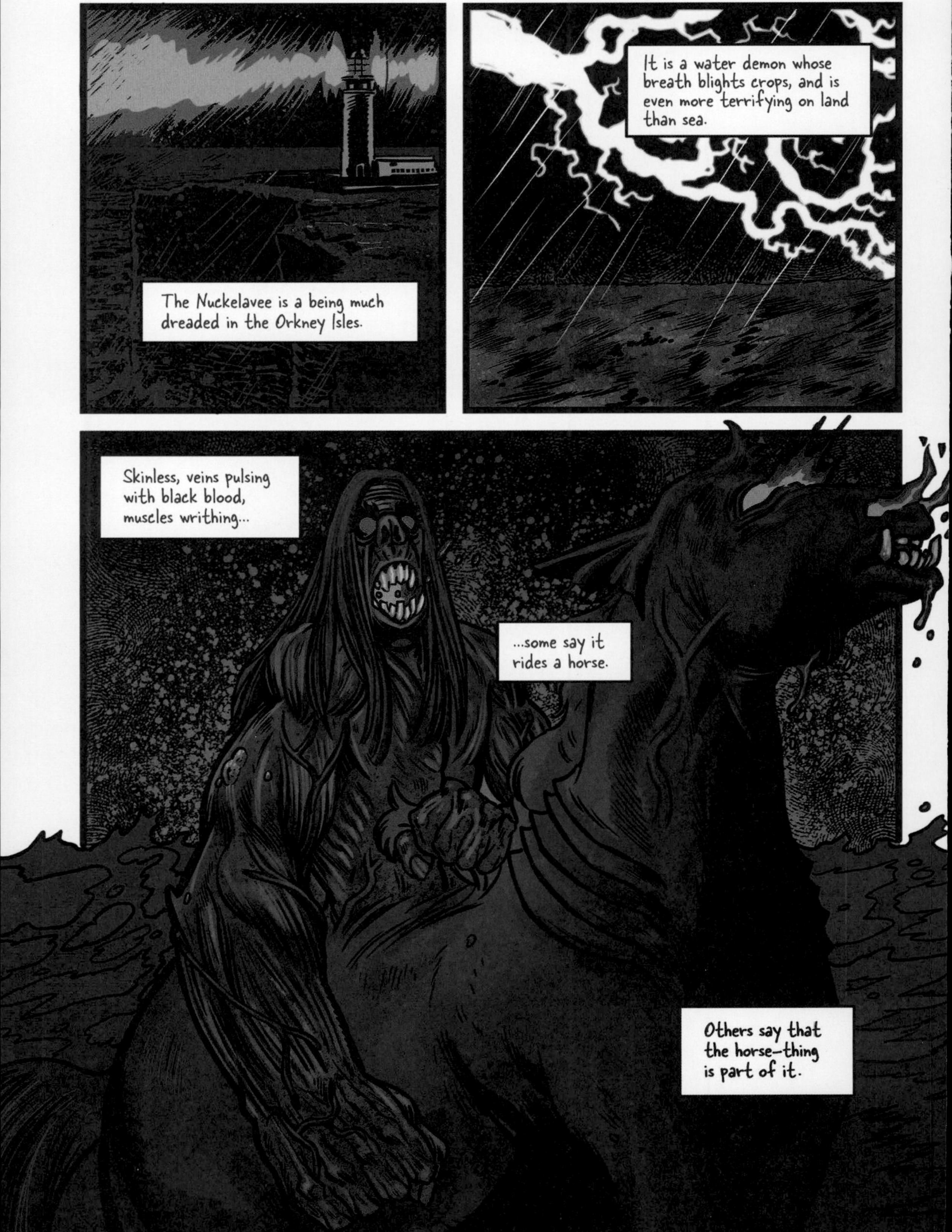
The Nuckelavee is a being much dreaded in the Orkney Isles.
It is a water demon whose breath blights crops, and is even more terrifying on land than sea.
Skinless, veins pulsing with black blood, muscles writhing...
...some say it rides a horse.
Others say that the horse-thing is part of it.

NUCKELAVEE

IN HER 1967 BOOK, *THE FAIRIES IN TRADITION AND LITERATURE*, THE RENOWNED FOLKLORIST Katharine Mary Briggs proclaimed the Nuckelavee the nastiest of all the demons of Scotland's Northern Isles. Living in the sea which surrounds the Isles of Orkney, the Nuckelavee was once often blamed for crop failures ("Nuckelavee's blight"), and animal and human illnesses, all said to be caused by the demon's foul, and poisonous, breath.

This Orcadian devil's direct opposition is the Mither o' the Sea – a life-giving mother goddess who bestows the blessings of spring and of the fruits of summer upon the islanders. Much more powerful than the Nuckelavee, she generally keeps the demon in check. Sometimes, however, the Nuckelavee is able to venture onto land, and it is then that the true horror of the creature may be glimpsed.

In 1891, the Orkney folklorist Walter Traill Dennison tracked down an islander named Tammas who had seen the Nuckelavee in the flesh and lived to tell the tale. Tammas was, apparently, reluctant to tell his tale to Dennison, but with much encouragement did so in the end. The creature Tammas encountered seemed to sit astride something like a huge horse with fins rather than hooves. This equine beast's mouth was "as wide as a whale's" and steam seemed to issue from it, like a boiling kettle. It had a single eye "as red as fire." On this horrific creature's back was something like a huge skinless man. Its head rolled from side to side, and Tammas said he could see black blood pumping through its exposed, yellow veins, and white sinews which twisted as the monster moved. Tammas eventually escaped the nightmarish Nuckelavee by crossing over a rivulet running from a nearby loch; the demon, like many folkloric beasts, apparently having a strange aversion to flowing fresh water.

Originally, it is thought that the horse-thing which the Nuckelavee rode on land may have been a local variation of kelpie, *ceffyl dŵr*, or *bäckahäst* – water-creatures which appear as horses on land to trick humans into mounting them so that they can drown and eat them. As tales of the Nuckelavee were told and re-told, however, the demon and its steed appear to have become permanently fused, resulting in a monster even more bizarre and terrifying than before.

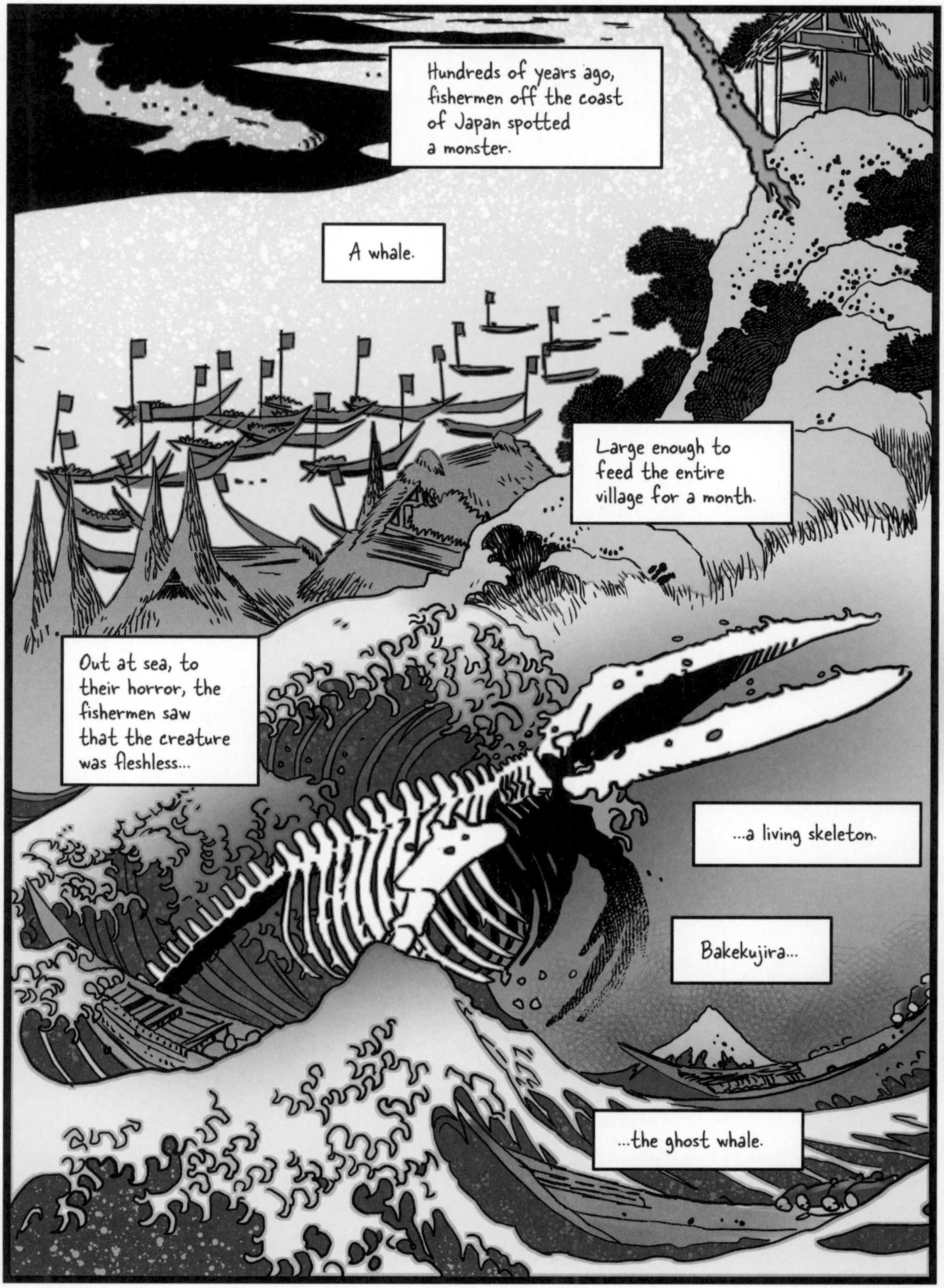
Hundreds of years ago, fishermen off the coast of Japan spotted a monster.
A whale.
Large enough to feed the entire village for a month.
Out at sea, to their horror, the fishermen saw that the creature was fleshless...
...a living skeleton.
Bakekujira...
...the ghost whale.

BAKEKUJIRA

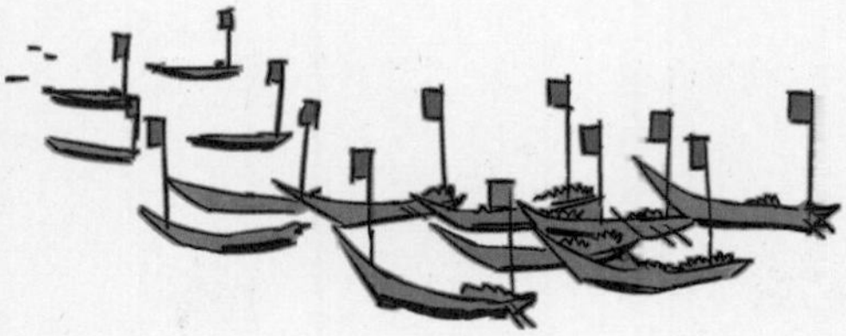

The Bakekujira is a Japanese *yōkai* – a class of supernatural beings which includes what we in the West think of as ghosts, or malevolent spirits. Bakekujira means "ghost whale."

The story goes that, one stormy night, a huge creature was sighted off the coast of Okino Island. Shoals of strange fish swarmed the ocean around the creature, seemingly fleeing ahead of it. Soon, the rain-filled sky above was crowded with strange birds, apparently doing likewise. Out in their boats, fishermen tried to harpoon the beast but, to their horror, their harpoons passed straight through it. The creature was the Bakekujira – a monstrous, fleshless, skeletal whale, somehow moving and swimming as if still alive. To everyone's relief, however, instead of beaching itself as appeared to be its original intention, the creature turned and swam back out to sea.

Japan has a long history of whaling but, up until the 16th century, they lacked the technology to hunt and harpoon whales out in the open ocean. Before this time, many coastal Japanese people practiced what is known as "passive whaling"; that is, they hunted (or in many cases, merely scavenged) whales which had become beached or trapped in shallow waters. The unexpected arrival of these colossal animals, and the vast shoals of fish they drove before them, were understandably seen as a gift from the gods. The whales' flesh, and that of the fleeing fish still swarming in the shallows, was enough for an entire community to feast upon for weeks, if not months.

Whale-based religions with names like Hyochakushin (漂着神 "Drifting Ashore God") and Yorikami Shinkyo (寄り神信仰 "Religion of the Visiting Kami") sprang up in many coastal villages. Kujira Tsuga was the name given to the burial mounds where the bones and other remains of the beached whales were given sacred burials. Monuments and shrines were constructed, sometimes of whale bone, and today more than one hundred whale graveyards (Kujira Haka 鯨墓) still exist across Japan.

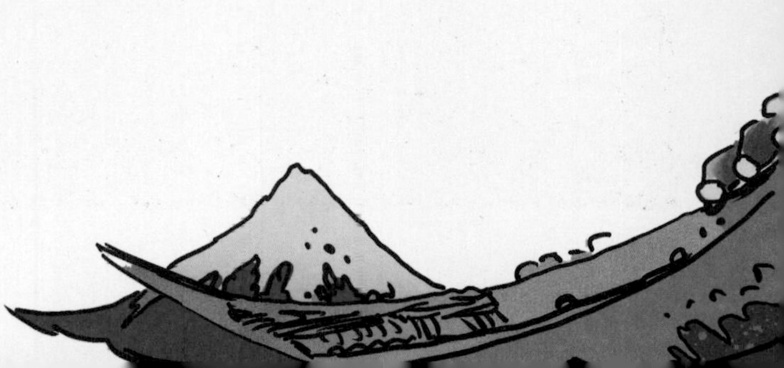

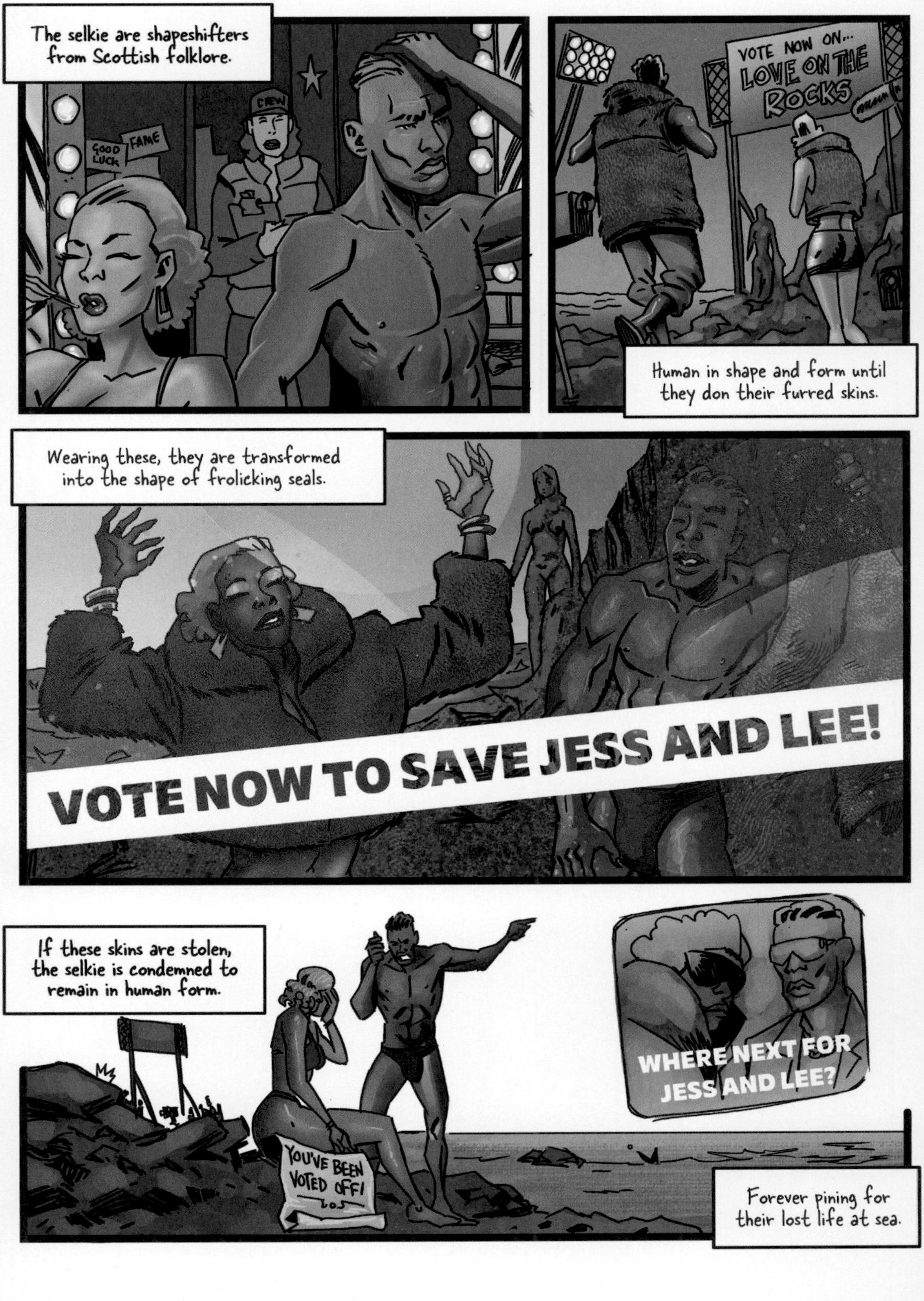
The selkie are shapeshifters from Scottish folklore.
CREW
FAME
GOOD LUCK
VOTE NOW ON... LOVE ON THE ROCKS
Human in shape and form until they don their furred skins.
Wearing these, they are transformed into the shape of frolicking seals.
VOTE NOW TO SAVE JESS AND LEE!
If these skins are stolen, the selkie is condemned to remain in human form.
YOU'VE BEEN VOTED OFF!
WHERE NEXT FOR JESS AND LEE?
Forever pining for their lost life at sea.

SELKIE

THE *SELKIE FOWK* ("SEAL FOLK") ARE SHAPESHIFTERS OF SCOTTISH FOLKLORE. The *merrow* ("sea-maid") of Irish mythology is sometimes also regarded as a seal-woman, as opposed to the more common notion of a mermaid. The 19th-century Scottish folklorist Walter Traill Dennison insisted in his writings that selkies were distinct from mer-folk, because they could transform from their human form into seals, rather than being a permanent terrestrial/aquatic hybrid. This was often done by physically removing the sealskin like a garment and leaving it in a hidden place, according to tales from the Faroe Islands which lie north-north-west of Scotland, and about halfway between Norway and Iceland. The tale was retold as *The Mermaid Wife* in George Douglas' *Scottish Fairy and Folk Tales* (1901):

> A story is told of an inhabitant of Unst, who, in walking on the sandy margin of a voe, saw a number of mermen and mermaids dancing by moonlight, and several seal-skins strewed beside them on the ground. At his approach they immediately fled to secure their garbs, and, taking upon themselves the form of seals, plunged immediately into the sea. But as the Shetlander perceived that one skin lay close to his feet, he snatched it up, bore it swiftly away, and placed it in concealment. On returning to the shore he met the fairest damsel that was ever gazed upon by mortal eyes, lamenting the robbery, by which she had become an exile from her submarine friends, and a tenant of the upper world. Vainly she implored the restitution of her property; the man had drunk deeply of love and was inexorable, but he offered her protection beneath his roof as his betrothed spouse. The merlady, perceiving that she must become an inhabitant of the earth, found that she could not do better than accept the offer.

As in most variants of the story, the seal-woman bears the children of her human captor/suitor, but ultimately deserts both him and them when she has an opportunity to return to the sea and the seal-people.

Folklore is sometimes like a conjuring trick: you desperately want to get to the bottom of it all, but when you do it only leaves you feeling disappointed and wishing you hadn't. In *The Testimony of Tradition*, Scottish folklorist and antiquarian David MacRitchie puts forward the theory that the sea-skins of the selkies were exactly what they appeared to be. Scandinavian fisher-folk, clad in sealskins and paddling seal-skin lined canoes, arrived long ago on the shores of Scotland and Ireland. Steal their boats and their weather-proof gear, and they would be unable to leave. Trapped. Forced to stay, they might become wives and husbands – mothers and fathers – but there will always be that longing to return to their people. To don their sealskins and plunge into the waves from whence they came.

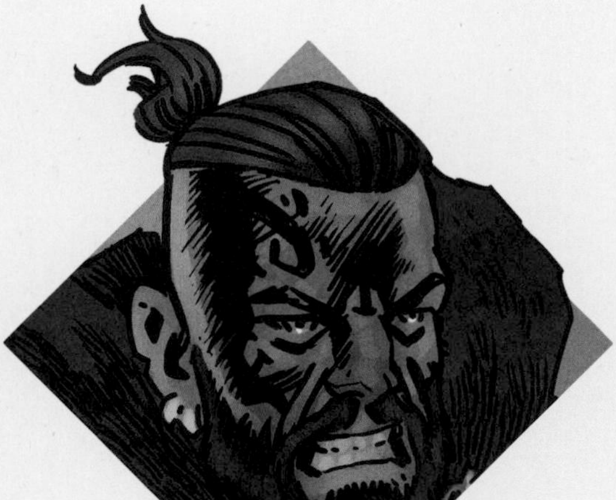

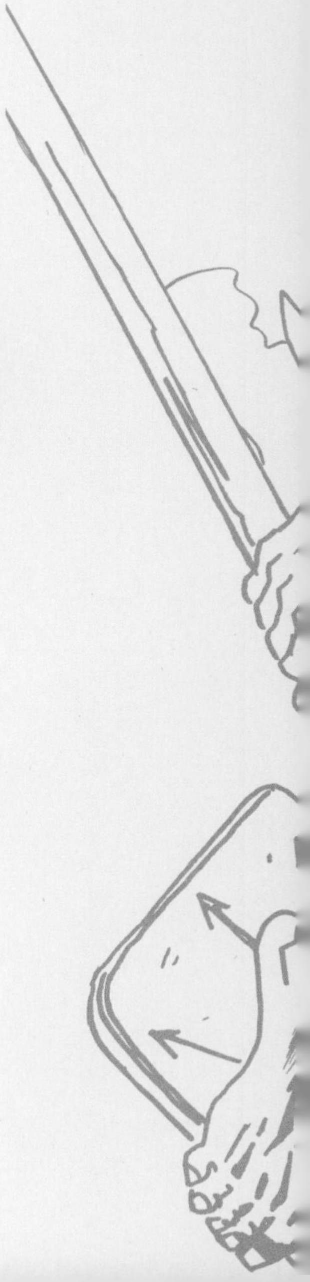

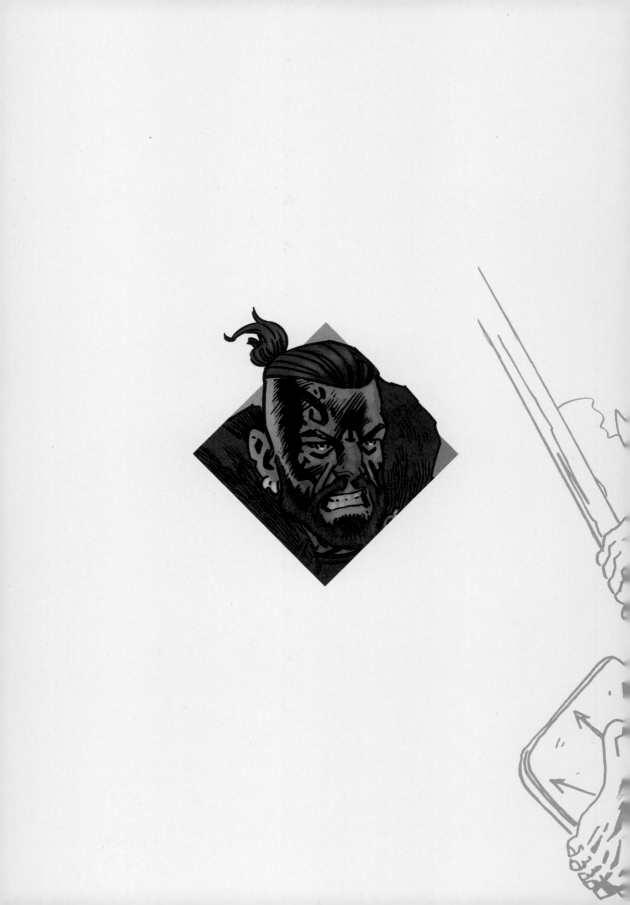

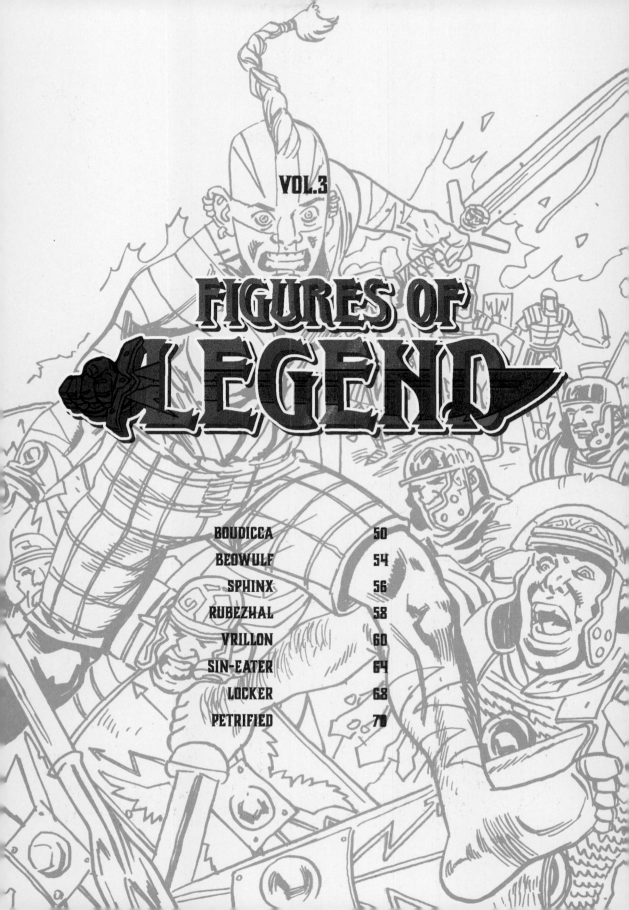

VOL.3

FIGURES OF LEGEND

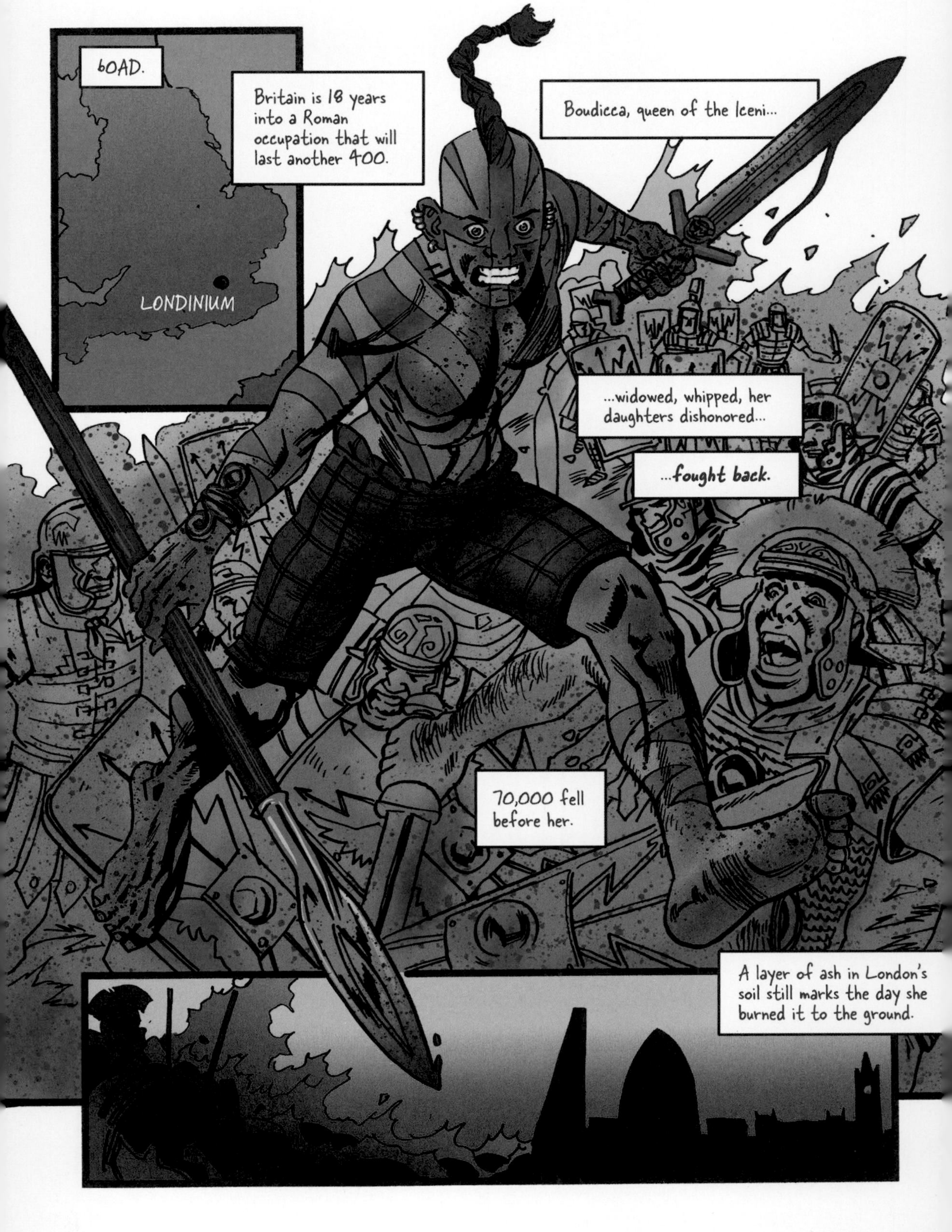
60AD.
Britain is 18 years into a Roman occupation that will last another 400.
LONDINIUM
Boudicca, queen of the Iceni...
...widowed, whipped, her daughters dishonored...
...fought back.
70,000 fell before her.
A layer of ash in London's soil still marks the day she burned it to the ground.

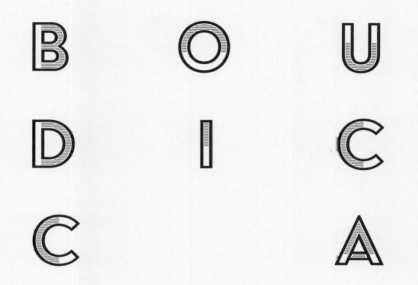

BOUDICCA

LITTLE IS KNOWN OF THE EARLY LIFE OF THE WARRIOR WE NOW KNOW AS BOUDICCA. It is believed that she was born into a noble family in what is now Eastern England around 25 CE. Around the age of twenty, Boudicca married Prasutagus, king of the Iceni tribe, who lived in what is now Norfolk. The Iceni were one of only six tribes who had allied themselves with Rome when Gaius Julius Caesar made the first attempts at conquering Britannia in 55 BCE. In 43 CE, under the fourth emperor, Claudius, what was to prove the final Roman invasion of Britain began. When the Romans arrived, the Iceni did not resist the occupation, ultimately believing they could coexist with, and benefit from, the Roman Empire.

Boudicca and Prasutagus had two daughters and, although Rome continued to make further gains and grew ever more tyrannical, all seemed well up until the king's death in 60 CE. Prasutagus had left instructions that his wife and daughters inherit his kingdom, but this was not the Roman way. Roman procurator, Decianus Catus, arrived at the Iceni court with his staff and a military guard. He proceeded to take inventory of the estate which now, as far as he was concerned, belonged to Rome. When Boudicca objected, Catus had her publicly flogged, and the princesses raped.

In 60 CE, while the Roman governor Gaius Suetonius Paullinus was occupied with a campaign on the island of Mona (modern Anglesey) in North Wales, Boudicca led her own force comprised of the Iceni, their neighbors the Trinovantes, and others, in a bloody rebellion. The Roman capital of Britain, Camulodunum (Colchester today), was the first place they attacked. The Roman veterans who had settled there mistreated the locals and had erected a temple to Emperor Claudius at local expense, making the city a focus for Celtic resentment. Boudicca and her army destroyed both the temple and the city itself, burning its buildings and killing everyone within. The Romans sent Legion IX Hispania (consisting of 4,000 well-trained men), under command of Quintus Petillius Cerialis, to quash the rebellion, but Boudicca's forces ambushed them and only the commander and some of his cavalry escaped.

The seemingly unstoppable rebel army next turned its wrath against the relatively new settlement of Londinium (London). Gaius Suetonius Paullinus, having heard of the rebellion, had already made his way there from Wales but concluded that the town was impossible to defend against such an army. The governor ordered an evacuation, but many stayed. All who did so were slain. Archaeological evidence shows a thick, red layer of burnt debris within the bounds of Roman Londinium. As it covers coins and pottery dating before 60 CE, this debris layer proves that Boudicca's forces burned the settlement to the ground. Next on her agenda was Verulamium (near Saint Albans), which was likewise destroyed and burned to the ground.

In all, some 75,000 to 80,000 Romans and Roman allies are thought to have been killed by Boudicca's forces. The Roman historian Publius Cornelius Tacitus recorded that the Britons took no prisoners whatsoever – they killed everyone and showed no mercy, just as the Romans had shown none to Boudicca and her daughters.

While the rebels were occupied with the destruction of Verulamium, however, governor Paullinus gathered a force of 10,000 Roman soldiers. In 61 CE, he took a stand at an unidentified location (probably in the West Midlands, somewhere along the Roman road now known as Watling Street) and went head-to-head with the rebel army thought to be some 200,000 strong by this time. Boudicca commanded her troops from her chariot, her daughters beside her. She is recorded to have made a speech saying that their cause was just, and the deities were on their side; the one legion that had dared to face them had been destroyed. She, a woman, was resolved to win or die. If the men wanted to live in slavery, that was their choice.

Despite being vastly outnumbered, through the use of superior weaponry and military tactics (including a well-chosen battleground), the Romans defeated the rebel army that day. Boudicca is said to have poisoned herself rather than face capture or death at the hands of Rome.

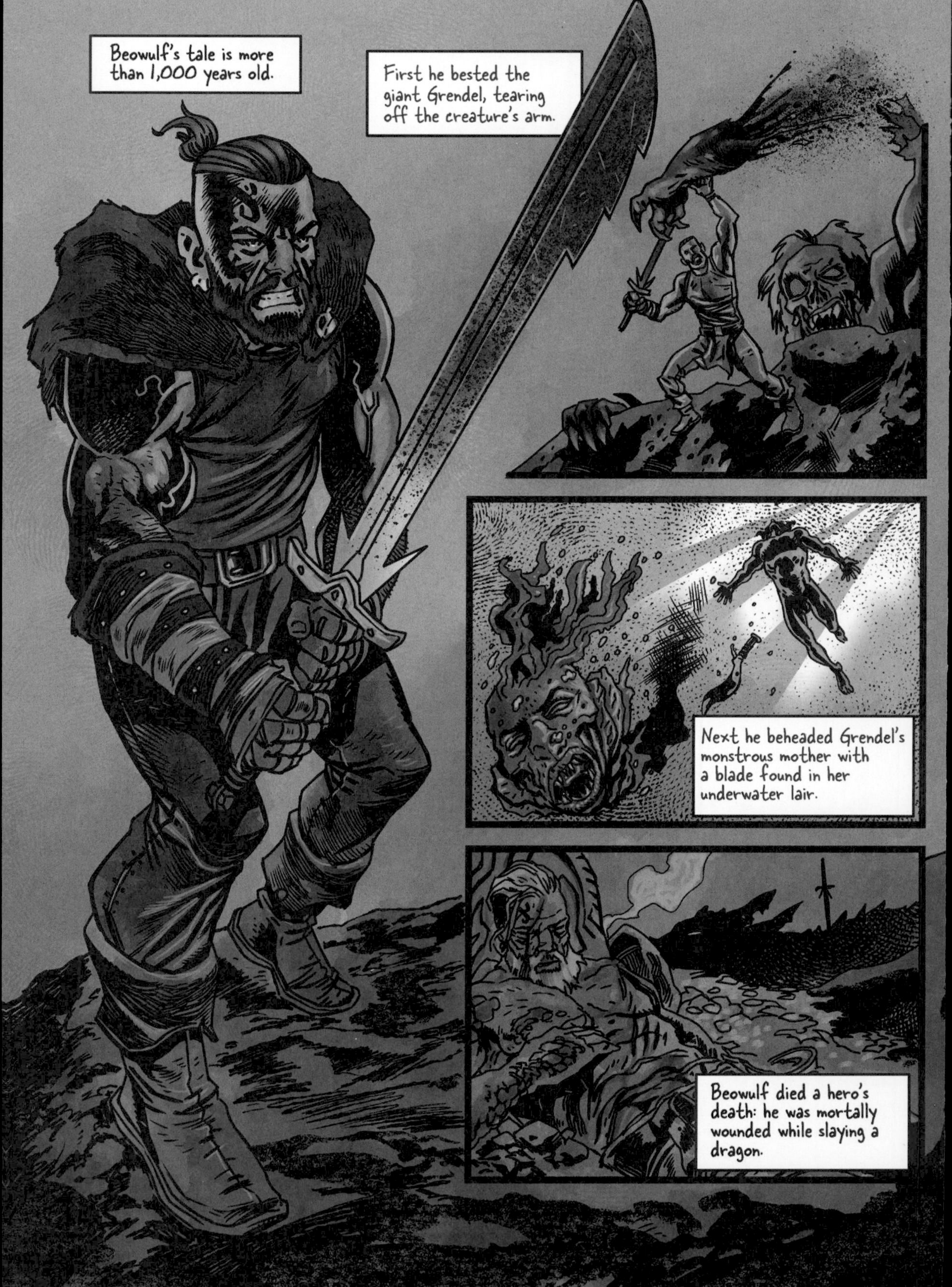
Beowulf's tale is more than 1,000 years old.
First he bested the giant Grendel, tearing off the creature's arm.
Next he beheaded Grendel's monstrous mother with a blade found in her underwater lair.
Beowulf died a hero's death: he was mortally wounded while slaying a dragon.

BEOWULF

The oldest extant version of the epic of Beowulf was written around 1000 CE, though the tale itself is believed to have originated circa 700 CE. Written in Old English, the 1000-CE text uses a mixture of dialects – Mercian, Northumbrian, Early West Saxon, Kentish and Late West Saxon – making it something of a linguistic patchwork.

The hero Beowulf was a member of the North Germanic tribe who inhabited Götaland, known as the Geats, or the Goths. In the poem, Beowulf came to the aid of King Hrothgar of the Danes who had built a vast mead-hall named Heorot where he, his wife, Wealhtheow, and his men drank and sang. Their music and merriment were loud enough to be overheard by Grendel – a troll-like monster, said to be descended from the biblical Cain – who could not stand the sound. Grendel attacked the hall while everyone slept and slaughtered many of Hrothgar's men, causing the king and his people to abandon the place.

Beowulf traveled to the hall and, refusing all weapons, lay in wait for Grendel, pretending to be asleep. When the monster entered Heorot, Beowulf's companions leapt to his aid, but none of their weapons could pierce Grendel's flesh. Wrestling with the beast, Beowulf tore off Grendel's arm at the shoulder using his bare hands.

Grendel retreated to the underwater cave from whence he came, and the arm was displayed in Heorot as a trophy. This angered Grendel's mother; described in the poem as "aglæc-wif," her title has been interpreted both as "wretch, or monster of a woman" but also as "warrior, or hero." She rose from the water to exact revenge, killing Hrothgar's most mighty fighter Æschere. So, Beowulf and his men returned to Hrothgar's land to hunt her down.

Beowulf jumped into the swamp, fought off a few water-monsters on the way down, and entered the cave where Grendel and his mother lived. Grendel's mother appeared impervious to all weapons and seemed certain to kill Beowulf until he laid his hand on a giant sword stored amongst the other loot in her cave. Beheading Grendel's mother, Beowulf also found the corpse of Grendel and removed its head. The mighty sword's blade melted away to nothing from the monster's corrosive blood. Beowulf emerged from the lake with Grendel's head in one hand, and the hilt of the gigantic sword in the other.

Beowulf, now a rich and famous hero, became king of the Geats. Fifty years after Beowulf's battle with Grendel's mother, a slave stole a golden cup from the treasure hoard of a dragon in Earnanæs, Sweden. The furious dragon went on a murderous rampage, and Beowulf was the only man who could stop it. Ever the hero, Beowulf said he would battle the dragon alone, but he was followed by a warrior named Wiglaf into the fight. Between the two, they slew the dragon, but Beowulf was mortally wounded. His body was ritually burned on a great pyre, and a barrow was built in memorial to the great hero, King Beowulf.

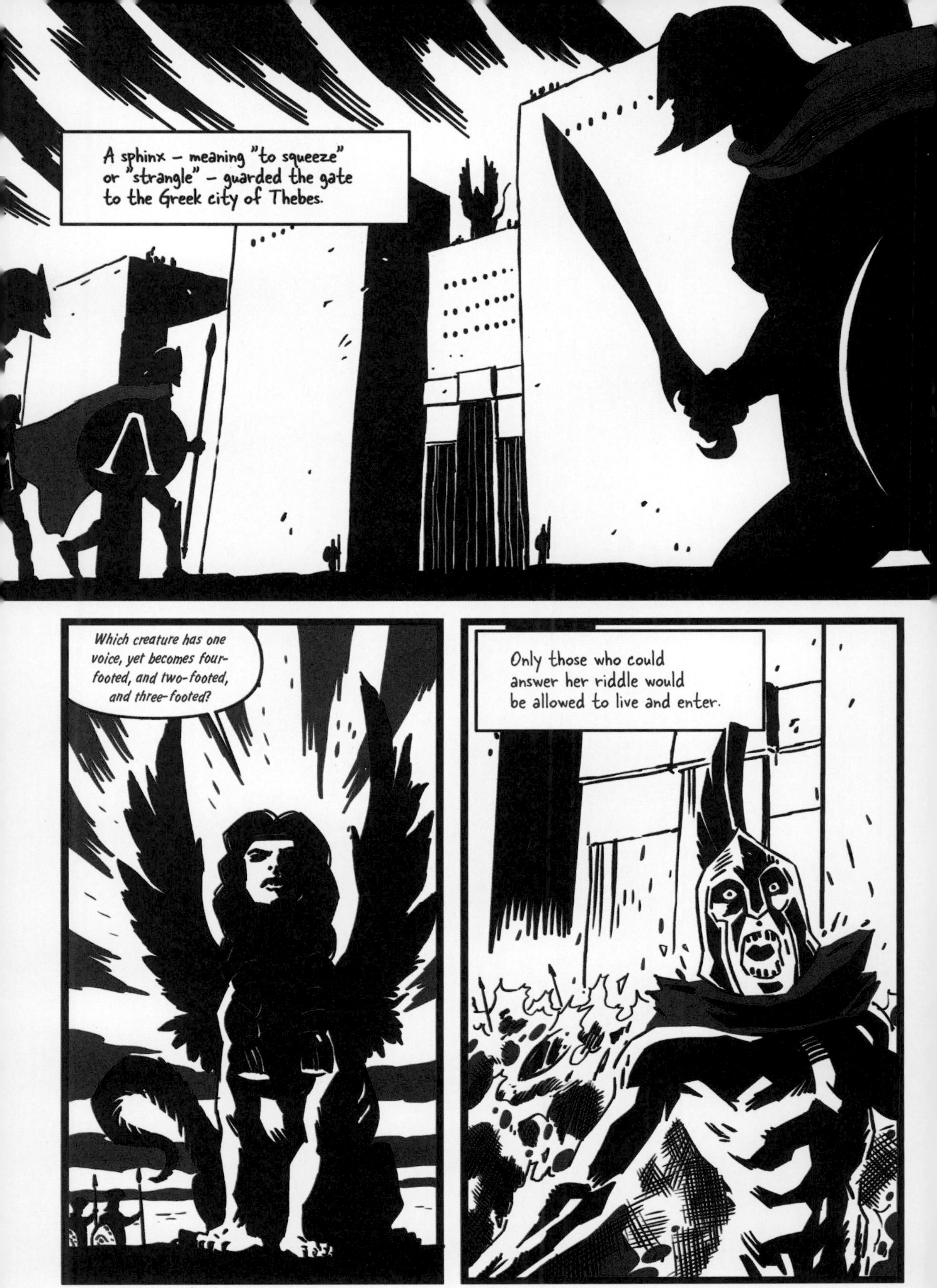
A sphinx – meaning "to squeeze" or "strangle" – guarded the gate to the Greek city of Thebes.
Which creature has one voice, yet becomes four-footed, and two-footed, and three-footed?
Only those who could answer her riddle would be allowed to live and enter.

THE WORD "SPHINX" MEANS "TO SQUEEZE OR STRANGLE" – modern terms like "asphyxia" having the same root. In Greek mythology, sphinxes are depicted as a chimera of human woman, lion, and falcon. Egyptian sphinxes, like those which famously guard the Great Pyramid at Giza, lack the falcon's wings, and are human/lion hybrids.

A sphinx features in *Oedipus Tyrannus*, a tragedy written by the ancient Greek playwright Sophocles, which was first performed in 429 BCE. Better known today as *Oedipus Rex*, it is the story of the mythical Greek king Oedipus, and his tragic adventures.

Oedipus encountered a sphinx en route to Thebes in Egypt. This sphinx would ask all travelers upon that road a riddle. Those who could not correctly answer the sphinx's riddle would be devoured by the monster. Those who could were allowed to go on their way. The sphinx asked Oedipus: "What walks on four feet in the morning, two in the afternoon, and three at night?" The tragic hero king knew that the answer was man, who crawls in the morning of his life, walks on two legs in the afternoon, and walks with the aid of a stick in his twilight years. And so, Oedipus was granted leave to continue on his journey.

Stylized sphinxes became a popular feature of sculpture and art in Europe from the 15th century onwards. The ancient-Egyptian architectural revivalism of 18th-century Europe saw an increase in sphinxes and pyramids as decorative motifs. Later, 19th- and 20th-century occultists like Aleister Crowley and Austin Osman Spare helped to popularize the magical significance of ancient Egyptian symbolism, the sphinx itself being officially adopted by the Freemasons as part of their iconography in the early 20th century.

The obelisk known as Cleopatra's Needle, originally constructed almost 4,000 years ago, today stands beside the river Thames in London, England. The monument – actually constructed in honor of Pharaoh Thutmose III – was transported from Egypt to London in 1878 and erected on the Thames Embankment. Two bronze Victorian sphinxes flank the ancient stone, watching over it just as the Great Sphinx still watches over the Great Pyramid in Egypt. The obelisk's twin was transported to the USA in 1881 and installed in Central Park, just west of Manhattan's Metropolitan Museum of Art.

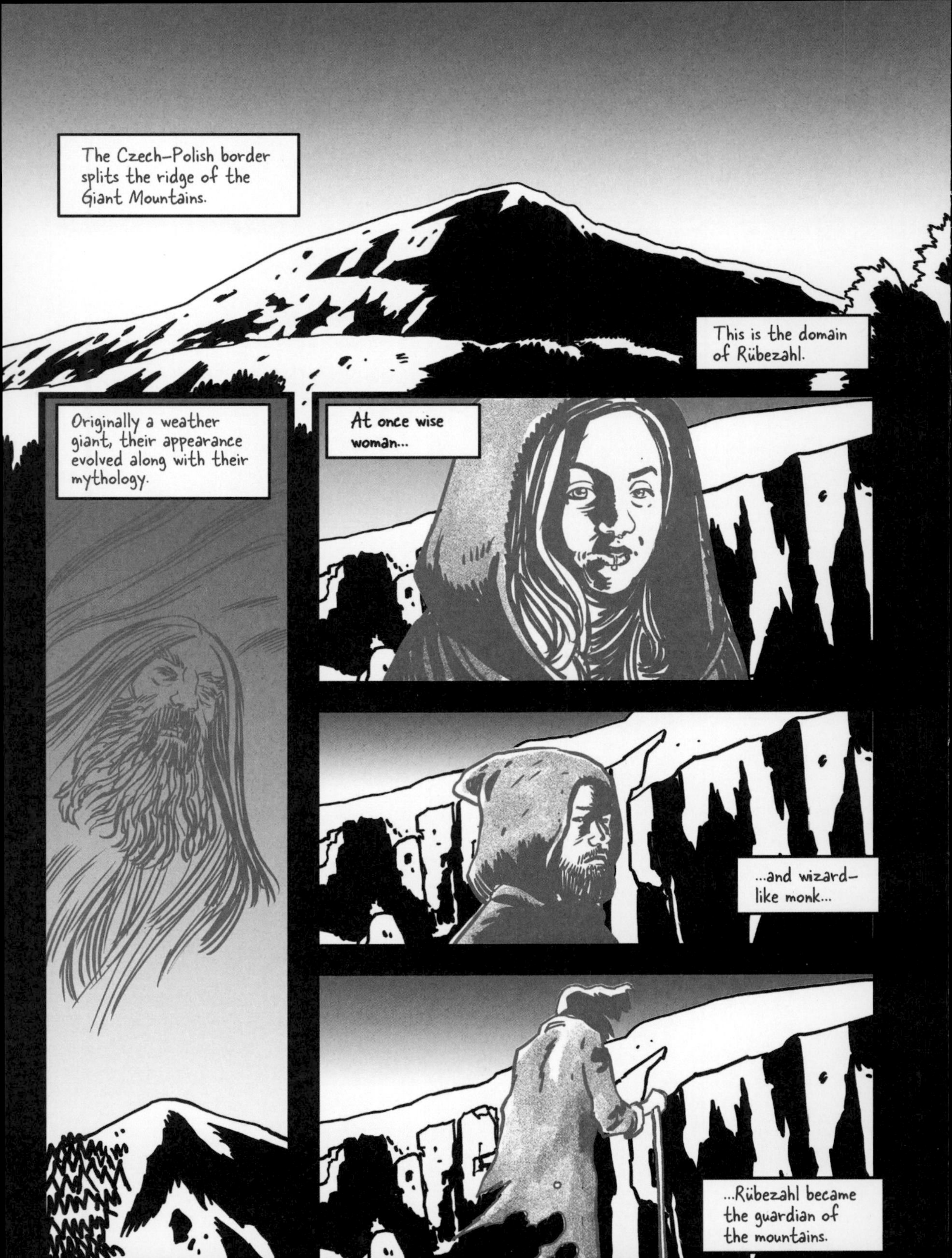
The Czech–Polish border splits the ridge of the Giant Mountains.
This is the domain of Rübezahl.
Originally a weather giant, their appearance evolved along with their mythology.
At once wise woman...
...and wizard-like monk...
...Rübezahl became the guardian of the mountains.

RÜBEZAHL

In 1561, the German cartographer Martin Helwig created a beautifully detailed map of Silesia (a historical region of Central Europe which is now mostly Poland, but also included parts of the Czech Republic and Germany). On the Riesengebirge mountain range (now known as the Giant Mountains) Helwig drew a strange figure: a shaggy-legged, stag-like creature, standing on two feet and holding a tall staff in its hands. Beneath it he wrote "Rübezahl."

In his 1904 book, *The Brown Fairy Book*, Andrew Lang retold an old Silesian story, 'Rübezahl', first recorded in print by Johann Karl August Musäus in his *Volksmärchen der Deutschen* ("Folktales of the Germans"), published in 1791. In Lang's story we learn that the being known as Rübezahl kidnaps a beautiful princess, trying to keep her entertained by using his magic to transform turnips into the likenesses of the friends and family she has left behind. As the enchanted vegetables wither their human forms also grow soft and weak, however, and so Rübezahl is forced to quest for more and more turnips. Eventually the princess makes good her escape while Rübezahl is busy counting all the turnips in a field, and this is where his nickname comes from: *rübe* ("turnips") *zählen* ("count") – "Turnip Counter." As such, the name is actually an insult, and a reminder of a time when the creature was outsmarted. More respectful terms of address include Lord of the Mountain, Treasure Keeper, Lord John, and Prince of the Gnomes.

It is believed that the creature or deity thought to inhabit the Giant Mountains began its life as a weather giant, like the Norse *jötnar*[1] (also known as trolls). The Norse god Odin was said to be a descendant of the jötnar, and soon the giant Rübezahl seems to have taken on the manner and appearance of his cousin, becoming a bearded, monk-like figure dressed all in gray (and making him, as some people theorize, the inspiration for Tolkien's Gandalf the Grey). Able to change shape at will, Rübezahl would sometimes take the form of animals and birds. Sometimes he becomes a she, taking up the mantle of wise woman, or the guise of a helpless old lady in distress in order to test the heart of any human she encounters. Strangely though, no extant tales of Rübezahl seem to even hint at the bizarre, demonic stag-like form as depicted by Martin Helwig in the 16th century.

---

1   See 'Skaði' (pg. 78)

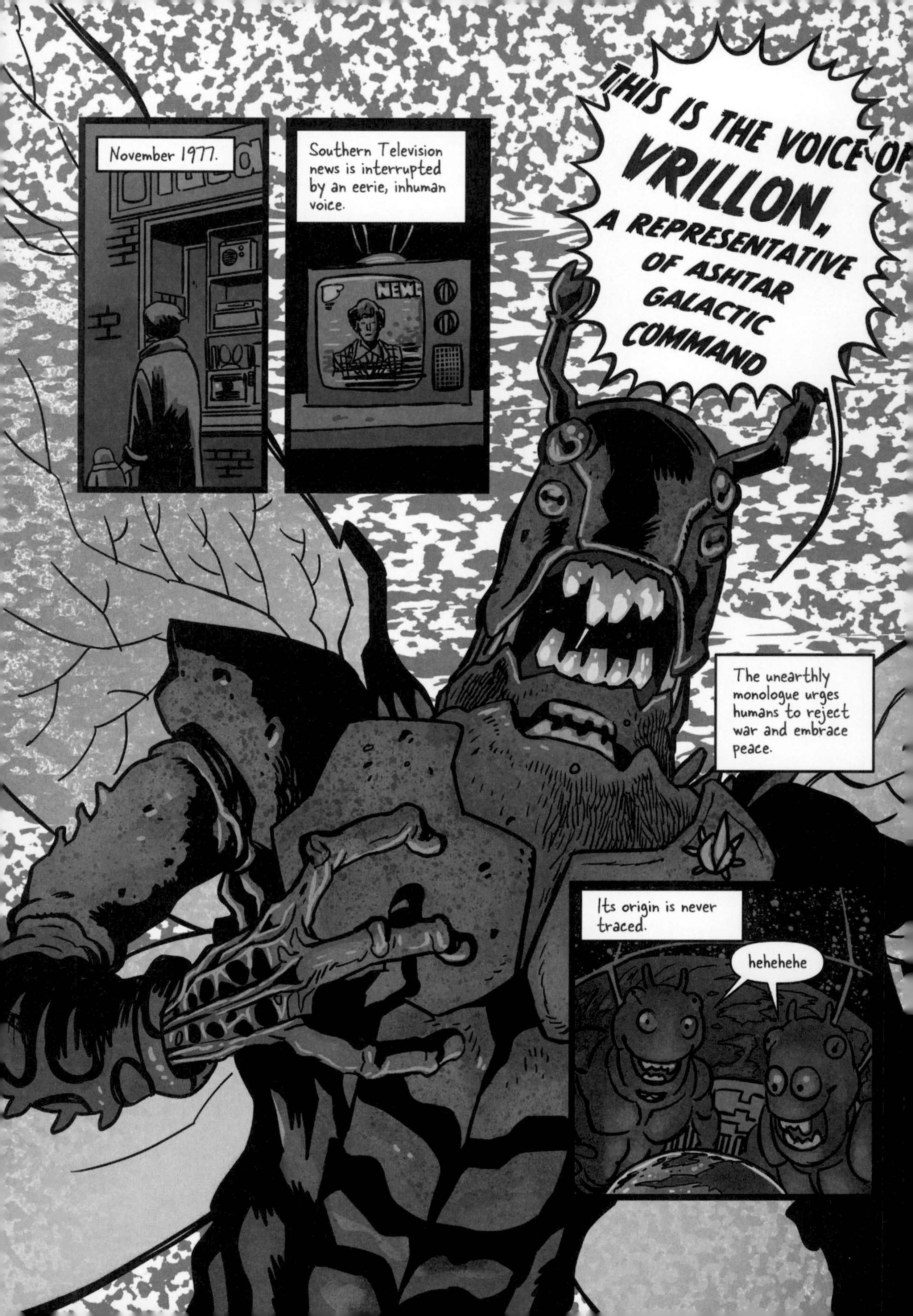
November 1977.
Southern Television news is interrupted by an eerie, inhuman voice.
NEWS
THIS IS THE VOICE OF VRILLON, A REPRESENTATIVE OF ASHTAR GALACTIC COMMAND
The unearthly monologue urges humans to reject war and embrace peace.
Its origin is never traced.
hehehehe

VRILLON

SOUTHERN TELEVISION WAS AN ENGLISH REGIONAL STATION, broadcasting to an area bordered by Weymouth in the west, Newbury in the north, and Brighton in the east. On Saturday the 26th of November 1977, at eleven minutes past five in the afternoon, news anchor Andrew Gardner was relating the headlines when viewers of the Southern Television broadcast noticed something strange. His image wavering, Gardner's sober tones were replaced with a gargling, unearthly voice, which began to relate the following message:

> This is the voice of Vrillon, a representative of the Ashtar Galactic Command, speaking to you. For many years you have seen us as lights in the skies. We speak to you now in peace and wisdom as we have done to your brothers and sisters all over this, your planet Earth. We come to warn you of the destiny of your race so that you may communicate to your fellow beings the course you must take to avoid the disaster which threatens your world, and the beings on our worlds around you.
>
> This is in order that you may share in the great awakening, as the planet passes into the New Age of Aquarius.

The Age of Aquarius refers to the heyday of the New Age and counter-cultural movements of the 1960s. Astronomically, the phrase is scientifically meaningless, the Age of Aquarius being a purely astrological idea. If the voice of Vrillon was that of an extra-terrestrial, it does seem strange for them to reference such an unscientific, earthly concept. Vrillon continued:

> All your weapons of evil must be removed. The time for conflict is now past and the race of which you are a part may proceed to the higher stages of its evolution if you show yourselves worthy to do this.

This warning would have been particularly relevant to a certain section of Southern TV's audience. Superimposed over a flickering yet oblivious Andrew Gardner, Vrillon's voice was broadcast to Aldermaston, Berkshire – home to the headquarters of the Atomic Weapons Research Establishment. Demonstrations against nuclear conflict took Aldermaston's name, to protest the research and testing of atomic weapons on the site. The Aldermaston Marches were organized by the Campaign for Nuclear Disarmament and occurred annually from the late 1950s onwards. During the 1960s, tens of thousands of protestors participated, but by Vrillon's broadcast in 1977, numbers had dwindled to mere hundreds. Other AWRE sites in West Berkshire and Reading also fell within Southern Television's broadcast area. Many viewers would, therefore, have understood what these "weapons of evil" were all too well – and may even have campaigned against the weapons themselves.

Vrillon went on to warn of false prophets who "suck the energy you call money and will put it to evil ends and give you worthless dross in return." Clearly then, the Ashtar Galactic Command was not only keen on horoscopes and nuclear disarmament but was also anti-capitalist. After reassuring viewers that the Ashtar Galactic Command would do all it could to help guide humankind onto its "path of evolution," Vrillon signed off, saying:

> May you be blessed by the supreme love and truth of the cosmos.

Operating in the pre-digital era, Southern Television used a series of masts to receive signals (via UHF and VHF radio waves) before relaying them on. It has been hypothesized that someone was able to place a transmitter within range of one of these masts, broadcasting audio which was then relayed by Southern Television's own technology. Homemade radio transmitters were already used by so-called "pirate radio" (illegal broadcasts). Pirate radio had enjoyed huge success during the 1960s in the UK but, thanks to new laws introduced at the end of the decade, pirate broadcasts were transformed into something much more guerilla, DIY, and subversive.

The source of Vrillon's voice has never been determined and no one (terrestrial or otherwise) has ever come forward to claim responsibility. But whoever broadcast the signal chose their time wisely: by interrupting the local news on Saturday afternoon, the voice of Vrillon was heard by as many people as possible. Sadly, however, their message of intergalactic peace and love did not have quite the history-altering impact they seem to have intended.

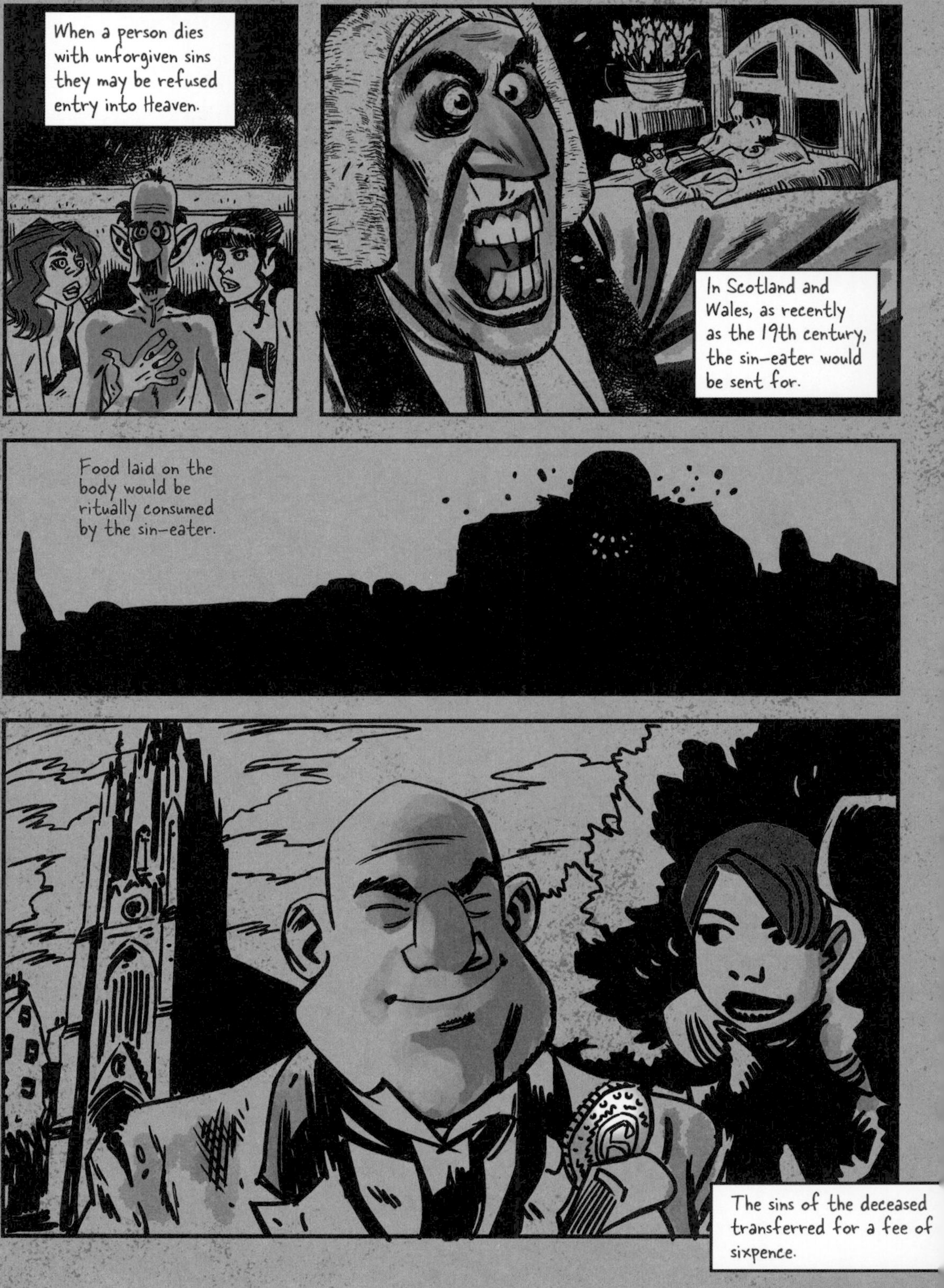
When a person dies with unforgiven sins they may be refused entry into Heaven.
In Scotland and Wales, as recently as the 19th century, the sin-eater would be sent for.
Food laid on the body would be ritually consumed by the sin-eater.
The sins of the deceased transferred for a fee of sixpence.

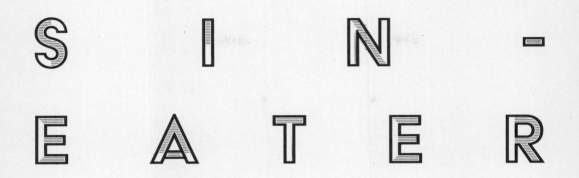

SIN-EATER

SIN-EATING WAS A RITUAL MEANS OF ABSORBING, RATHER THAN ABSOLVING, THE SINS OF THE dying or newly deceased[1], and was once practiced in parts of England, Wales, and Scotland. In his 1926 work, *Funeral Customs: Their Origin and Development*, Bertram S. Puckle outlined the (by then already endangered) role of the professional sin-eater:

> A less known but even more remarkable functionary, whose professional services were once considered necessary to the dead, is the sin-eater. [...] It was the province of the human scapegoat to take upon himself the moral trespasses of his client – and whatever the consequences might be in the after life – in return for a miserable fee and a scanty meal.

In his 1895 essay, *Burial Customs*, England Howlett F.S.A. recorded the following details of the ritual, and its purpose:

> The corpse being taken out of the house, and laid on a bier, a loaf of bread was given to the sin-eater over the corpse, also a maga-bowl of maple, full of beer. These consumed, a fee of sixpence was given him for the consideration of his taking upon himself the sins of the deceased, who, thus freed, would not walk after death.

Their sins absorbed by the sin-eater, the soul of the deceased would therefore be guaranteed entry into the heavenly hereafter. The sin-eater, on the other hand, carried the sins of many with them, and so lived as an outcast. Puckle recorded a (second-hand) meeting with a Welsh sin-eater, which had occurred a century earlier:

> Professor Evans of the Presbyterian College, Carmarthen, actually saw a sin-eater about the year 1825, who was then living near Llanwenog, Cardiganshire. Abhorred by the superstitious villagers as a thing unclean, the sin-eater cut himself off from all social intercourse with his fellow creatures by reason of the life he had chosen; he lived as a rule in a remote place by himself, and those who chanced to meet him avoided him as they would a leper.

This unfortunate was held to be the associate of evil spirits, and given to witchcraft,

---

1   For more funeral and gravesite customs, see 'Willow' (pg. 22) and 'Hallowe'en' (pg. 100).

incantations and unholy practices; only when a death took place did they seek him out, and when his purpose was accomplished they burned the wooden bowl and platter from which he had eaten the food handed across, or placed on the corpse for his consumption.

While Puckle wrote of sin-eating as a practice already all-but-extinct by the end of the 19th century, and concurrent sources repeat the idea that sin-eaters were pariahs, there appears to be some evidence to the contrary.

Richard Munslow was buried in Ratlinghope village, Shropshire, England in 1906. Munslow was a well-respected farmer in the area, but he was also a sin-eater: possibly the very last sin-eater in England. In 2010, locals raised £1000 to restore Munslow's grave which had fallen into disrepair.

The Reverend Norman Morris, the vicar of Ratlinghope, led a service for Munslow at St Margaret's Church on the day the restored headstone was placed. Interviewed at the time, the Reverend told the BBC that, though sin-eating would not have been officially approved by the Church, it was likely that reverends had turned a blind eye to the practice at the time. He went on to say that, although the custom was an important and fascinating one, he had no desire to see the ritual restored in modern times.

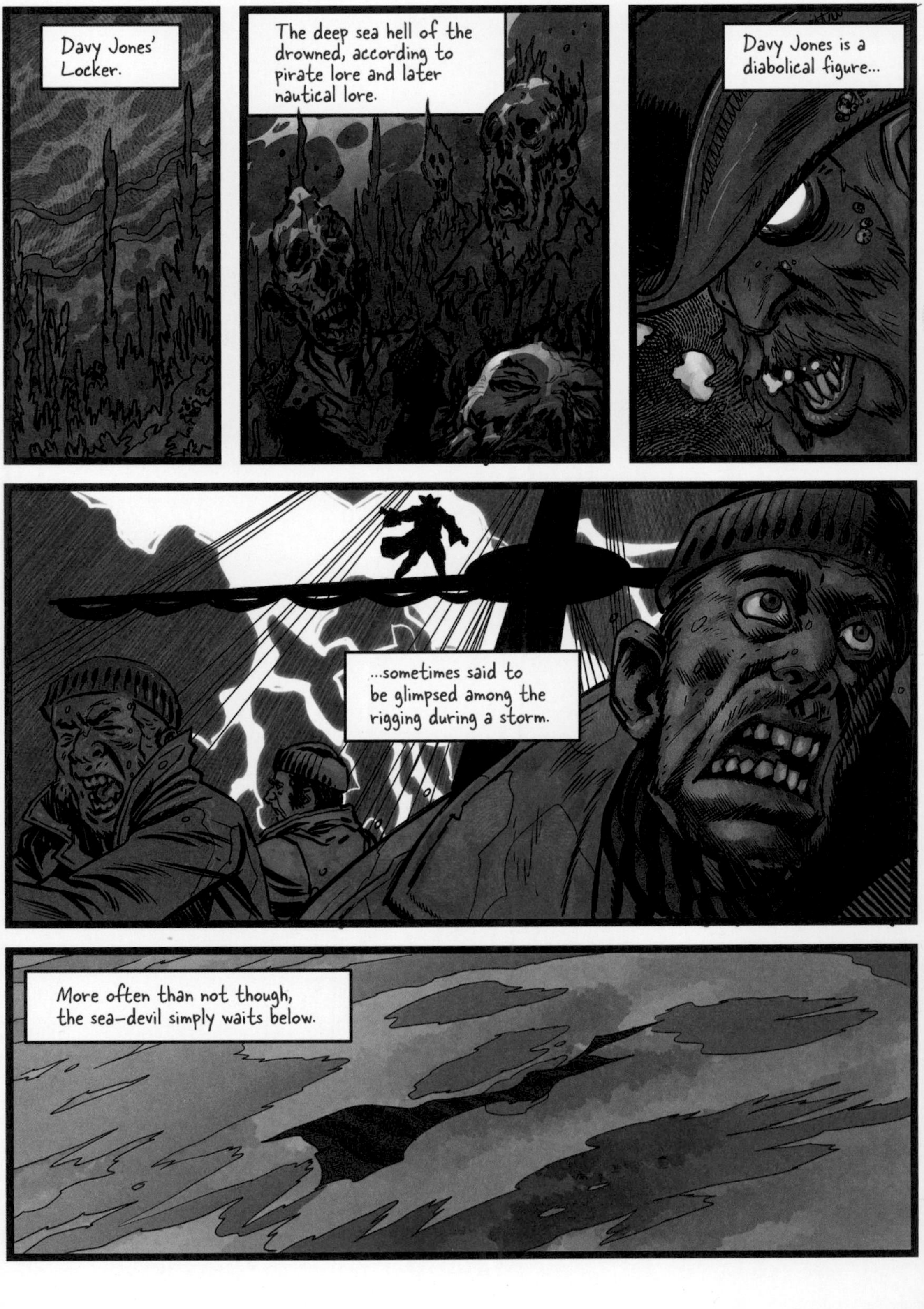
Davy Jones' Locker.
The deep sea hell of the drowned, according to pirate lore and later nautical lore.
Davy Jones is a diabolical figure...
...sometimes said to be glimpsed among the rigging during a storm.
More often than not though, the sea-devil simply waits below.

L

O

C

K

E

R

WHO WAS DAVY JONES? A ghost? A demon? A maritime deity? Perhaps he's a modernized incarnation of the Norse sea goddess Rán, whose very name meant "plunder," "theft," or "robbery." Rán would cast her gigantic net, dragging sailors and ships down to a watery grave upon the ocean bed – so it's easy to see how she could have influenced later tales of nautical fiends.

The name "Davy Jones" was first recorded in print in reference to the deep-sea graveyard known as "Davy Jones' locker" – a term that also could have referred to Hell itself — in Daniel Defoe's *Four Years Voyages of Captain George Roberts* (1726). The locker, and the fiend himself, were described in more detail in Tobias Smollett's *The Adventures of Peregrine Pickle* (1751):

> I know him by his saucer-eyes, his three rows of teeth, his horns and tail, and the blue smoke that came out of his nostrils. [...] This same Davy Jones, according to sailors, is the fiend that presides over all the evil spirits of the deep, and is often seen in various shapes, perching among the rigging on the eve of hurricanes:, ship-wrecks, and other disasters to which sea-faring life is exposed, warning the devoted wretch of death and woe.

It has been hypothesized that the name Davy Jones may derive from the Welsh patron saint, David, whose name would often have been invoked by sailors from that country. Jones is, of course, one of the most popular surnames in Wales, so Davy Jones may have originated as a kind of joke. Others argue that Davy Jones could be a corruption of Jonah – the biblical figure who was famously swallowed by a whale, or giant fish. The term "a Jonah" has long been used by seamen, meaning someone whose presence on board brings bad luck to the ship and her crew.

All in all, Davy Jones remains something of a mystery; a piece of 18th-century folklore whose origin is obscured by vague and conflicting sources. The fact that Jones is seen as a hoarder of treasures, cargoes, and souls, suggests to me that he is a personification of greed, or perhaps hubris. He is a warning to those who would dare to overload their ships, and think that they could best the mighty ocean, and defy its power.

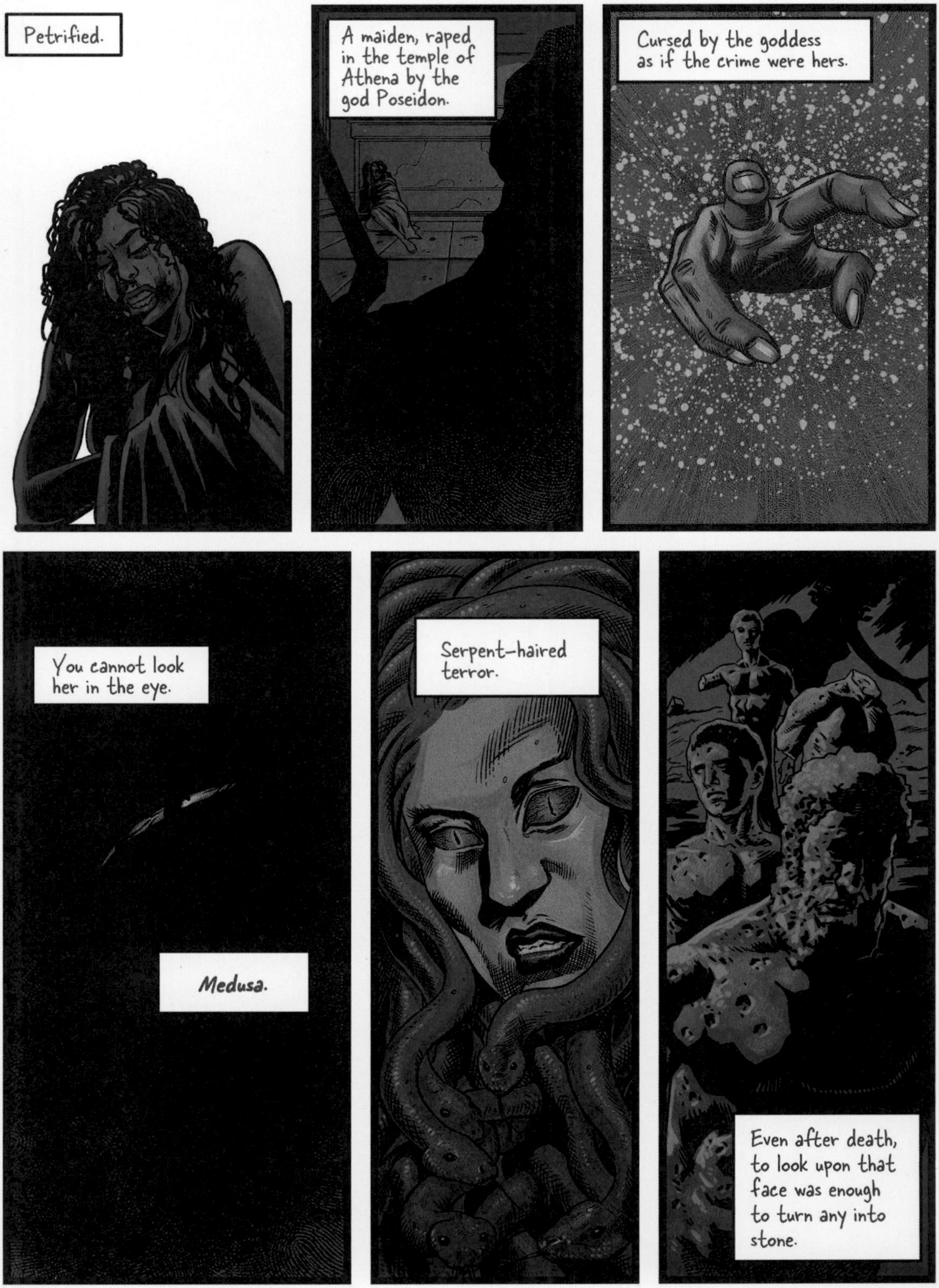
Petrified.
A maiden, raped in the temple of Athena by the god Poseidon.
Cursed by the goddess as if the crime were hers.
You cannot look her in the eye.
Medusa.
Serpent-haired terror.
Even after death, to look upon that face was enough to turn any into stone.

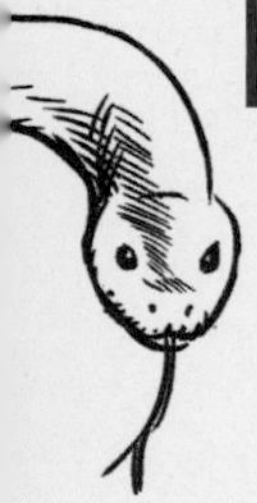

PETRIFIED

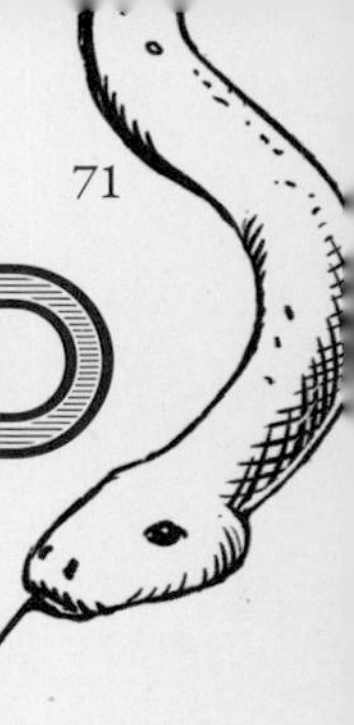

> "Medusa once had charms; to gain her love
> A rival crowd of envious lovers strove.
> Her Neptune saw, and with such beauties fir'd,
> Resolv'd to compass, what his soul desir'd.
> In chaste Minerva's fane, he, lustful, stay'd,
> And seiz'd, and rifled the young, blushing maid.
> But on the ravish'd virgin vengeance takes,
> Her shining hair is chang'd to hissing snakes.
> These in her Aegis Pallas joys to bear,
> The hissing snakes her foes more sure ensnare,
> Than they did lovers once, when shining hair."

The above is Ovid's account of how the human Medusa came to be transformed into the serpent-haired gorgon we all know today. It is taken from his *Metamorphoses, Book the Fourth*, published in 8 CE. In Ovid's version, it is the new, Roman god Neptune who attacks the young maiden, rather than his older Greek equivalent Poseidon, and the goddess Minerva, rather than Athena, who takes it upon herself to curse the victim, instead of the perpetrator.

Medusa (meaning "guardian" or "protectress") was one of three siblings: the gorgons, whose name translates as "grim" or "dreadful." Daughters of the primordial sea god and goddess, Phorcys and Ceto, the sisters were born in the caverns beneath Mount Olympus. In the oldest legends, the gorgons were monstrous from birth – chimeric creatures with wings, boar tusks, bronze clawed hands, and yes, snakes for hair – but, as the myth evolved, so did the sisters.

Medusa was the youngest of the three; Euryale (whose name meant "far roaming") was the middle sister; Stheno (whose name meant "forceful"), the eldest. Not only was Medusa the last to be born, but she was also born mortal, which only made her sisters all the more protective of her. With Medusa having been raped by the sea god, and then cursed by the goddess of wisdom, her sisters naturally stood up for her, and so they too were cursed and transformed, given snakes for hair, and eyes which would turn any who looked into them to stone.

Perseus, son of Zeus, was tricked into promising to bring back the head of Medusa as a gift for King Polydectes, who wished to wed Perseus' mother. Perseus did not favor the union, so Polydectes concocted this quest to occupy Perseus. Aided by the goddess Athena (evidently not yet satisfied with the level of suffering she had caused Medusa and her sisters), and his father, Zeus, Perseus set out on an epic quest to behead the youngest gorgon. Using a highly polished shield as a mirror, Perseus was able to look at Medusa without turning to stone. Like a coward, he struck while she slept. From the body of the gorgon sprang forth Pegasus ("he who sprang") and Chrysaor ("sword of gold") – chimeric children, they were proof of Poseidon's rape of Medusa.

Hearing of their sister's murder, Euryale and Stheno pursued her killer, but Perseus escaped their wrath using a magical helmet of invisibility. Medusa's eyes retained their petrifying power even after death, and Perseus wielded her severed head as a weapon, turning all manner of beings to stone – not least King Polydectes, who in Perseus' absence had raped his mother.

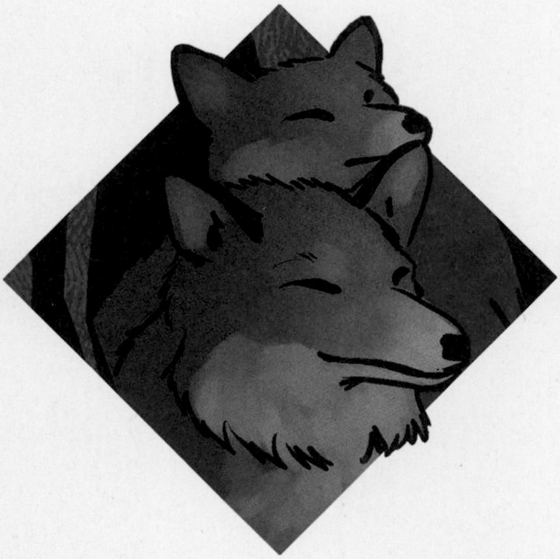

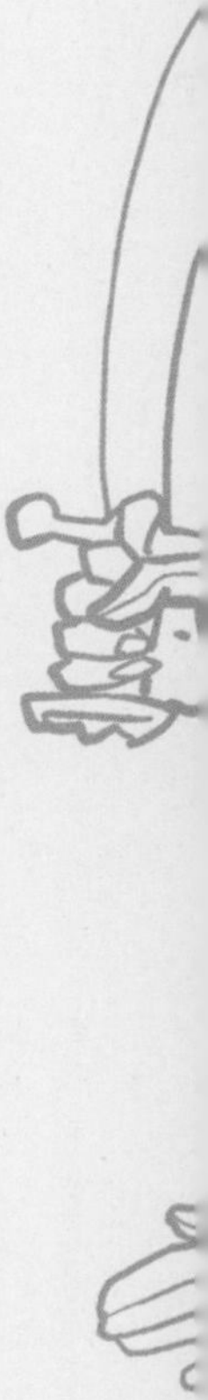

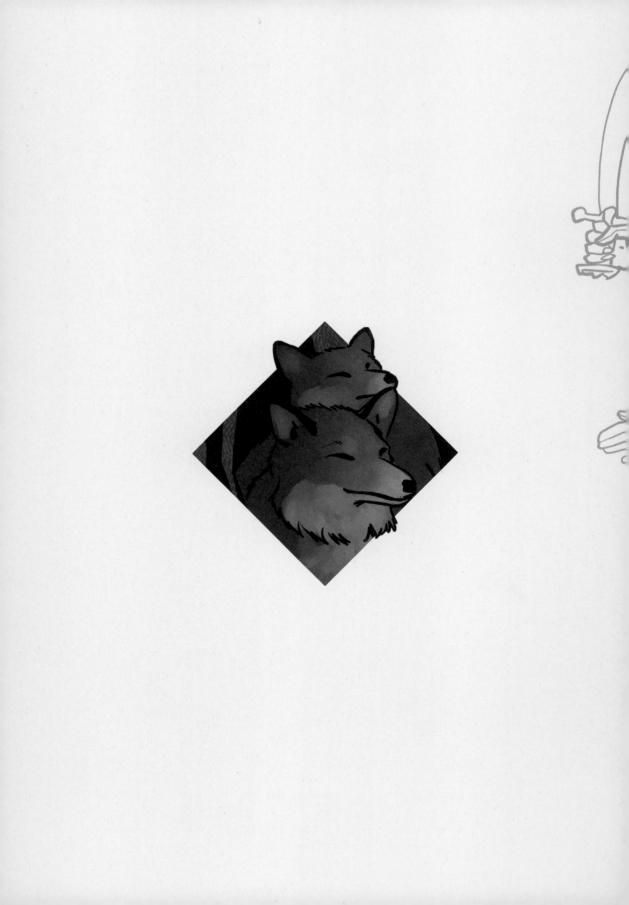

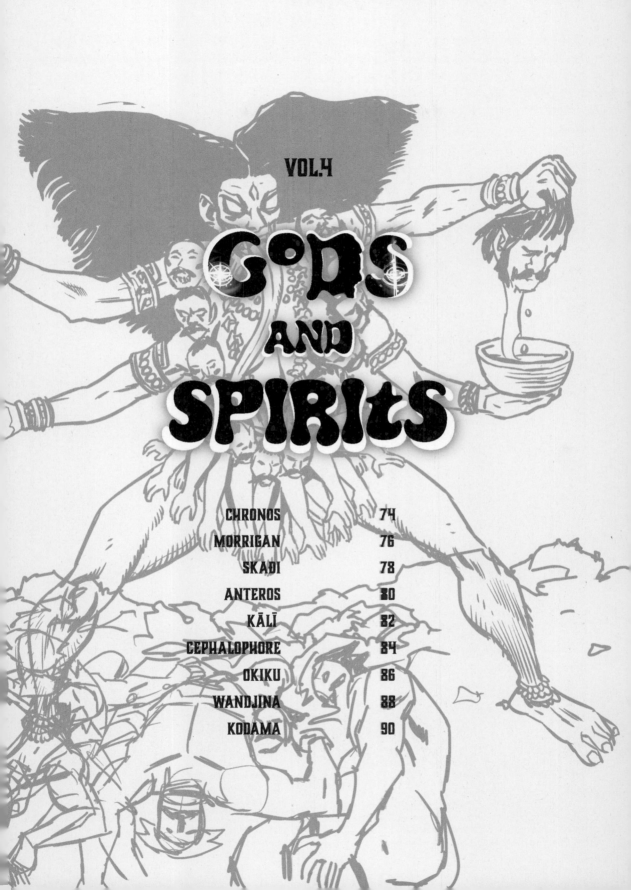

VOL.4

GODS AND SPIRITS

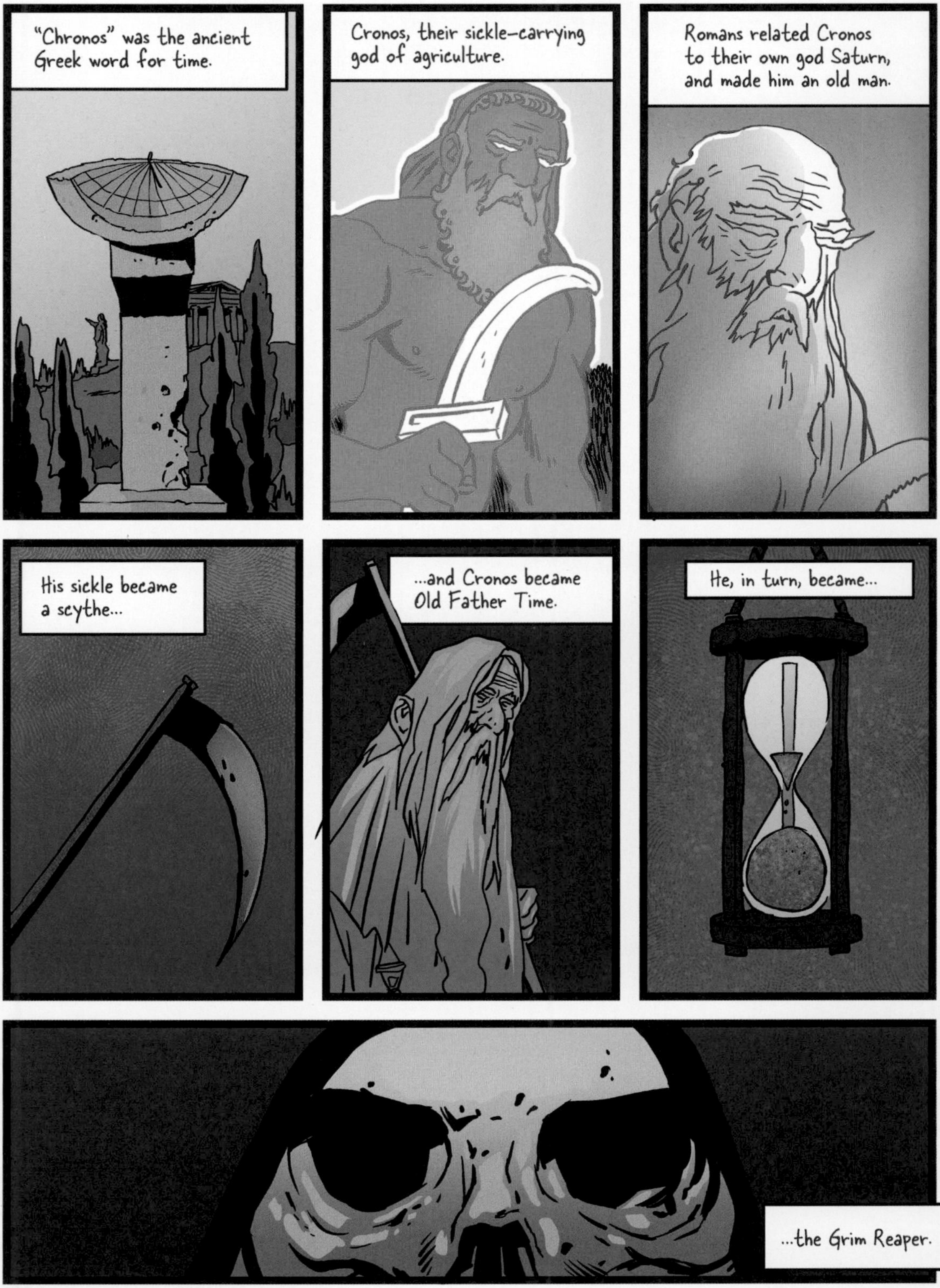
"Chronos" was the ancient Greek word for time.
Cronos, their sickle-carrying god of agriculture.
Romans related Cronos to their own god Saturn, and made him an old man.
His sickle became a scythe...
...and Cronos became Old Father Time.
He, in turn, became...
...the Grim Reaper.

WITH THANKS @JUSTRENA FOR BRONZE AGE ADVICE

CHRONOS MEANS "TIME" IN ANCIENT GREEK, AND CHRONOS himself was the personification of time in early Greek philosophy, usually depicted as an aged, bearded man. He is often conflated with the Titan Cronos, the god of agriculture, who may have been worshiped as a separate aspect of the time god Chronos. In classical Athens, a harvest festival called Kronia was held in Cronos' honor. Cronos carried a sickle, although this was a weapon used to castrate his father, Uranus, rather than for harvesting.

In classical antiquity, Cronos was identified with the Roman Saturn, another harvest deity, who also carried a sickle. Saturn, too, was depicted as an aged, bearded man and, in time, his sickle was replaced with a scythe. Saturnalia[1] – Saturn's own festival – was held in December and marked the new year. Saturn's increasingly aged appearance came to represent the old year about to meet its end. Within his mythology, Saturn famously devoured his own children and, allegorically, this has been interpreted as the passage of the seasons – time devouring the year, piece by piece.

Between the 16th and 18th centuries, the figure of a "Father Time" became a popular subject in European art. Father Time, essentially a de-deified Chronos, was time personified; an old man with a long beard, carrying a scythe. During the Renaissance, he was also often depicted with an hourglass, and sometimes with wings. Father Time began to feature regularly in end-of-year editorial newspaper cartoons during the 19th century, often accompanied by the infant Baby New Year. Baby New Year was, of course, the cute and full-of-potential personification of the year to come, but whose roots are nevertheless easily traced back to Saturn's cannibalized offspring.

Death, like time, has been personified in many forms throughout human history, but the figure we now know as the Grim Reaper seems to be a direct descendant of Chronos and an earlier, darker, alter ego of Father Time. The Danse Macabre was a Christian artistic trope originating around the 15th century wherein emaciated and skeletal resurrected dead were depicted, often alongside the bony figure of Death. The Middle Ages were a time of mass death; a bubonic plague pandemic killing as many as 200 million in the mid-1300s and recurring for centuries. Soon, the skeletal figure of Death as depicted in the Danse Macabre began, like Saturn and Father Time, to wield a scythe; a necessary piece of equipment when one is reaping souls, not one by one, but en masse.

Time and death are, of course, one and the same, and always have been. As the old Latin motto runs, *tempus edax rerum* – "time devours all things."

1   See 'Saturnalia' (pg. 106).

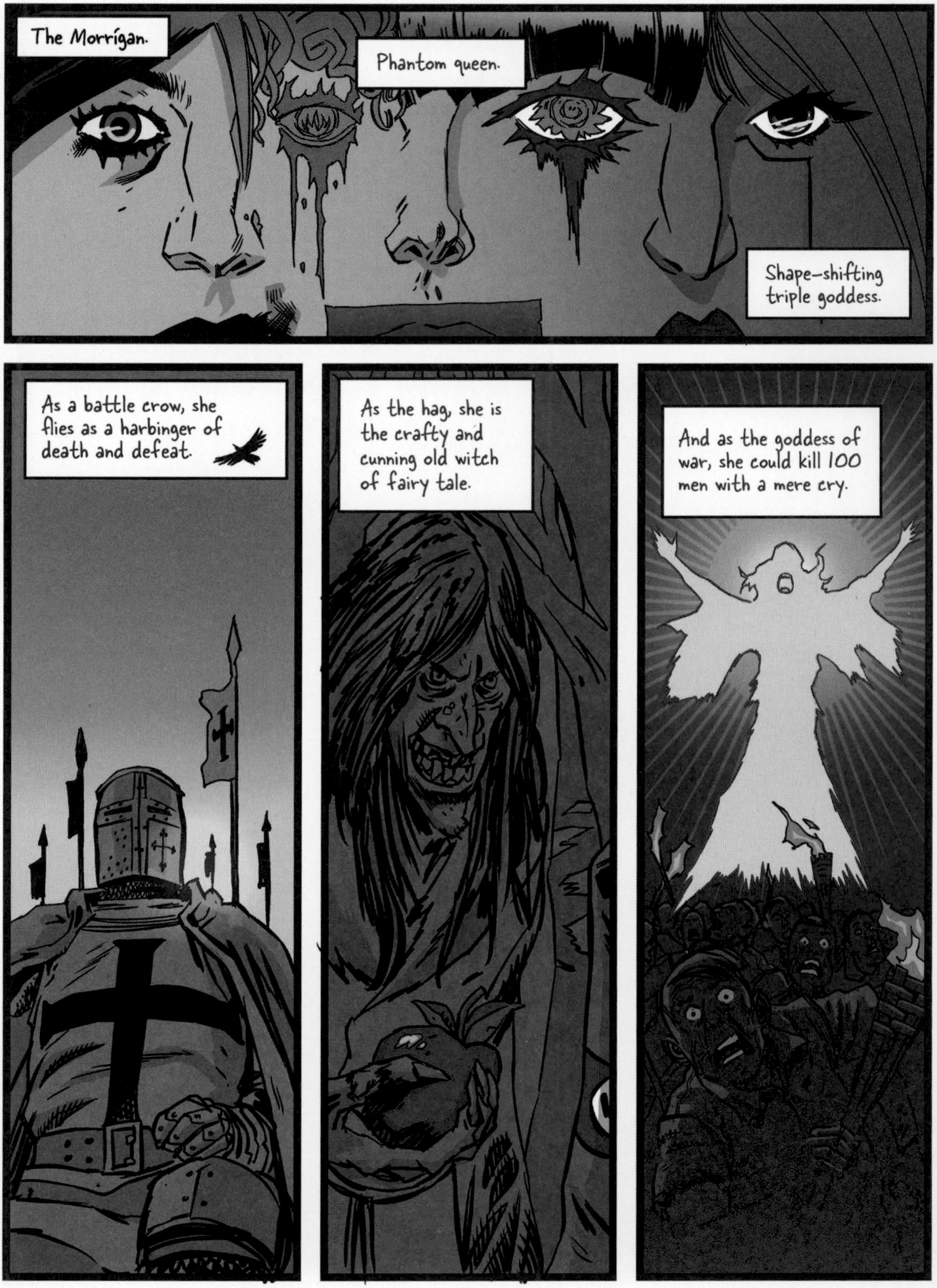

The Morrígan.
Phantom queen.
Shape-shifting triple goddess.
As a battle crow, she flies as a harbinger of death and defeat.
As the hag, she is the crafty and cunning old witch of fairy tale.
And as the goddess of war, she could kill 100 men with a mere cry.

MORRIGAN

The Morrígan is perhaps one of the strangest deities in Irish Celtic mythology. As a tripartite goddess of war, she is made up of three separate personalities or aspects. These are Morrígu, Badb, and Nemain. There is some debate as to whether "Morrígan" is merely a title these separate figures shared (like the gorgons of Greek mythology), or whether they were all different forms of the one goddess.

The Morrígan's appearance would foreshadow battle; on the field of war, as Badb the battle crow, she would spread fear and confusion among enemy soldiers. Indeed, some Celtic literature refers to the battlefield as "the garden of the Badb." In this avian form, the Morrígan alighted on the shoulder of the mortally wounded demigod Cú Chulainn, indicating to Lugaid, son of one of the many slain by the warrior, that it was safe to approach and strike his fatal blow.

The Morrígan was also a goddess of divination and prophecy. In the grand Irish epic *Tain Bo Cuailnge*, the Morrígan forecast a bloody battle to come:

> The raven ravenous
> Among corpses of men
> Affliction and outcry
> And war everlasting
> Raging over Cúailgne
> Death of sons
> Death of kinsmen
> Death! Death!

On that battlefield, in the form of Nemain – personification of the frenzy and havoc of warfare – the Morrígan confused the combatants, causing them to fight and kill their own.

> Then the Nemain attacked them, and that was not the most comfortable night with them, from the uproar of the giant Dubtach through his sleep. The bands were immediately startled, and the army confounded, until Medb went to check the confusion.

According to the medieval text *Cath Maighe Tuireadh*, Morrígan was the consort of the mighty Dagda, the gigantic demigod chief of the Tuatha dé Danann. The text tells of a meeting between the two around the time of Samhain, down by the riverside. There, after making love, the Morrígan prophesied that the Tuatha dé Danann would be victorious in their coming battle with the evil, supernatural Fomorians. There would, however, be a heavy toll to pay for the victory.

Fighting alongside Dagda, the Morrígan used her influence to send the Tuatha dé Danann into a frenzy of bloodlust, driving the Fomorians into the sea in terror before her. Though the battle was indeed won, the Morrígan's prophecy came true: Dagda perished afterwards from a wound inflicted by Cethlenn, wife of Balor of the Fomorians.

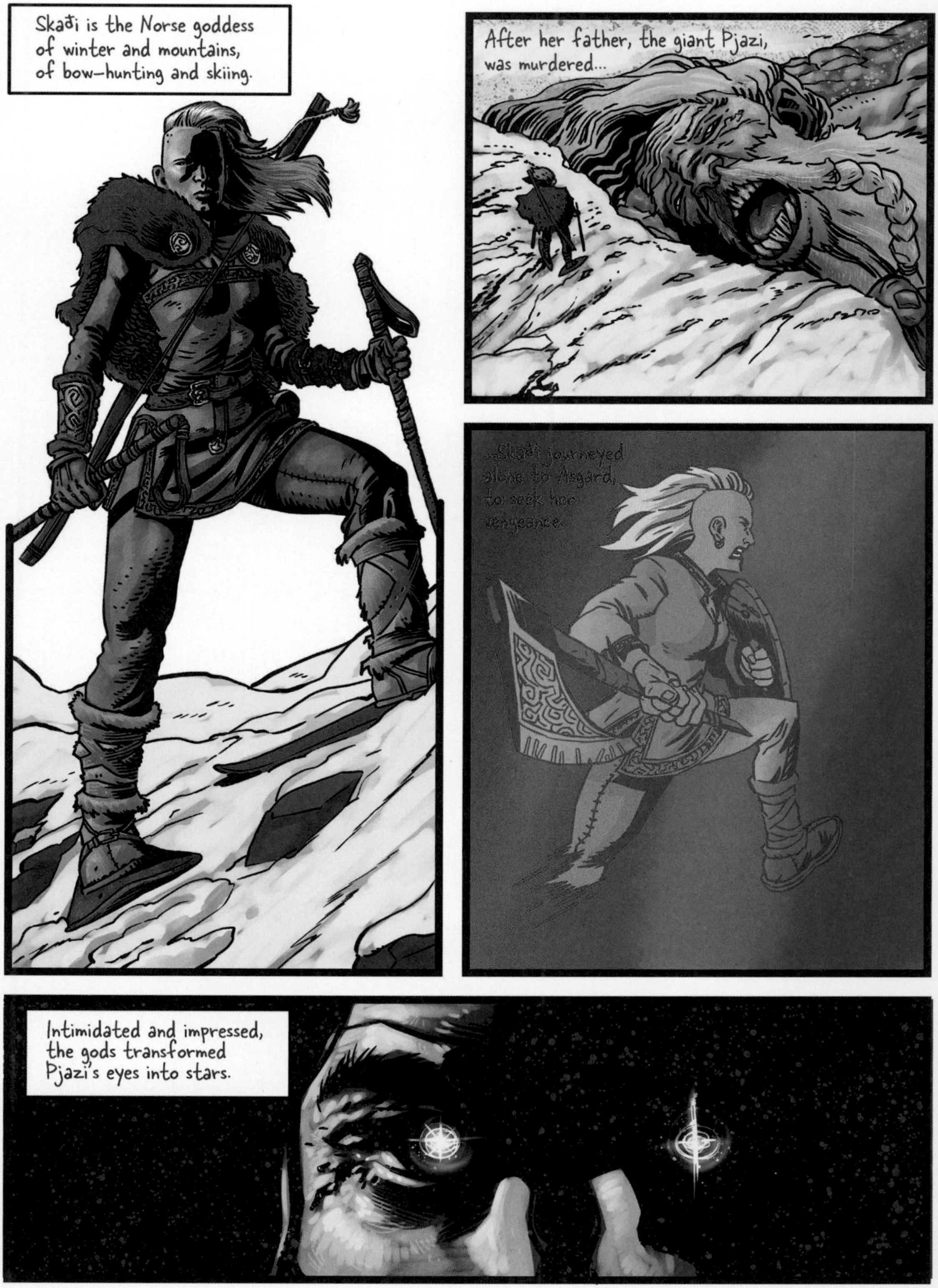

Skaði is the Norse goddess of winter and mountains, of bow–hunting and skiing.
After her father, the giant Pjazi, was murdered...
...Skaði journeyed alone to Asgard, to seek her vengeance.
Intimidated and impressed, the gods transformed Pjazi's eyes into stars.

Skaði (Skathee) was the Norse goddess of bow-hunting, skiing, winter, and mountains. As the daughter of the Frost Giant Þjazi (Thiassi), Skaði was also a *jötunn*, a word often translated into English as "giant" or "troll," though a more literal translation is "devourer." The *jötnar* inhabited Jotunheim; one of the nine worlds of Norse cosmology. Jotunheim was the wilderness: the untamed forest and the wild, inaccessible mountains where mere mortals feared to tread. On those mountains, the snow never melted, and so Skaði hunted with her bow on skis, or sometimes wearing snowshoes.

As one story goes, Skaði's father Þjazi, under orders of the ever-mischievous Loki, transformed himself into a gigantic eagle and kidnapped Iðunn, goddess of apples. Iðunn's disappearance caused the Aesir (gods) to grow old and gray, and soon they realized that Loki was to blame. To avoid the wrath of the gods, Loki kidnapped Iðunn back from Þjazi who, in turn, gave chase in his eagle form. In Asgard, the gods built a great fire which Loki flew towards but stopped short of. Þjazi, however, found his feathers singed by the flames, and fell to the ground where he was set upon and murdered by the gods.

Hearing of Þjazi's murder, Skaði vowed to avenge her father. Donning her armor and all available weapons, she journeyed to Asgard to challenge the gods. Intimidated, the gods were reluctant to battle the fierce warrior Skaði. Instead, they offered her compensation. Odin took Þjazi's eyes and placed them in the night sky, where they would shine down forever as stars. Skaði was also offered her pick of husband from the gods, although she was (for some reason) only permitted to look at their feet while making her choice. This resulted in her choosing the sea god Njörðr, mistaking his feet for those of the beautiful Baldr, son of Odin. Before she would accept any compensation, however, Skaði decreed that the gods must make her laugh. This was accomplished by Loki who tied a goat's beard around his testicles and allowed the beast to drag him around, eventually landing in the goddess's lap. This, quite understandably, did raise a chuckle from Skaði.

Njörðr and Skaði's marriage was not a happy one, he wishing to live in the sea, and she only happy in the snow-capped domain of the Frost Giants. Some tales say that their marriage went unconsummated and that Skaði was eventually wed to Odin himself.

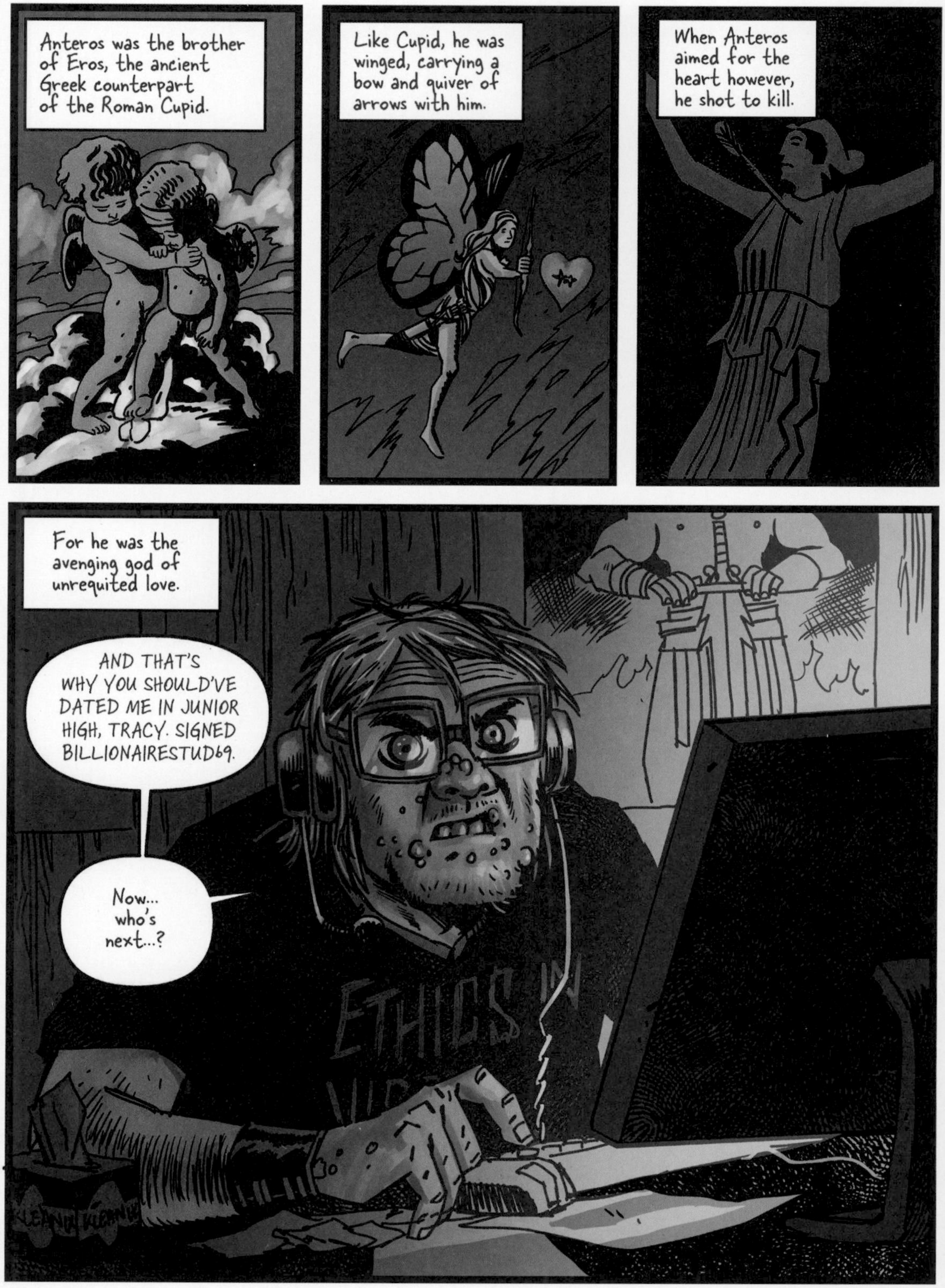
Anteros was the brother of Eros, the ancient Greek counterpart of the Roman Cupid.
Like Cupid, he was winged, carrying a bow and quiver of arrows with him.
When Anteros aimed for the heart however, he shot to kill.
For he was the avenging god of unrequited love.
AND THAT'S WHY YOU SHOULD'VE DATED ME IN JUNIOR HIGH, TRACY. SIGNED BILLIONAIRESTUD69.
ETHICS IN
Now... who's next...?

ANTEROS

MOST OF US HAVE HEARD OF EROS – WINGED GOD OF DESIRE WHO EVOLVED INTO THE infantilized CUPID adorning Valentine's cards – but his brother, Anteros, is significantly less well known.

Aphrodite was the ancient Greek goddess of love, beauty, pleasure, passion, and procreation. As might be expected, she had quite a few children. With Ares, god of war, she had (at least) eight children, and (at least) four of these were known as the Erotes. The Erotes were winged gods who helped their mother with her earthly duties, serving as love deities.

Eros, the most famous of the Erotes, was the god of love and sex, which seems fairly straightforward. His brothers, however, had slightly more specific roles. Hedylogos was the god of sweet talk and flattery; Pothos, the god of longing and yearning; Hymenaeus, the god of weddings and marriage; Hermaphroditus, the androgynous, intersex deity of fertility. Anteros' name means "love returned," and he was charged with the task of punishing those who did not return the affections of another.

A Manual of Classical Mythology, written by Thomas Swinburne Carr and published in 1846, gives us the following entry on Anteros:

> ANTEROS is the Deity who avenges slighted love (Deus ultor); hence, in the palaestra at Elis, he is represented as contending with Eros or Cupid. This conflict, however, was also considered as a rivalry existing between two lovers; and thus Anteros may in some respect be considered as forwarding the schemes of Cupid. And hence we may explain the fable that, on the birth of Anteros, Cupid felt his strength increase and his wings enlarge, and that, whenever his brother is at a distance, he finds himself reduced to his ancient shape.

As the avenger of unrequited, or slighted, love, Anteros was armed with arrows made of lead, or sometimes with a club of solid gold.

Similarities between Anteros and his brother are so striking that one is often mistaken for the other. The famous statue which stands at the top of the Shaftesbury Memorial Fountain in Piccadilly Circus, London, has been widely known as Eros for decades. The first sculpture in the world to be cast in aluminum, in 1892, the figure represented is actually that of Anteros. The god was chosen to represent love given blindly, or without expectation of return, as a metaphor for the philanthropy of Lord Shaftesbury, to whom it is dedicated.

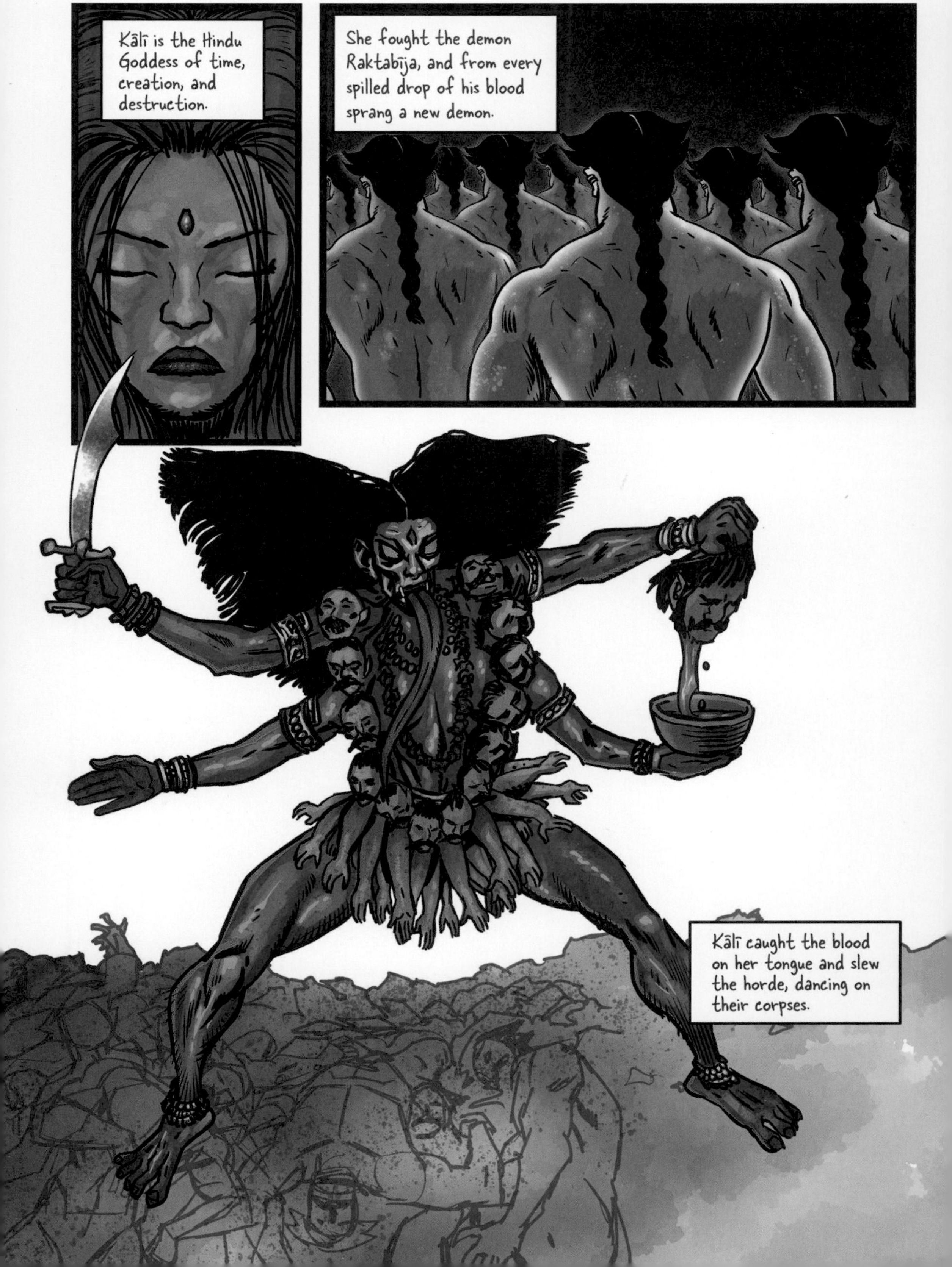
Kālī is the Hindu Goddess of time, creation, and destruction.
She fought the demon Raktabīja, and from every spilled drop of his blood sprang a new demon.
Kālī caught the blood on her tongue and slew the horde, dancing on their corpses.

KĀLĪ

The goddess Kālī is one of the Mahāvidyā ("Great Wisdoms"): a group of ten Hindu tantric goddesses. They consist of Tārā, "guide and protector"; Sundarī, "beautiful in the three worlds"; Bhuvaneśvarī, "world mother"; Bhairavī, "the fierce"; Chinnamastā, goddess of self-sacrifice; Dhūmāvatī, the "widow goddess"; Bagalāmukhī, "paralyzer of enemies"; Mātaṅgī, goddess of the arts; Kamalā, the "lotus goddess"; and Kālī, the midnight-skinned "devourer of time."

The goddess Kālī appears in the sacred Hindu text the *Devi Mahatmyam* ("Glory to the Goddess"), written circa 500 CE. In this telling, Kālī is the personification of the wrath of the goddess Durgā– herself an aspect of the mother goddess, Mahādevī – upon the battlefield. Kālī is the slayer of the demons Chanda and Munda, though the demon she fought is named elsewhere as Raktabīja. Raktabīja, whose name translates as "blood seed," was said to be unkillable. Just as the Lernaean Hydra of Greek myth is said to have grown two heads in place of each one severed, so every drop of Raktabīja's blood that was spilled birthed a new, fully formed version of the demon. The *Devi Mahatmyam* describes the creation/birth of Kālī as the goddess Durga, who faced the demon(s):

> Out of the surface of her [Durga's] forehead, fierce with frown, issued suddenly from Kālī of terrible countenance, armed with a sword and noose. Bearing the strange khaṭvāṅga (skull-topped staff), decorated with a garland of skulls, clad in a tiger's skin, very appalling owing to her emaciated flesh, with gaping mouth, fearful with her tongue lolling out, having deep reddish eyes, filling the regions of the sky with her roars, falling upon impetuously and slaughtering the great asuras in that army, she devoured those hordes of the foes of the devas.

Kālī is said to have bested the demon(s) by catching every drop of blood she spilled upon her long, crimson tongue, thus preventing any more of the horrors being birthed. The clone horde slain, Kālī danced for victory upon a mountain of their corpses.

Kālī's associations with battle, blood, and death, and her title of "devourer of time," are often misinterpreted by non-Hindus. She is the end of all things: of war, of ignorance, of suffering, but she is also a mother and a protector of the innocent. In order for there to be rebirth and renewal, there must first be death. New beginnings are impossible without endings.

Cephalophore means "head carrier" and is used to describe a group of Christian Saints martyred by beheading.

Tales of these decapitated saints often tell of them picking up their severed heads, carrying them under their arms to a suitably holy burial place.

CEP HAL OPH ORE

CEPHALOPHORE MEANS "HEAD CARRIER," AND THE TERM IS USED TO REFER TO ANY OF A NUMBER of beheaded Catholic saints. In his 1916 work *Saint's Legends*, medievalist Gordon Hall Gerould wrote the following:

> It is clear that the whole company of martyrs, of whom legend relates that they carried their heads after death, the céphalophores, arose from a widely known form of iconography.

Saint Denis is a 3rd-century Christian martyr who was executed by Romans by beheading. After his head was severed from his body, it is said that Saint Denis picked it up. A sermon was delivered from the lips of the severed head as Saint Denis' body carried it to the summit of a hill, where a shrine was subsequently built in his honor. That shrine became the Basilica of Saint-Denis, in Paris, where the kings of France were buried from then on. Saint Denys's Church in York, England, depicts the head-carrying saint in a 15th-century stained glass window. The church is built upon the site of a Roman temple dedicated to Arciaco – a god, or deity, whose name is not recorded anywhere else.

Other saintly cephalophores include Saint Just, Saint Ginés de la Jara, Saint Firmin, Saint Minias, the siblings Saints Felix and Regula, Saint Exuperantius, Saint Valerie, Saint Maxien, Saint Lucien, Saint Julian, Saint Chéron, and Saint Osyth. Saint Cuthbert is also often depicted carrying a severed head, though in this case the head belongs to another saint. It is the head of Saint Oswald, which was interred with the body of Saint Cuthbert at Durham Cathedral.

Edmund the Martyr, king of East Anglia and first patron saint of England, was murdered by Northlanders in the 9th century. Bound to a tree, Edmund was shot with arrows, his head then struck from his lifeless body. Though Edmund did not become a head-carrying saint, legend records that something strange did happen to his head. When Edmund's followers came in search of him, one of them called out, "Where are you?" "Here! Here! Here!" came the answer. Following the voice, the men found themselves face-to-face with a huge wolf, between whose forepaws sat the severed head of their king. Whether the guiding words issued from the wolf's jaws or from Edmund's own lips cannot be said for certain.

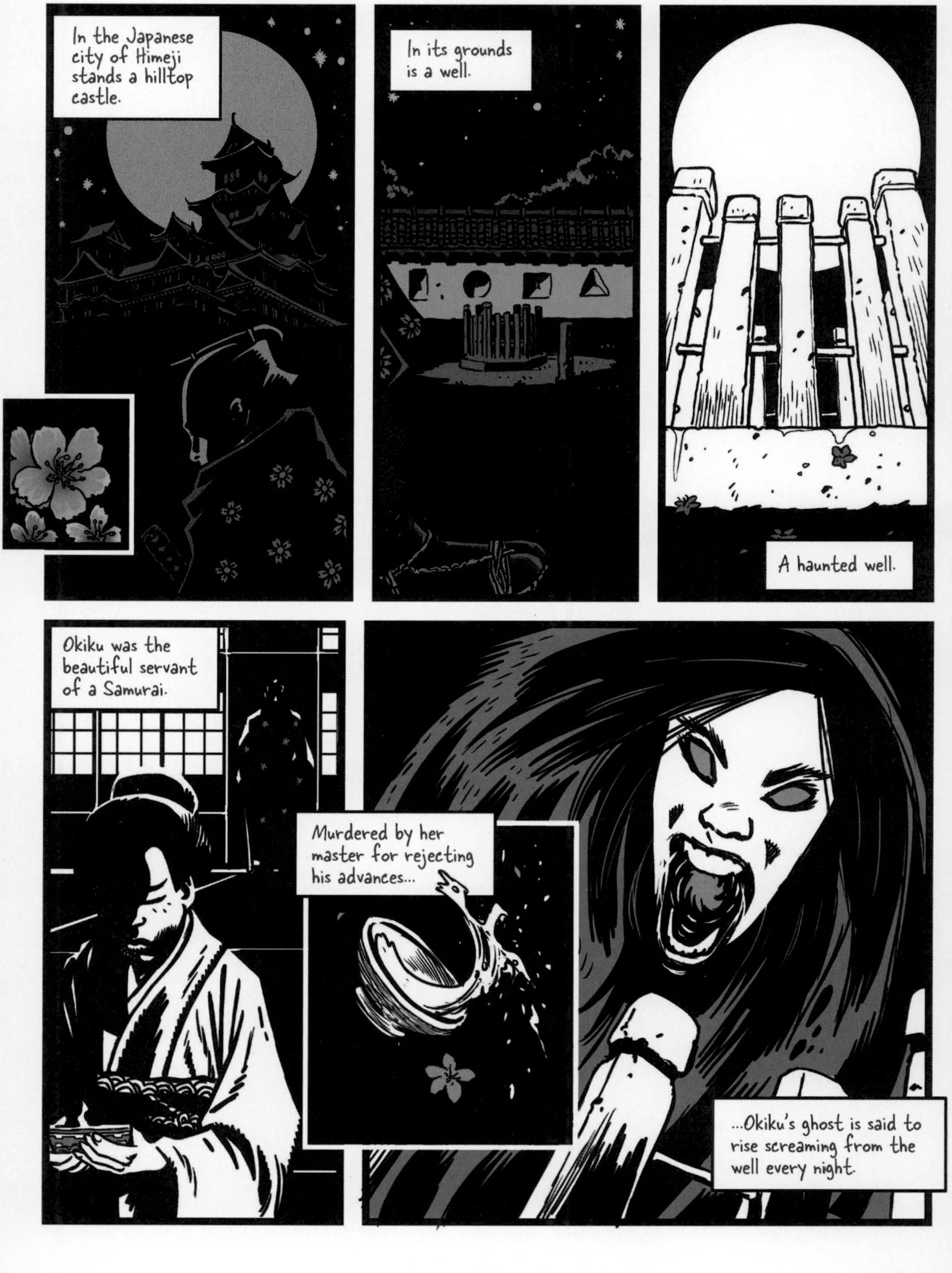
In the Japanese city of Himeji stands a hilltop castle.
In its grounds is a well.
A haunted well.
Okiku was the beautiful servant of a Samurai.
Murdered by her master for rejecting his advances...
...Okiku's ghost is said to rise screaming from the well every night.

O K I K U

Onryō (怨霊) is a Japanese word meaning "vengeful spirit" or "wrathful spirit." More than mere apparitions, these angry ghosts are capable of affecting the physical realm and causing harm, or even death, to the living. It is recorded (and widely believed) that Genbō, the Japanese scholar-monk and bureaucrat of the Imperial Court at Nara, was murdered by the vengeful ghost of his enemy, Fujiwara no Hirotsugu, in the year 746. The onryō has become a staple of J-horror, featuring in many internationally successful films. Their appearance therein – long black hair, often partly obscuring their face, flowing white burial robes, pale faces and dark rimmed eyes – comes directly from the Japanese Kabuki theater tradition.

Himeji Castle is regarded as one of the finest surviving Japanese castles of its era. Constructed on the site of a fort in the 14th century, the castle was extensively expanded and remodeled in the 16th century. The story goes that a beautiful young servant named Okiku once lived and worked in the castle for the samurai Aoyama Tessan. Aoyama found Okiku very attractive, but the servant spurned her master's advances. In a deeply unpleasant plot to force Okiku to submit to his desires, Aoyama hid one of his family's ten prized delft plates, and accused the servant of losing or breaking it. When Okiku could not find the tenth plate and was forced to admit this to her master, he gave her a choice: she could suffer death, or she could become his lover. Still Okiku refused the advances of the samurai and so, in a fury, Aoyama threw her down the castle's well, to her death. Soon after, the onryō of Okiku began to haunt the castle, rising from the well. Tearfully, her voice could be heard counting "One... two... three..." but when it came to the missing tenth plate the ghost would let out a terrible scream.

In some versions of the folktale, the ghost of Okiku is laid to rest by being presented with the tenth plate, and her haunting of Aoyama Tessan is brought to an end. In others, the samurai is harrowed to death by the vengeful spirit. Okiku's well still stands in the grounds of Himeji Castle, and stories persist of her spirit rising from its depths nightly. Still searching for the lost plate. Still counting. "One... two... three..."

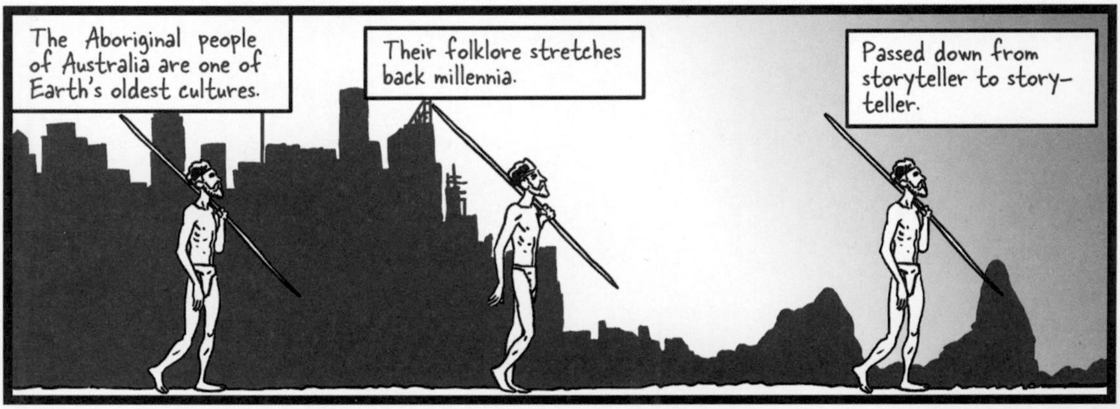
The Aboriginal people of Australia are one of Earth's oldest cultures.
Their folklore stretches back millennia.
Passed down from storyteller to story-teller.

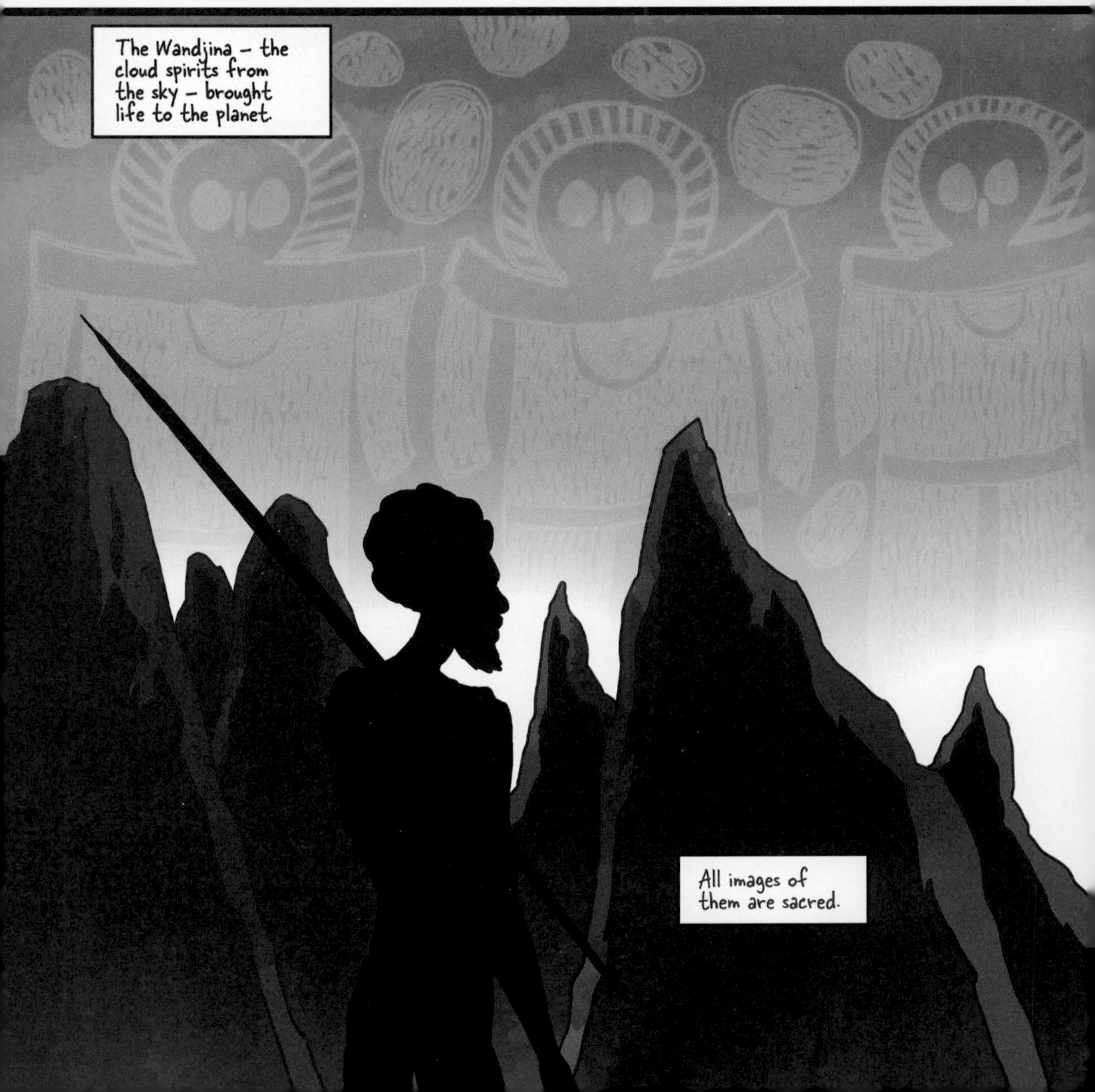
The Wandjina – the cloud spirits from the sky – brought life to the planet.
All images of them are sacred.

HUMANS FIRST ARRIVED IN AUSTRALIA SOME 65,000 YEARS AGO, migrating by sea from East Asia. The descendants of these Ice Age pioneers became the Aboriginal peoples of the Australian mainland and Tasmania, and the Torres Strait Islander peoples from the seas between Queensland and Papua New Guinea.

Indigenous Australians lived in harmony with nature for millennia, understanding the signs and cycles of their environment and passing this knowledge down through folktales and oral history. Across Australia's different indigenous cultural groups, nature is often considered sacred. Many First Nation cultures have distinct deities, but just as there is an overlap of words between Australia's indigenous languages, there is also an overlap of beliefs between communities. The Wandjina spirits in the northern Kimberley region of Western Australia belong to the Ngarinyin, Worora, and Wunambal communities. Some extant painted depictions of these cloud-spirits date back to 2000 BCE. These Wandjina spirits are responsible for bringing the wet season rains, as well as laying down many of the laws for the people. As one travels east, this function is taken over by Yagjagbula and Jabirringgi – the Lightning Brothers of the Wardaman group in the Victoria River district of the Northern Territory; then by Nargorkun, also known as Bula, in the upper Katherine River area; and by Namarrgun, the Lightning Man in the Kakadu and western Arnhem Land regions.

Spirituality often intersects with human activity, and stewardship of the environment was not left to the spirits and deities of local folklore. Fire-stick farming was once practiced widely by First Australians as a means of managing the land. Controlled burnings created firebreaks, halting the spread of the wildfires which occur naturally in the hot, dry Australian climate. The 2019–20 bushfire season was among the worst in documented Australian history, exacerbated in no small part by a lack of rain. 95,000 square miles of land burned, and an estimated three billion animals, many of which are now endangered species, died. In the wake of this disaster, many environmental experts called for a reintroduction of fire-stick farming. Workshops in which First Australians demonstrated their methods to landowners and communities were set up. In May 2021, representatives of the Kaurna people conducted a 'cultural burn' within the Adelaide Park Lands. This represented the first time in hundreds of years that First Australians had been able to do so within that area.

Yet, it's not just humans who have returned to these ancient methods of stewardship. The 2021–22 wet season (November to April) saw some of the highest rainfall since Australian records officially began. Perhaps the ancient, benevolent cloud-spirits saw fit to bless the parched red earth with their life-giving waters once more.

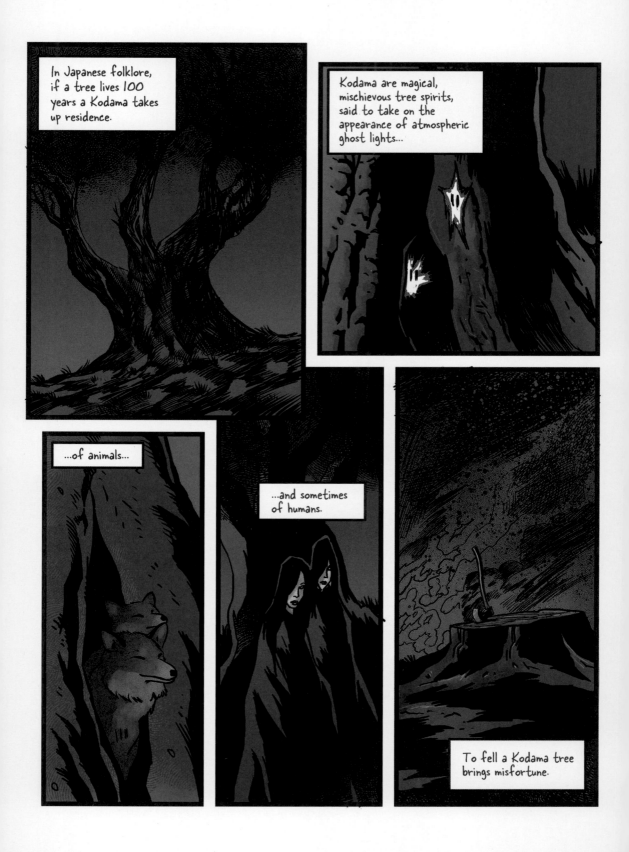

In Japanese folklore, if a tree lives 100 years a Kodama takes up residence.

Kodama are magical, mischievous tree spirits, said to take on the appearance of atmospheric ghost lights...

...of animals...

...and sometimes of humans.

To fell a Kodama tree brings misfortune.

KODAMA

In Japanese folklore, if a tree lives for one hundred years, it is said that *KODAMA* take up residence in it. Kodama are tree spirits with similarities to the Greek dryads. They are magical, occasionally mischievous demi-gods, said to take on the appearance of atmospheric ghost lights, of animals, and sometimes of humans. Cutting down a tree which houses a kodama is thought to bring misfortune[1], and such trees often have a length of sacred rope (*shimenawa)* tied around their trunks, both to mark them out and to protect them.

In the Japanese religion of Shinto, plants, landscape, and nature form a core part of the belief system. Forest and tree spirits are especially prevalent within Shinto beliefs, and kodama are just one example of these.

In the mountains of Aogashima, in the Izu Islands, the *kidama-sama*, or *kodama-sama*, are honored at shrines at the base of the vast Cryptomeria trees which grow there. On Okinawa Island – the largest of the six Okinawa islands off Japan's southeastern coast – tree spirits are known as *kiinushii*. These spirits must be prayed to and appeased before a tree can be felled. If the sound of a falling tree is heard, but no fallen tree can be found, it is believed to have been a kiinushii who made the sound. This sound is believed to herald the death of the tree in which the kiinushii had taken up residence, which can be seen to wither and die within days of its call.

Gazu Hyakki Yagyō (画図百鬼夜行 "Night Parade of One Hundred Demons") is a Japanese bestiary, published in 1776. Artist Toriyama Sekien (a pseudonym of poet, artist, and scholar Sano Toyofusa) used woodblock printing to depict various gods, monsters, and spirits of Japanese folklore. In the volume, there appears an illustration of an ancient tree with an elderly man and woman beside it, each wielding a broom. A note written by the artist in the upper right of the image reads:

> **"** Kami are said to appear in ancient trees. **"**

Kami is the name given in Shinto to the gods, demi-gods, and spirits which inhabit the natural world. For this reason, the religion is also known as *kami-no-michi* – "the way of the spirits." The kami depicted in Sekien's illustration is named in its title as "Kodama."

---

1   A similar belief is present in other cultures: see also 'Hawthorn' (pg. 10) and 'Mushroom' (pg. 12).

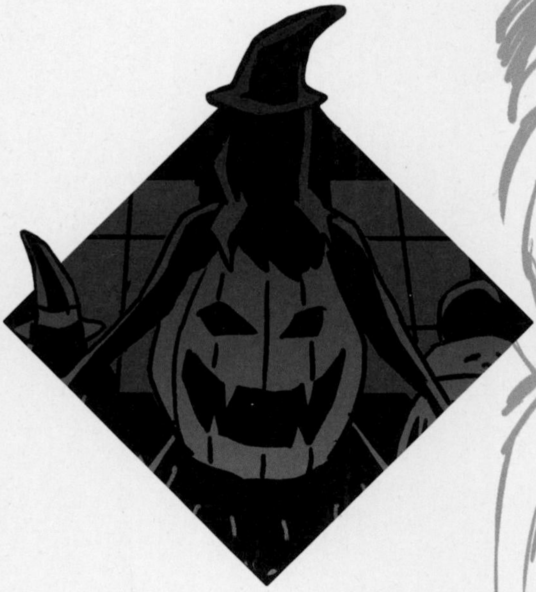
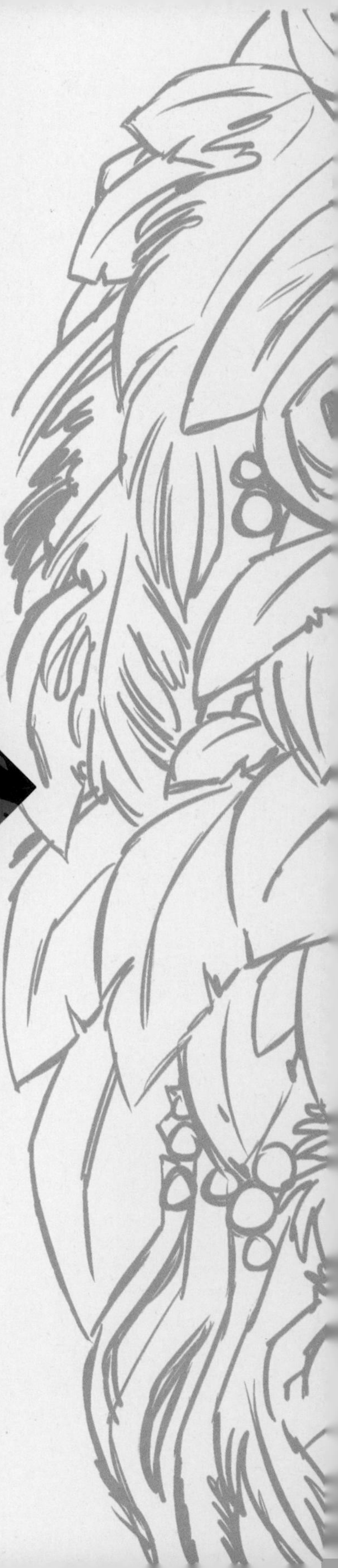

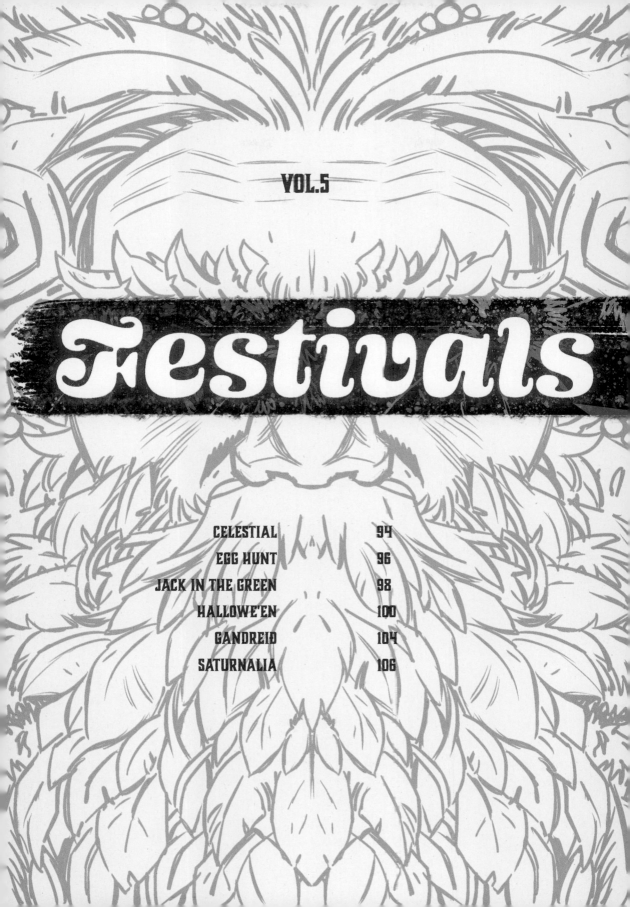

VOL.5

Festivals

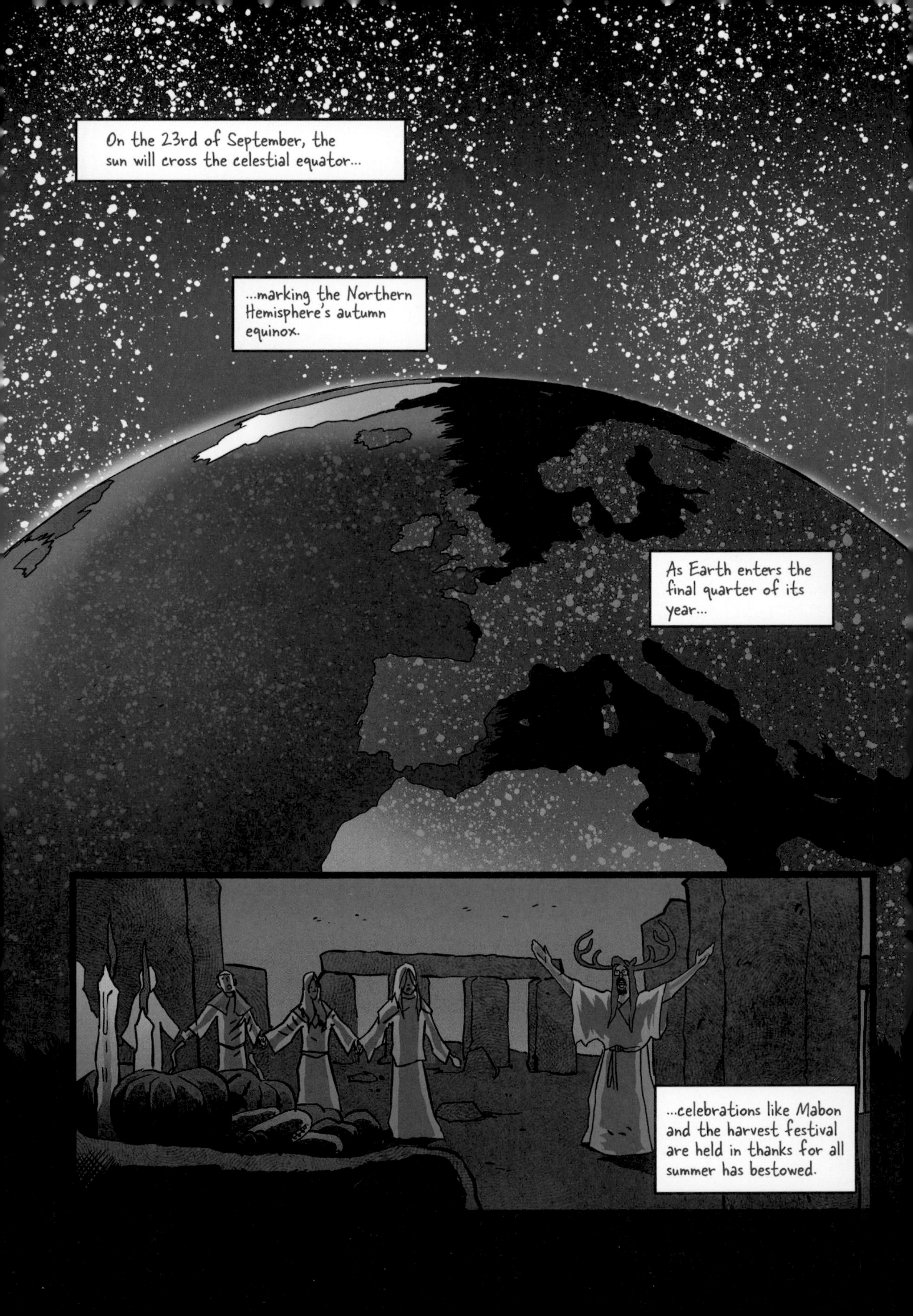
On the 23rd of September, the sun will cross the celestial equator...
...marking the Northern Hemisphere's autumn equinox.
As Earth enters the final quarter of its year...
...celebrations like Mabon and the harvest festival are held in thanks for all summer has bestowed.

C
E
L
E
S
T
I
A
L

THE CELESTIAL EQUATOR FOLLOWS THE SAME PLANE AS THE terrestrial equator – the line which divides Earth into its northern and southern hemispheres – but it is the projection of a greater circle which stretches out into space. When the plane of Earth's terrestrial equator passes through the geometric center of the Sun's disk – which it does twice a year – we call this an equinox.

The word equinox means "equal night" and it commonly refers to the two days of the year when night and day are of equal length. Each year on Earth is divided into four quarters, marked by the two equinoxes – the vernal, or spring equinox, and the autumnal equinox – and the two solstices, summer and winter. These four events, called by a host of different names, have held significance for as long as humans have been humans. For those of us who follow the Gregorian calendar, and who reside in Earth's Northern Hemisphere, the autumnal equinox takes place around the 23rd of September.

The huge sarsen stones and smaller bluestones which form the prehistoric monument of Stonehenge are aligned to frame two particular celestial events: the sunrise of the summer solstice, and the sunset of the winter solstice. The stone circle which stands on Salisbury Plain in Wiltshire, England, is thought to have been constructed circa 2500 BCE. From the early 20th century onward, a revival of interest in Stonehenge as a site of religious significance has taken place, championed by adherents of neopaganism, New Age beliefs, and particularly by neo-druids. Around 1970, American academic and neopagan Aiden A. Kelly gave the autumn equinox its own name within paganism: Mabon. This festival is now celebrated with a ritual of thanksgiving by followers of neopaganism and Wicca each year. Today, Wiccans, neopagans, and others gather in great numbers at Stonehenge to observe the Mabon sunset.

Irrespective of faith, the autumnal equinox marks a time of balance, not just between the hours of darkness and light, but of all things. Now is the time when we may reap what we have sown, both literally and figuratively. We may reflect upon all that has been achieved and give thanks. We may look ahead to what must be done in the future to ensure that, by the next time our planet – an uneven, and insignificant sphere of rock and water, adrift in the celestial sea – has orbited its sun, there is something else to be thankful for.

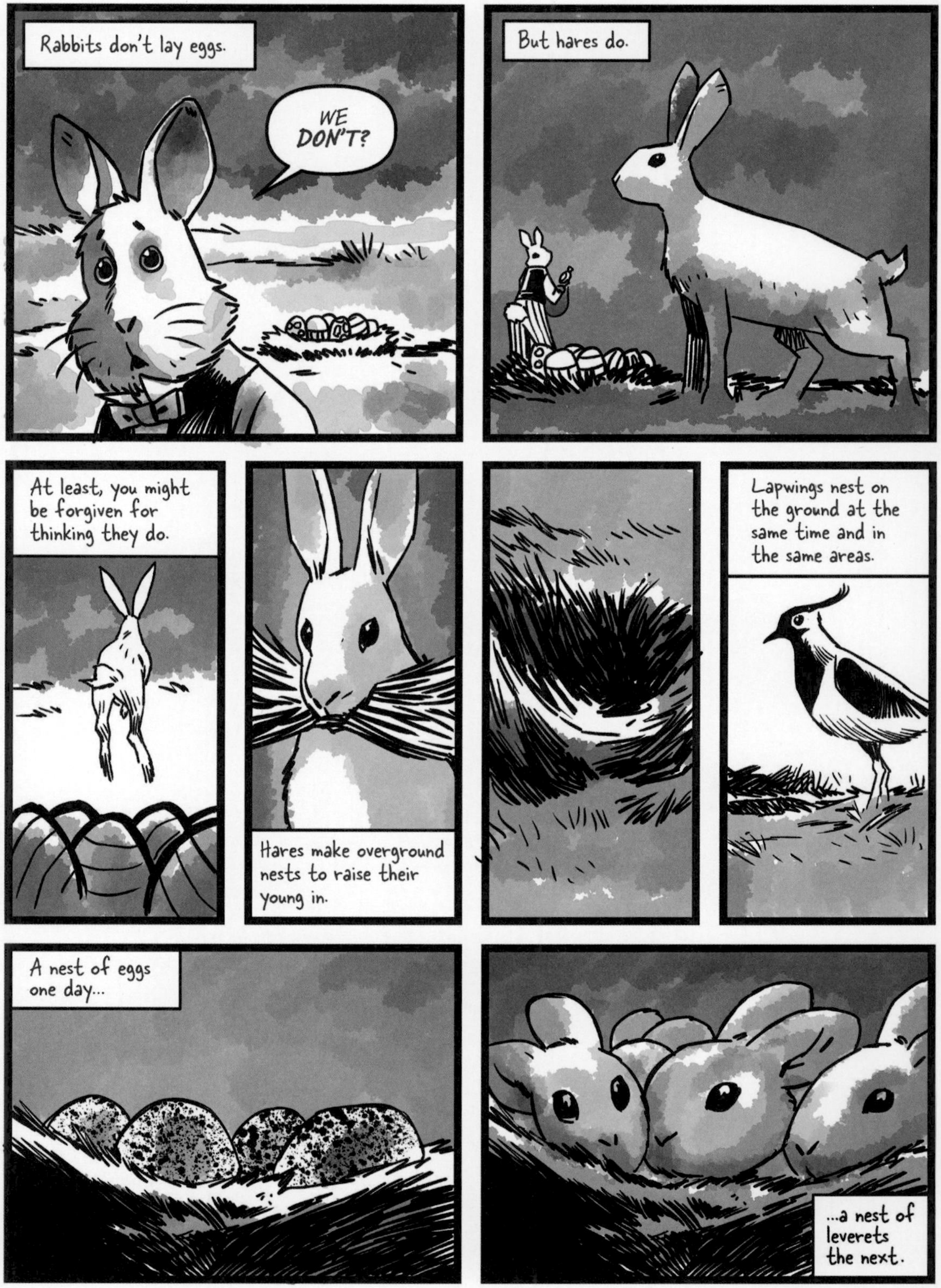
Rabbits don't lay eggs.
WE DON'T?
But hares do.
At least, you might be forgiven for thinking they do.
Hares make overground nests to raise their young in.
Lapwings nest on the ground at the same time and in the same areas.
A nest of eggs one day...
...a nest of leverets the next.

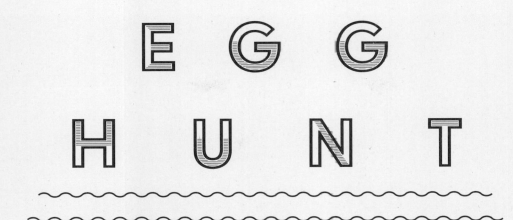

E G G
H U N T

THE EASTER BUNNY IS A FAMILIAR FIGURE OF MODERN WESTERN FOLKLORE AS A LARGE rabbit (though apparently a hare in earlier times) who gifts colorful, patterned eggs to good little boys and girls. These eggs are often hidden outside amongst the springtime grasses and flowers, so that they must be hunted for. Much like the Tooth Fairy and Santa Claus, the Easter Bunny seems so commonplace that its folkloric roots are barely considered by many of us. Some claims about the "true" origins of Easter, and of the Easter Bunny, do circulate, however.

In his 8th-century writings, Bede the Venerable recorded the following:

> Eosturmonath has a name which is now translated "Paschal month," and which was once called after a goddess of theirs named Eostre, in whose honour feasts were celebrated in that month.

Today, many report as a matter of fact that the Anglo-Saxon goddess Eostre had as her consort a magical hare. This hare was, therefore, the forerunner of the modern Easter Bunny. In truth, Bede's brief mentions of Eostre and Eosturmonath are the earliest extant records of either. No historic images or descriptions of Eostre exist, and her connection with hares/rabbits is at best a wild speculation, at worst a pure fabrication.

There does, however, seem to be another very real and natural connection between Eastertide, hares, and brightly colored eggs. Hares do not raise their leverets below ground as rabbits do their kittens, rather, they build shallow little nests for them among the grass. These nests are called "forms" and look remarkably like the nests of lapwings and other ground-level-nesting birds. In the spring (around the time of Easter) in certain parts of Britain, it is possible to find forms filled with tiny baby hares, pretty much directly alongside nests containing beautifully speckled and patterned birds' eggs.

As the theory goes, perhaps, long ago, someone saw a hare tending its young in a form, having previously seen eggs in a very similar-looking nest in more or less the same location. Naturally then, they might come to the conclusion that, around Eastertide, a hare or large rabbit might be seen to hide brightly colored eggs amongst the springtime grasses and flowers. This theory appears to have emerged online circa 2009 but, perhaps surprisingly, it does not seem to have had anything like the same impact as the claim that the Easter Bunny was once Eostre's hare companion.

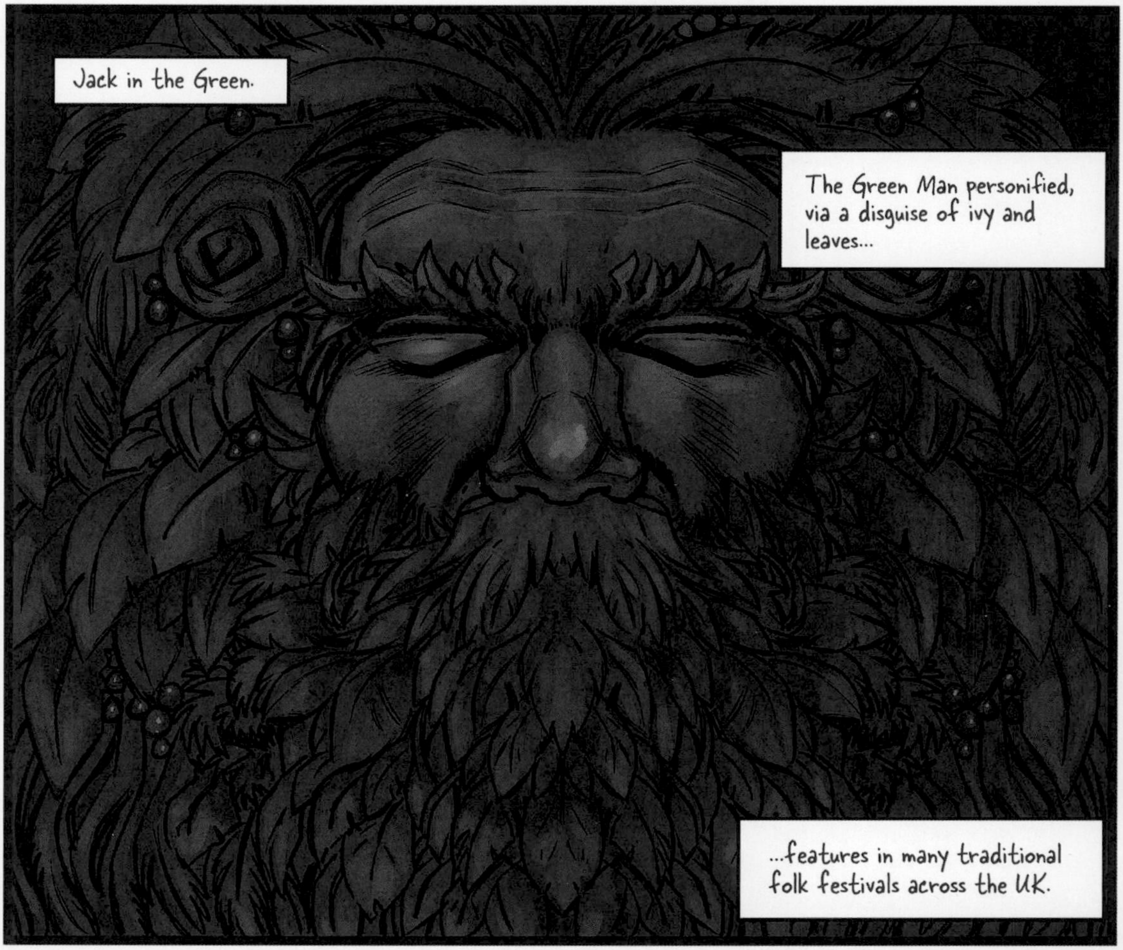
Jack in the Green.
The Green Man personified, via a disguise of ivy and leaves...
...features in many traditional folk festivals across the UK.
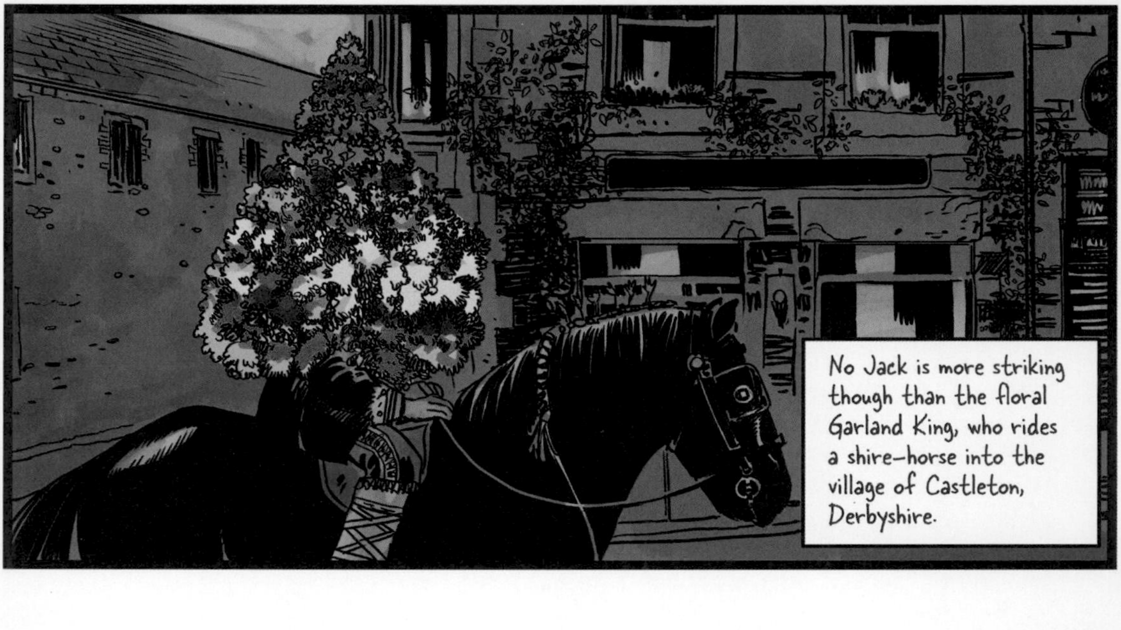
No Jack is more striking though than the floral Garland King, who rides a shire-horse into the village of Castleton, Derbyshire.

JACK IN THE GREEN

May is an important month in the British folklore calendar, falling as it does midway between the spring equinox and summer solstice. It is the month when the rising sap reaches its culmination; buds become blooms, lambs are in the field, and chicks are in the nest. Many of England's folk customs take place on May Day at the start of the month (celebrated in Scotland, Ireland, on the Isle of Mann, and by modern pagans as Beltane).

Dating back to at least the 16th century, one old English custom sees a young woman crowned as the Summer Queen, or May Queen. The young, beautiful, and virtuous May Queen leads the May Day procession, acting as a personification of the holiday, of springtime, and of summer. Since the 18th century, and increasingly since the 1970s, the May Queen has been accompanied in many of these regional processions by a figure known as "Jack in the Green."

In Castleton, Derbyshire, May the 29th is known as Garland King Day. The Garland King – Castleton's own Jack in the Green – rides a cart horse which is donned with a large wooden frame completely covered in flowers and greenery, so that only its legs are visible. At the apex of the King's floral finery is fixed a posy of especially fine flowers, and this is known as the Queen. Following the King is a second Queen, on horseback like himself. Up until 1956, the Queen (or the Woman, as she was known then) was always a man in female dress. The Garland King leads a procession which makes its way through the village, via the six public houses, into the churchyard. There, the great garland is hoisted up on ropes to the top of the church tower, and the Queen posy is laid at the foot of the village war memorial.

Although the custom of dressing Jack in the Green in leaves and flowers can be reliably traced back to the 18th century, some folklorists have argued that the tradition harks back to much older beliefs and practices. Links between Jack and the ancient yet elusive figure of the Green Man have been postulated (and likewise disputed) by many. The idea that the Green Man – a foliage-faced figure depicted on church carvings across Europe since the Middle Ages – represents a pre-Christian nature god continues to fascinate many, but remains unproven.

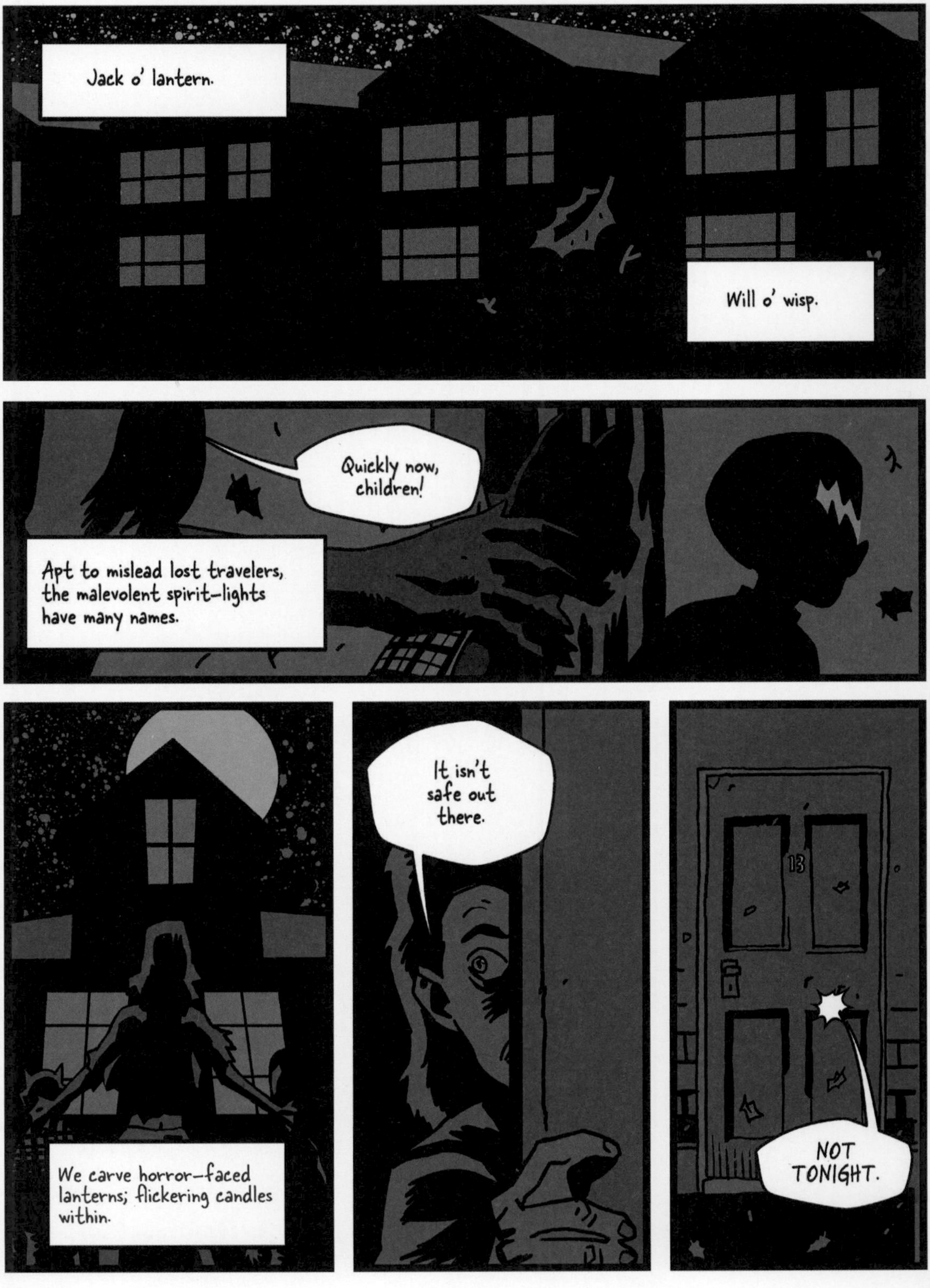
Jack o' lantern.
Will o' wisp.
Quickly now, children!
Apt to mislead lost travelers, the malevolent spirit-lights have many names.
We carve horror-faced lanterns; flickering candles within.
It isn't safe out there.
13
NOT TONIGHT.

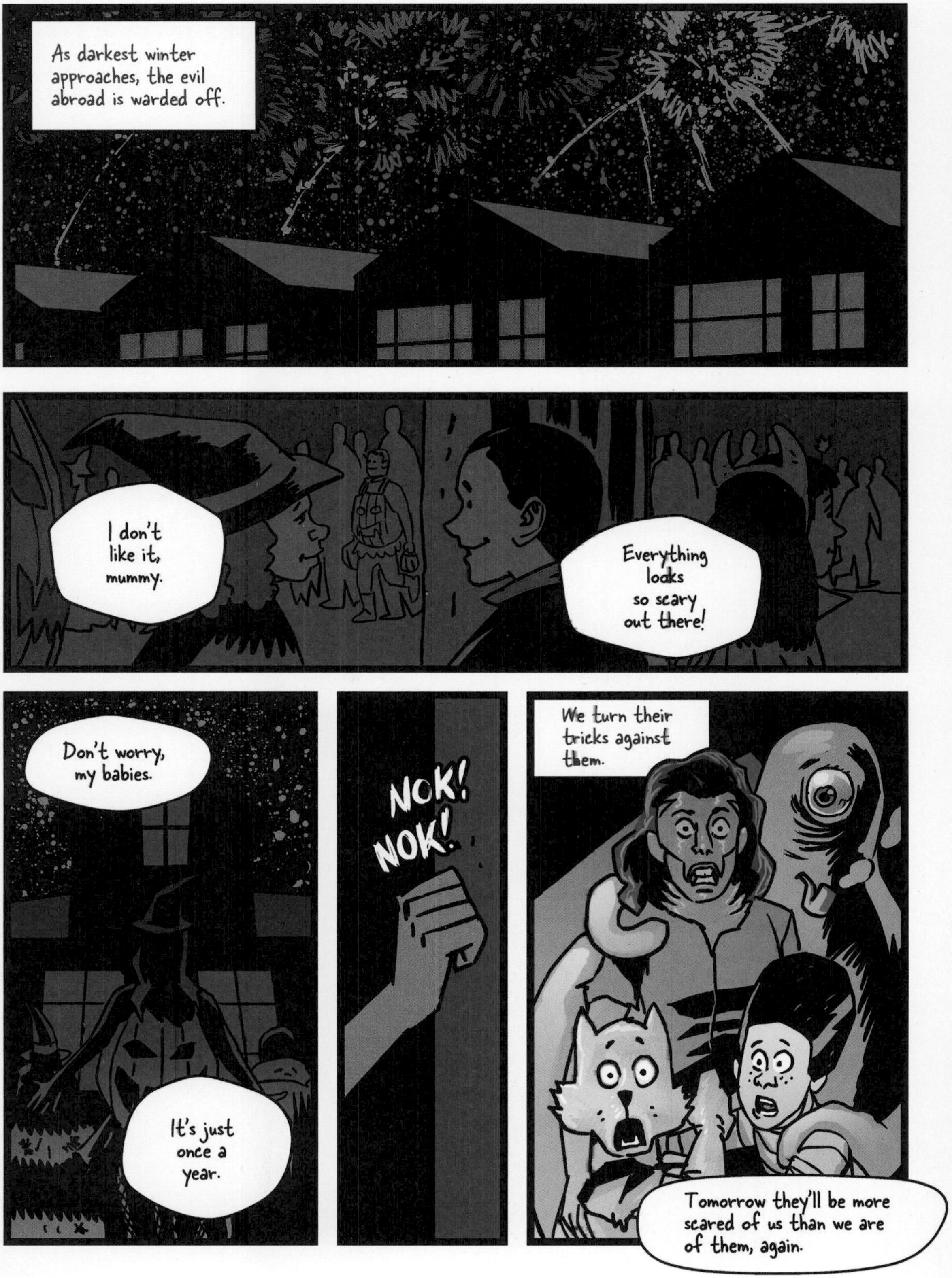
As darkest winter approaches, the evil abroad is warded off.
I don't like it, mummy.
Everything looks so scary out there!
Don't worry, my babies.
It's just once a year.
NOK! NOK!
We turn their tricks against them.
Tomorrow they'll be more scared of us than we are of them, again.

HALLOWE'EN

THE NAME HALLOWE'EN IS A CONTRACTION OF ALL Hallow's Eve. All Hallows' Day is an event in the Christian calendar commemorating all Christian martyrs. Since the 8th century, All Hallows' Day has been celebrated on the 1st of November by the Roman Catholic, Protestant, Anglican, and Methodist churches, as well as many other Christian sects. These churches also celebrate All Souls' Day, aka the Day of the Dead, on the 2nd of November. Together, these three days are referred to as Allhallowtide.

In Mexico, Día de los Muertos ("the Day of the Dead") festivities take place throughout Allhallowtide. Friends and family gather together to honor and remember the dead, making offerings of marigold flowers [1] on graves and home altars. Decorative skulls (*calavera*) feature heavily in Día de los Muertos, giving the celebrations a macabre yet festive air. Similar festivals take place at this time in Brazil, Costa Rica, and across much of Latin America.

Many modern day pagans (neopagans) refer to the night of October 31st and day of November 1st as Samhain – one of the four "quarter days" of the pagan Wheel of the Year. Samhain is the modern Gaelic name for a festival dating back to at least the 1st century BCE, marking the beginning of winter and the coming of the long, dark nights. Certain extant Neolithic burial sites in Ireland – such as the Hill of Tārā and the Mound of Hostages in County Meath – are believed by some to have been deliberately aligned with the Samhain sunrise. This has been put forward as evidence that this transitional time may have held significance for many thousands of years.

The medieval Irish text *Acallam na Senórach* ("Tales of the Elders of Ireland") records that the cave of Cruachan, in County Roscommon, served as a portal to the "Other Realm," from which "certain pigs of paganism," a trio of female werewolves, and other strange, supernatural creatures were said to have emerged on different Samhains. Such writings have long been taken as evidence that Samhain was believed to be a time when the barrier which separated the human realm and the Other Realm – the place of the fae, of the dead, and of other paranormal beings – was somehow at its thinnest.

1   For similar customs, see 'Willow' (pg. 22).

Trick-or-treating is probably the most familiar and widely practiced Hallowe'en custom for many of us. Trick-or-treating as we know it today has its roots in the Middle-Ages British-Catholic "souling" tradition. Soulers were typically children and poor adults who went door to door during Allhallowtide, offering songs and prayers for the dead, and especially for those trapped in Purgatory. In exchange for their songs and prayers, soulers received specially baked "soul cakes" made with dried fruits and winter spices, and marked with the sign of the cross. Soulers sometimes wore disguises to hide their identities, and traditionally carried lanterns made from hollowed-out turnips.

The earliest surviving record of the association between pumpkin carving and All Hallows' Eve comes from a 1st-of-November-1866 edition of the Canadian newspaper the *Daily News*:

> The old time custom of keeping up Hallowe'en was not forgotten last night by the youngsters of the city. They had their maskings and their merry-makings, and perambulated the streets after dark in a way which was no doubt amusing to themselves. There was a great sacrifice of pumpkins from which to make transparent heads and face, lighted up by the unfailing two inches of tallow candle.

The carved pumpkins we have come to associate with Hallowe'en are the American descendants of the old souling turnip lanterns. According to Professor Ronald Hutton's *The Stations of the Sun* (1996), hollowed-out turnip lanterns with faces carved into them were already a part of Allhallowtide custom in Ireland and Scotland by the 19th century. Some believe that the purpose of these lanterns was to ward off those from the Other Realm who might be abroad at this time of year, or else to fool them that the carriers were their associates and therefore should be left alone. For these same reasons, these carved lanterns would be displayed on windowsills and next to doorways, in order to dissuade wandering spirits from entering buildings.

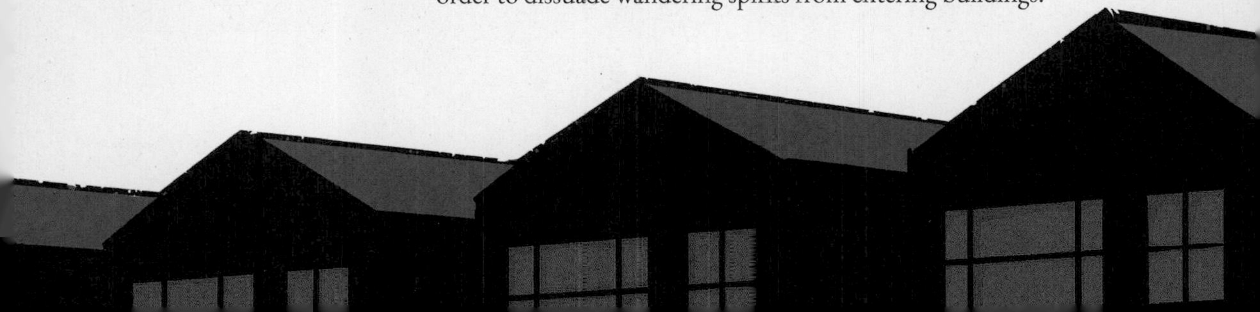

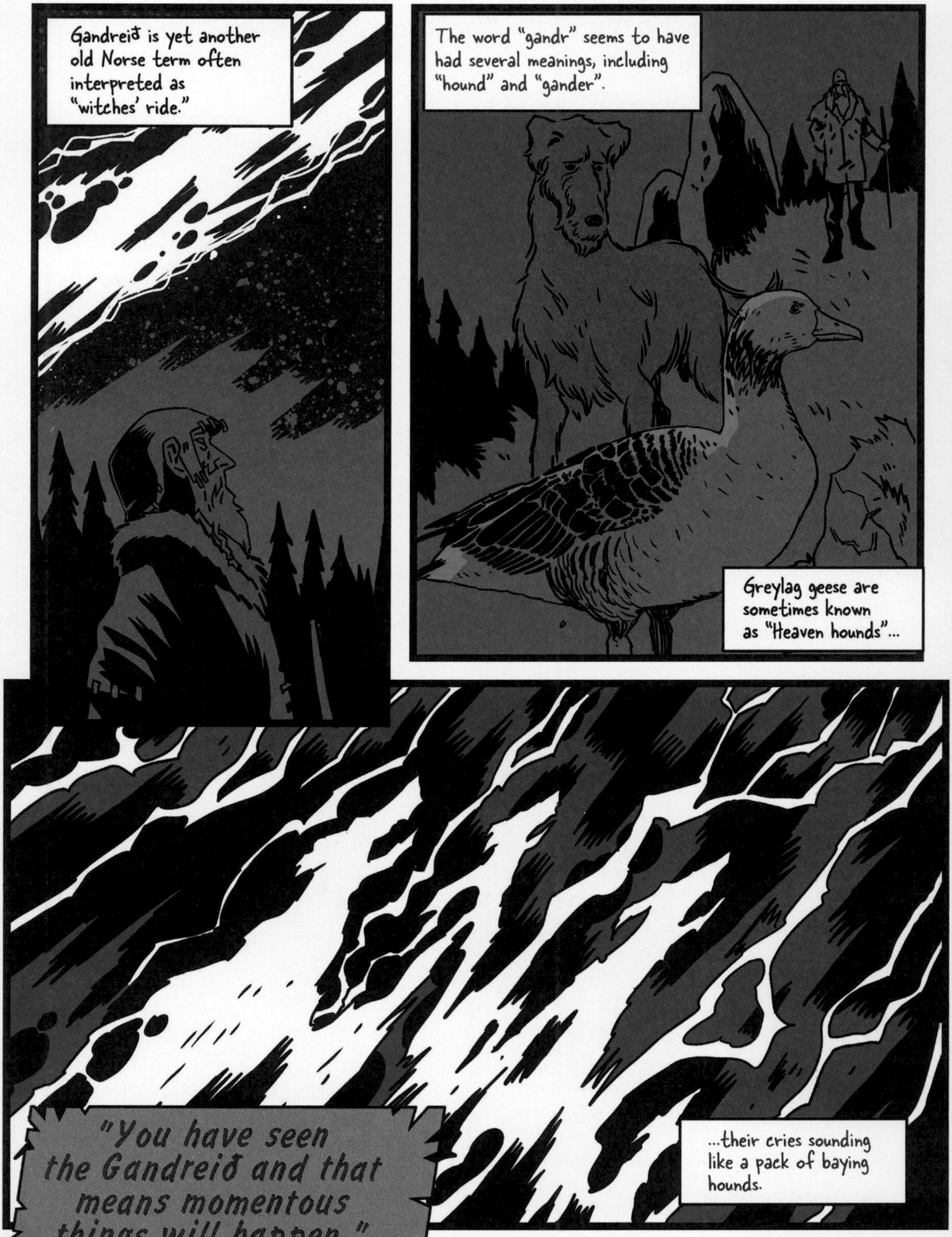
Gandreið is yet another old Norse term often interpreted as "witches' ride."
The word "gandr" seems to have had several meanings, including "hound" and "gander".
Greylag geese are sometimes known as "Heaven hounds"...
"You have seen the Gandreið and that means momentous things will happen."
...their cries sounding like a pack of baying hounds.

GANDREIÐ

THE WILD HUNT (*WILDE JAGD*, IN THE ORIGINAL GERMAN) IS A TERM POPULARIZED BY THE folklorist Jacob Grimm in his 1835 work *Deutsche Mythologie*. There are many variations of the Wild Hunt, dating back centuries and varying according to their location, but all share certain characteristics:

> On certain nights, a supernatural party travels noisily through the air [...] In many stories an uncanny pack of hunting hounds or wolves accompanies the party.

Grimm believed that the Wild Hunt had its root in Old Norse pagan beliefs, formed between the 2nd and 8th centuries. Odin – Father of the Slain, and god of wind – was its original leader. Yet, Grimm's Wild Hunt had nothing to do with the noble recruitment of supernatural champions: instead, it was something to be feared. Grimm's Wild Hunt was a heathen "furious host" comprised not of Valkyries, but of the ghosts of the unbaptized, of baying black hounds, and worse. Even back when Odin led the hunt, the cult of Christ was already spreading across Europe. While it may be difficult to substantiate claims that the Wild Hunt is pre-Christian in any true sense, it has always been "un-Christian." The old pagan gods were demonized by the Christian church, their skybound hunt becoming monstrous. The restless spirits of Grimm's Wild Hunt were the unbaptized, witches, faeries, revealing their "connexion with heathenism," as Grimm put it.

The Wild Hunt has had many names, including Odensjakt ("Odin's Hunt"), Oskoreia ("Terrifying Ride"), and Gandreið. Although Gandreið is often interpreted as meaning "Witches' Ride," the Old Norse word *gandr* actually seems to have had several meanings, including "staff," "hound," "swift horse," and "gander," as in a male goose. The word *gandr* survives today in Scandinavian languages, meaning a "magical gust of wind." Witches, of course, were known to ride all of these things, including geese, through the sky on their way to their Black Sabbats.

Greylag geese – the larger, wild ancestors of the domestic European goose – are, in certain British locations, nicknamed "Heaven hounds," or "Gabriel's hounds." They share these names with the spectral black dogs of folklore and legend in the same areas. The cries of Greylag geese are said to sound like a pack of baying hounds. Because the birds migrate to and from different parts of Europe at the turn of the season, their calls are only heard at certain times of year – just as the Wild Hunt, with its pack of hunting hounds, may only be heard overhead on certain nights.

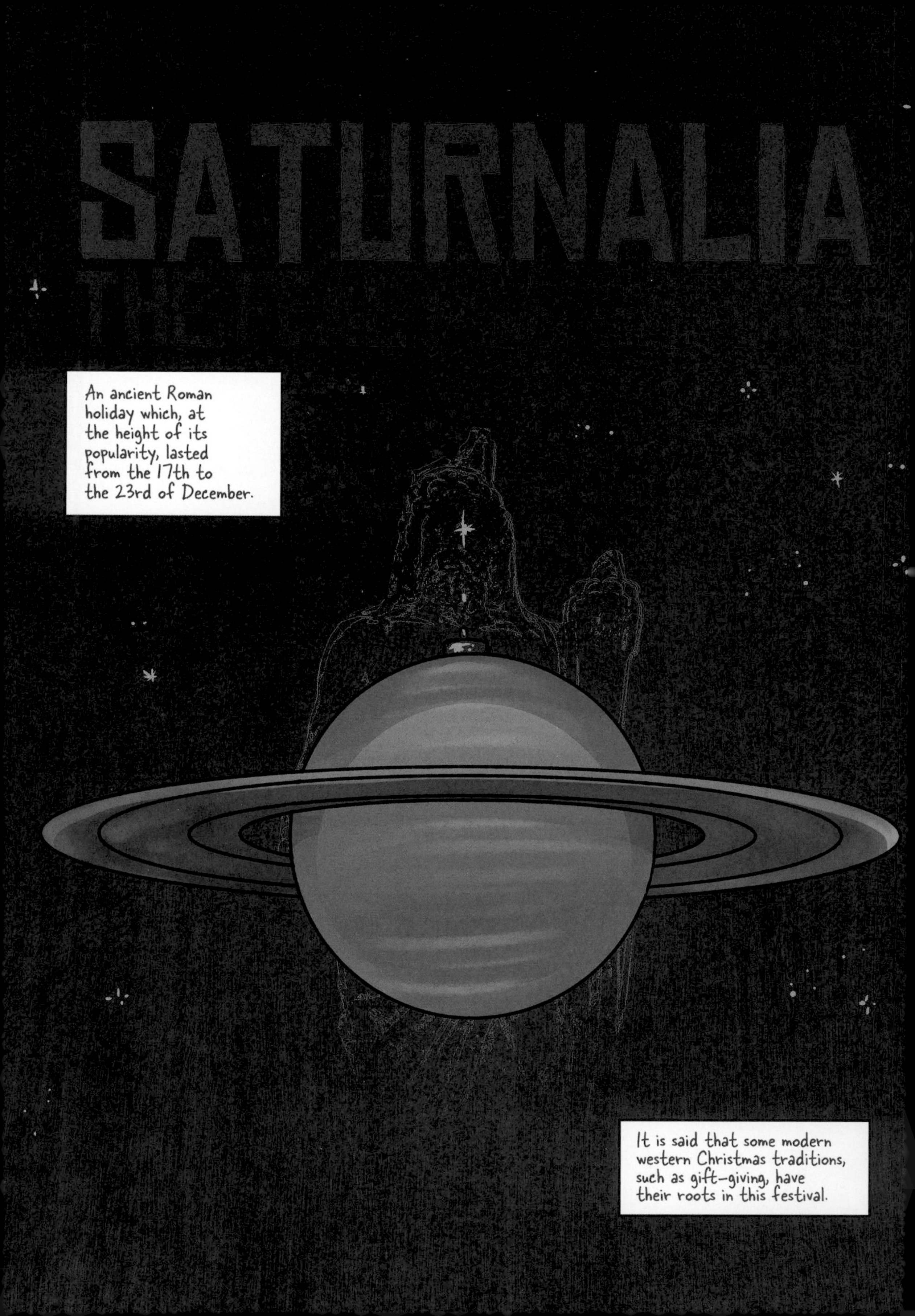
SATURNALIA
An ancient Roman holiday which, at the height of its popularity, lasted from the 17th to the 23rd of December.
It is said that some modern western Christmas traditions, such as gift-giving, have their roots in this festival.

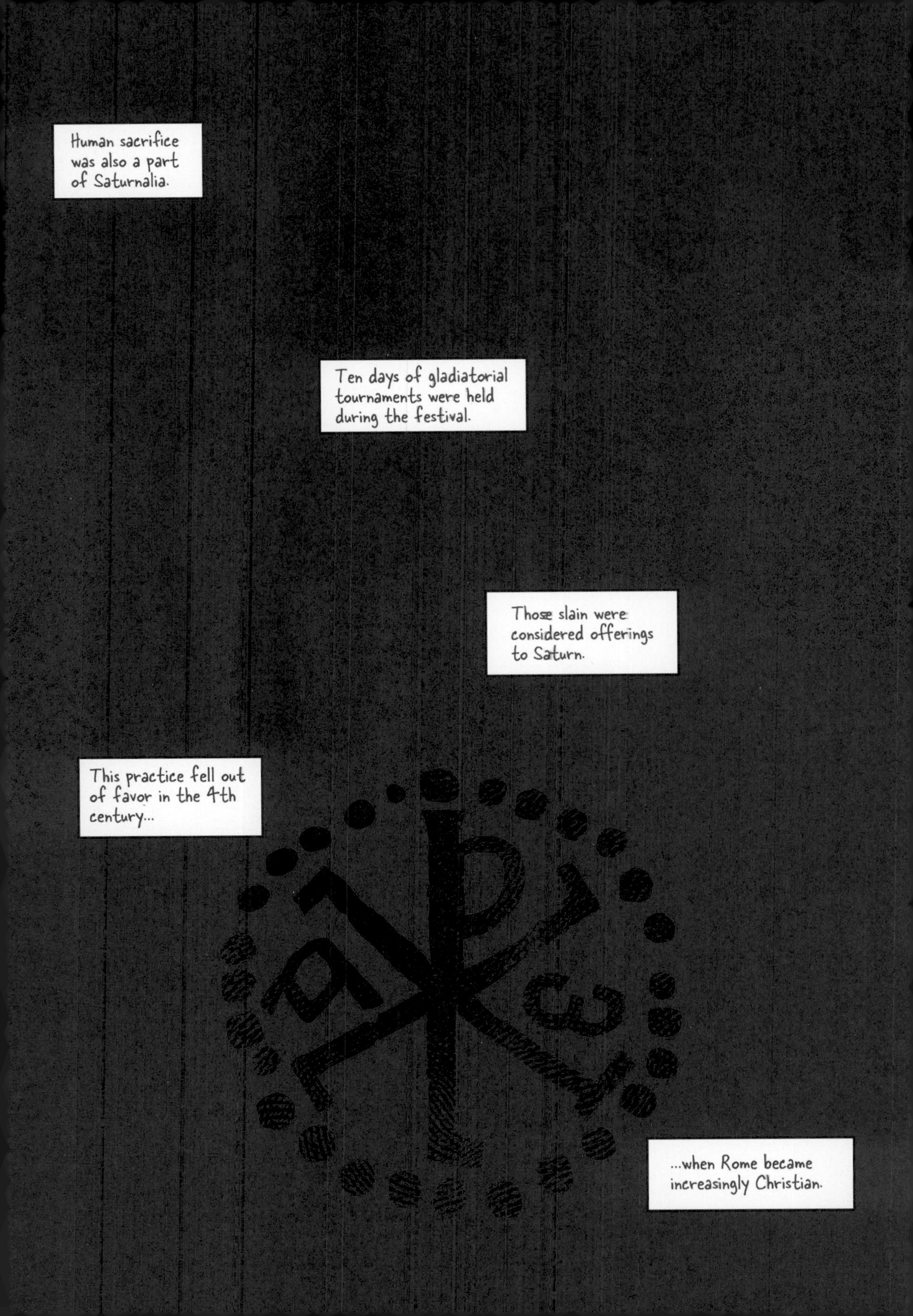
Human sacrifice was also a part of Saturnalia.
Ten days of gladiatorial tournaments were held during the festival.
Those slain were considered offerings to Saturn.
This practice fell out of favor in the 4th century...
...when Rome became increasingly Christian.

SATURNALIA WAS A DECEMBER FESTIVAL HELD IN HONOR OF THE ANCIENT ROMAN GOD SATURN.
Saturn, and the ritual practices pertaining to him, were believed to have their roots in the mythical Golden Age when the Titans ruled the earth. The Greek Titan Cronos[1] became the Roman Titan Saturn, who was said to have ruled over Rome in the long-ago as the first emperor. Saturn was worshiped as a god of wealth and abundance, but also of dissolution and renewal.

The festival of Saturnalia has a complex history. Originally taking place on the 17th of December, over centuries, Saturnalia evolved into a week-long festival. Prior to 217 BCE, Saturnalian customs adhered to what were considered the contemporary, acceptable Roman ways of honoring the gods. However, following Rome's defeat at Carthage, Rome adopted a different approach to the festival, increasingly influenced by (what they believed to have been) ancient Greek rites and practices. After this time, public banquets became part of the celebration as, increasingly, did the concept of "misrule."

A *Saturnalicius princeps*, or "Lord of Saturnalia," was appointed by lot and presided over the festivities, often ordering participants to engage in comical and humiliating deeds. In his (now much disputed) 1890 work *The Golden Bough*, anthropologist and folklorist James Frazer claimed that the Lord of Saturnalia may have at one time (pre-1st century BCE) been ritually killed at the end of his mock reign, as an offering to Saturn. Frazer and others have noted parallels between the Lord of Saturnalia and the Medieval French *Prince des Sots* ("Prince of Fools") and his English and Scots equivalents, the Lord of Misrule and Abbot of Unreason. These temporary rulers presided over the Christian Fools Day – also known as the Feast of Fools – during the Middle Ages, in which comedy, debauchery, and mayhem were likewise encouraged. Like Saturnalia, and our own modern April Fool's Day, the Feast of Fools was an "inversion ritual": a special occasion on which it is understood by all that cultural and societal norms have been temporarily suspended or reversed.

As part of the inversion festivities during Saturnalia, all slaves and servants were given leave to act as freemen, as their masters even served food at some feasts. Gambling (usually forbidden) was permitted at the time of the festival, and brightly colored clothes (usually seen as vulgar) were worn by all throughout. Gifts were privately given and received, and a general atmosphere of fun and frivolity seems to have pervaded the whole celebration; the 1st century BCE Roman poet Gaius Valerius Catullus referred to Saturnalia as "the best of days."

---

1   See 'Chronos' (pg. 74).

N A L I A

Animal sacrifice to Saturn did form an undisputed part of Saturnalian rites, but by 97 BCE cultural norms had shifted, and Rome formally banned human sacrifice, now viewing it as a (literally) barbaric practice. Nevertheless, a loophole was included in this ancient law, allowing for ritual killing under certain religious conditions. Ten days of gladiatorial tournaments were held during Saturnalia and the blood spilled, and lives lost, were all dedicated to Saturn.

The celebration of Saturnalia fell out of favor post-4th century CE, as Rome and its customs became increasingly Christianized. Indeed, in 350 CE, Pope Julius I officially decreed that Jesus Christ's day of birth was the 25th of December – the date on which the festival of Saturnalia had previously culminated. The century-faded echoes of that ancient Roman festival can still be detected, however faintly, within modern Christmas and New Year's festivities.

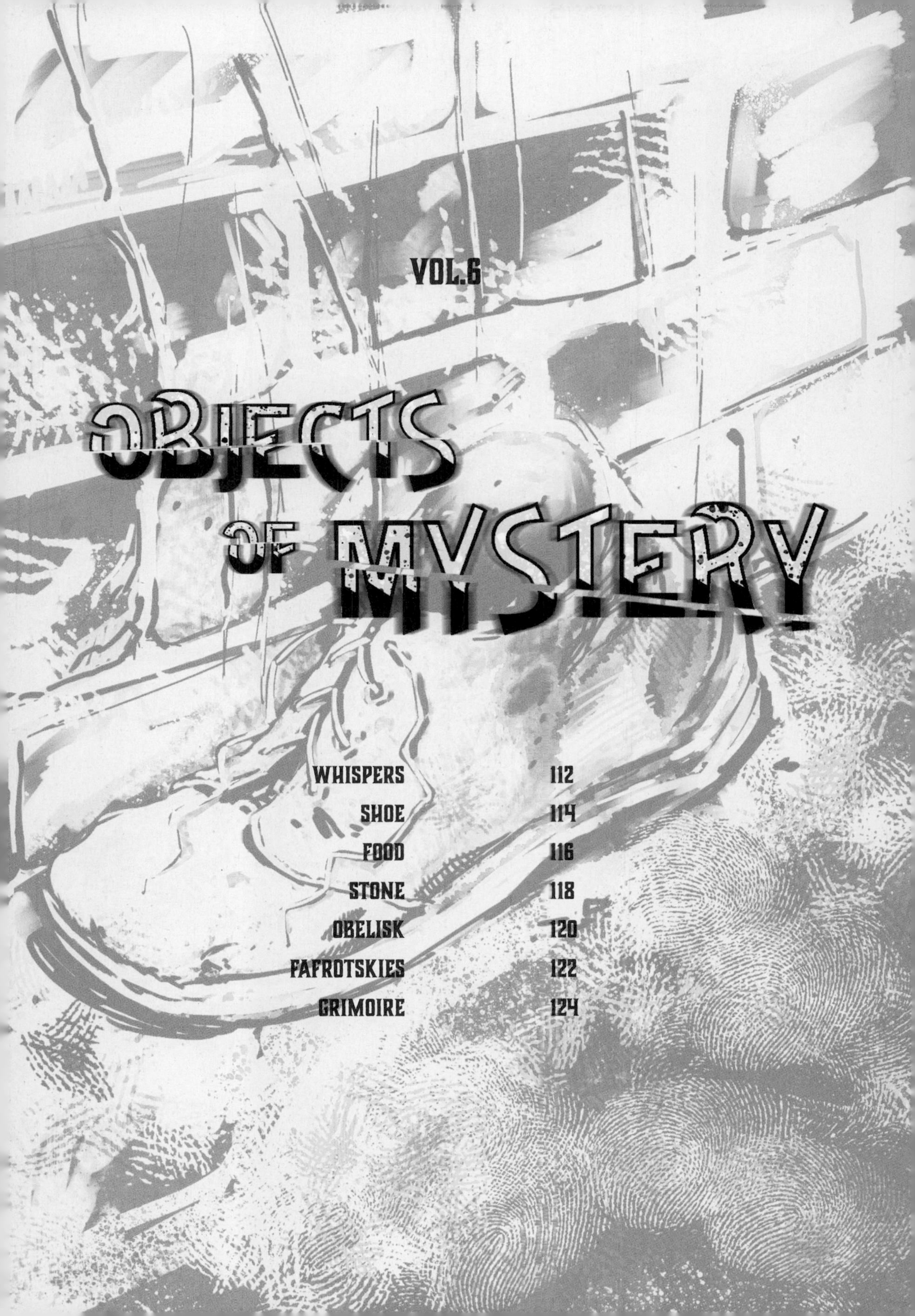

VOL.6

OBJECTS OF MYSTERY

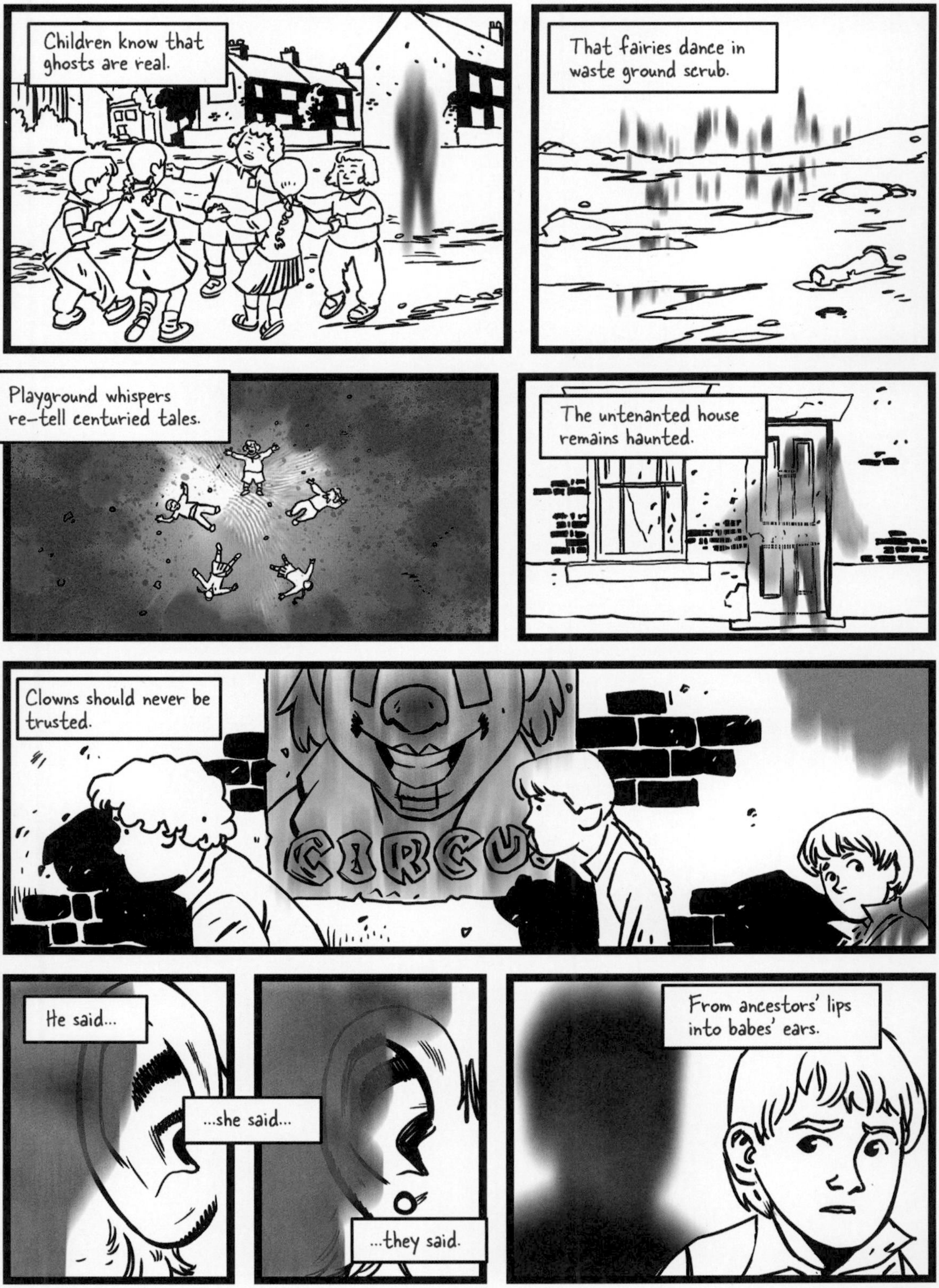
Children know that ghosts are real.
That fairies dance in waste ground scrub.
Playground whispers re-tell centuried tales.
The untenanted house remains haunted.
Clowns should never be trusted.
CIRCU
He said...
...she said...
...they said.
From ancestors' lips into babes' ears.

W
H
I
S
P
E
R
S

Children are natural storytellers. Unlike most adults, they weave tales in a way which incorporates them into the fabric of their reality. Mistakes in retellings are corrected by older kids, or by kids with older siblings from whom they have already heard the stories. Because of this, childlore[1] – the folklore of the playground – survives through oral tradition. Games and rhymes acted and chanted out in modern tarmac school-yards are survivors from previous generations of children, and some were first created centuries ago.

> " Lizzie Borden took an ax
> She gave her mother forty whacks
> When she saw what she had done
> She gave her father forty one "

This skipping rhyme, sung in American playgrounds on a daily basis, memorializes a grisly crime committed in 1892. More than a century and half later, Lizzie Borden's name is still on the lips of children.

Much of what we call childlore remains all-but-unknowable to adults, shrinking away to nothing under the harsh lens of academic or critical analysis. Children see and believe things which grown ups are positive they cannot be right about, even though they saw and knew them too when they were kids. The internet gives us a strange glimpse into some of those ideas though, because it amplifies rumors which adults pick up from children.

During the 1980s there were schoolyard whispers of Killer Clowns at large across America, the UK, and beyond. Vaguely remembered now by many of us born in the 1970s, these child-to-child tales were barely noticed, or else quickly dismissed by any adults who caught a whiff of them. 2016's "Great Clown Panic," by contrast, became something quite different. Driven by social media, hundreds of creepy clown sightings were not just reported, but photographed and filmed, and shared around the globe.

Although these clown hoaxes were not perpetrated by children, those responsible were certainly immature in the truest sense of the word; they were functioning at a level above that of childish magic, and awe, and below that of adult responsibility and stoic realism. Many involved may, in truth, have been trying to recapture that childlike thrill of believing by making others believe. There is something profoundly tragic about the idea that the closest some adults will ever get to that sense of wonder and reverence of knowing monsters were real, as they did when they were children, is to become the monsters themselves.

1   See 'Food' (pg. 116).

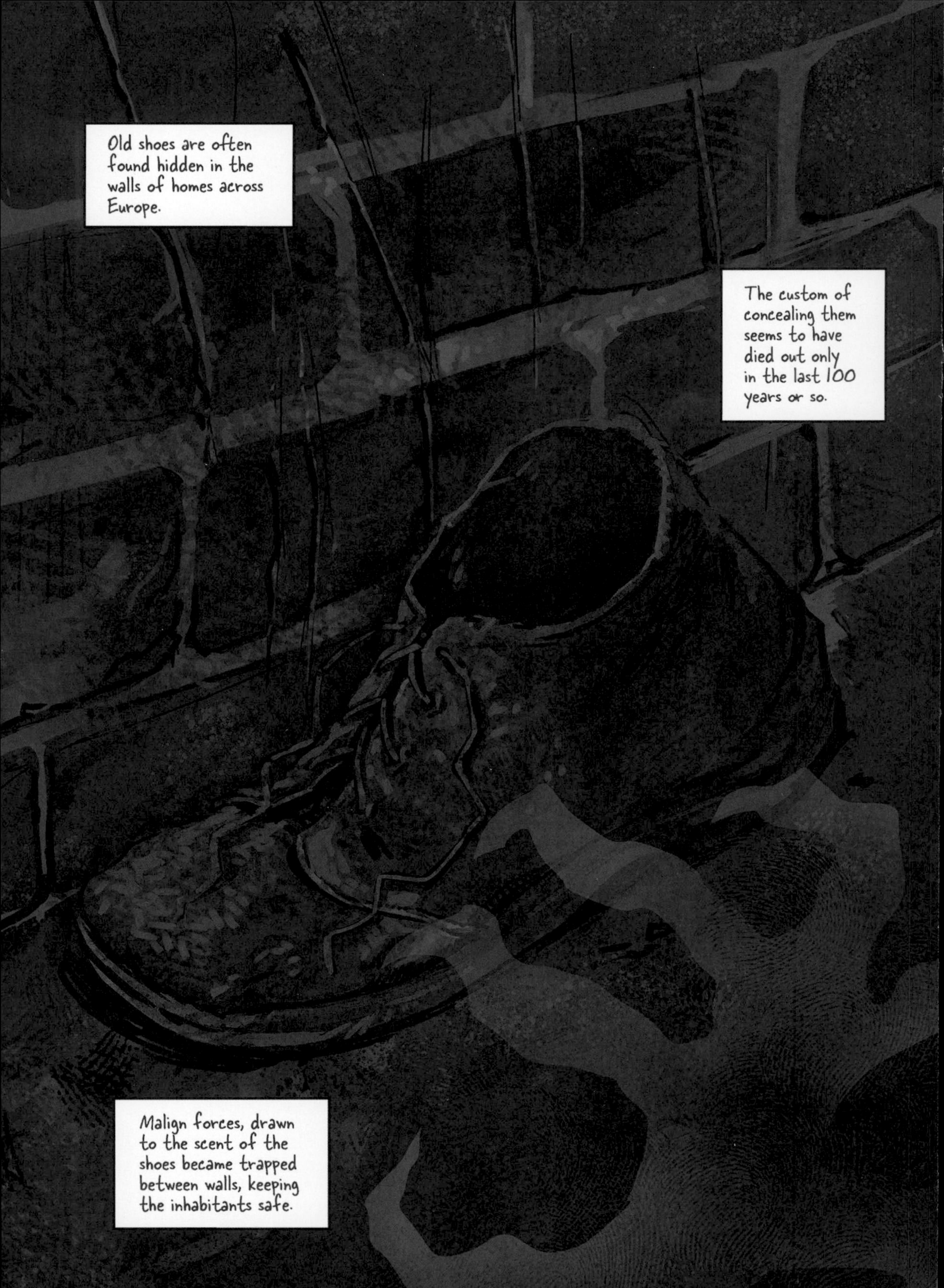
Old shoes are often found hidden in the walls of homes across Europe.
The custom of concealing them seems to have died out only in the last 100 years or so.
Malign forces, drawn to the scent of the shoes became trapped between walls, keeping the inhabitants safe.

S H E

APOTROPAIC MAGIC (FROM GREEK *ἀποτρέπειν* MEANING "TO WARD OFF") IS A FORM OF protective magic using charms. Practiced since at least ancient Egyptian times, when boar tusks were used to ward off evil influences from children and expectant mothers, apotropaic magic takes many forms, as do the charms used. Horseshoes, gargoyles, crucifixes on walls, dreamcatchers, painted eyes – all of these are familiar examples of apotropaic charms still used in the 21st century.

In early modern Europe, the practice of walling up a protective charm to protect against evil influences and black magic became widespread. The mummified corpses of cats, the skulls of horses, and specially prepared "witch bottles" were all common charms used, but the most widespread was shoes. Found during renovation and conservation, these shoes – almost always single shoes, rather than a pair – are secreted under floorboards, within the fabric of walls, up chimneys, and around doors and windows, in countless buildings.

In the 1950s, Miss June Swann was the keeper of the Boot and Shoe Museum in Northampton, England. Miss Swan noted that people were often bringing shoes into the museum which they had found hidden in parts of their home, or place of business. She began to keep a distinct record of these finds. By 1969, Miss Swan had recorded 129 such discoveries, and by 1986, that number had grown to 700. Today, the Northampton museum's Concealed Shoe Index contains records of over 2,000 such finds, with three or four new entries being made each month.

The exact reason behind the hiding of shoes within the fabric of a building remains a topic of much discussion and conjecture. The ensuring of fertility is one theory, the idea being that the worn shoe of a mother, or of a healthy child, might somehow imbue the building it was hidden in with fertility and maternal health. Some have gone on to claim links to the much darker Carthagian and Roman practice of interring the body of an infant in the foundations of a building. The most popular theory, however, is that the shoes were intended to ward off malign influences. Whether these were literal witches, ghosts, malicious fae and household spirits, or simply ill health and bad luck, remains a topic of debate.

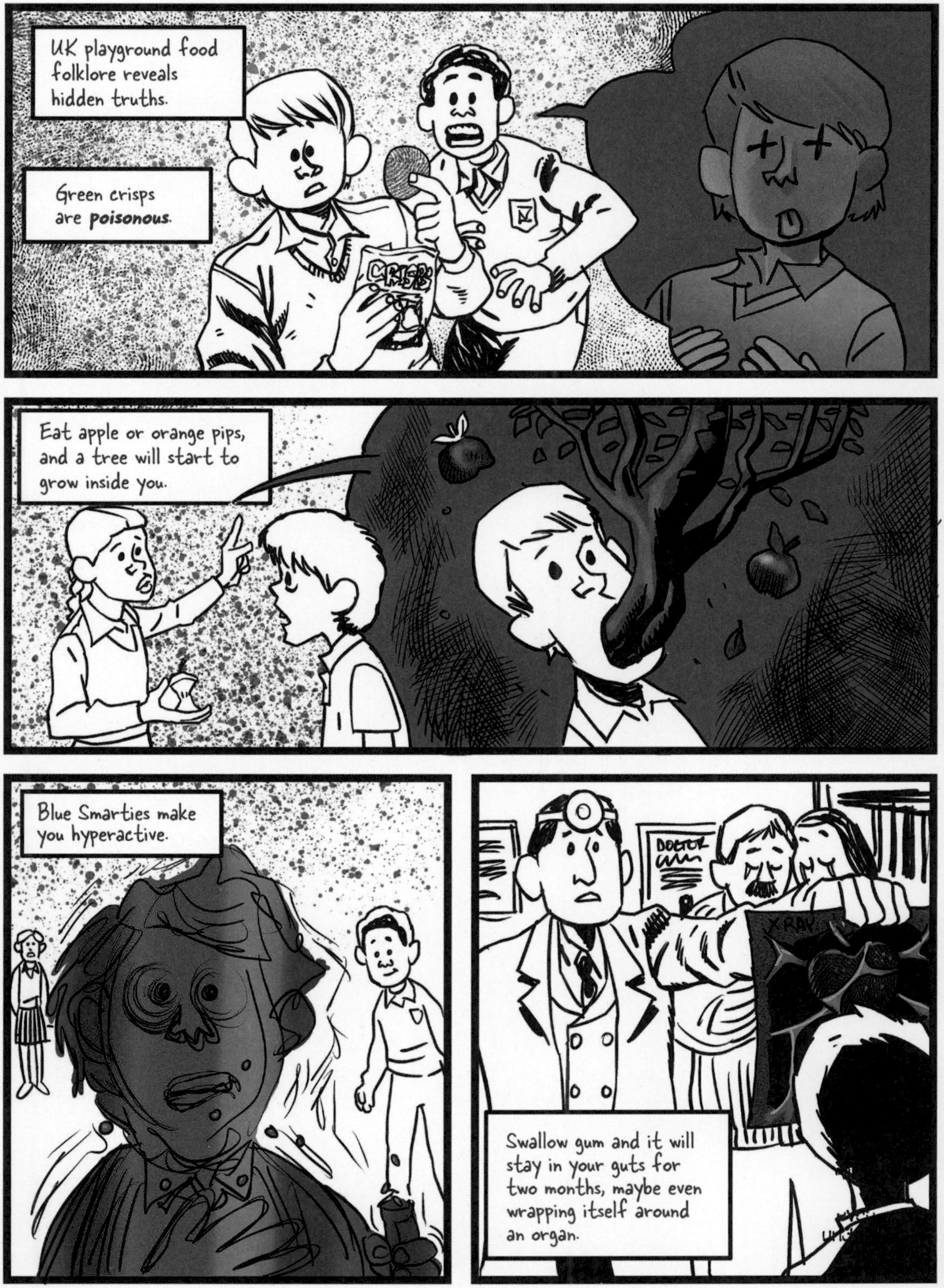
UK playground food folklore reveals hidden truths.
Green crisps are **poisonous**.
Eat apple or orange pips, and a tree will start to grow inside you.
Blue Smarties make you hyperactive.
DOCTOR
X-RAY
Swallow gum and it will stay in your guts for two months, maybe even wrapping itself around an organ.

F

O

D

EVERY CHILD KNOWS IT TO BE TRUE. Passed down from class to class, from year to year, children learn the cold, hard facts about potential dangers lurking in the lunchbox.

LESSON 1. Green crisps are poisonous.

The reason some crisps (potato chips) end up with a green edge is due to sunlight. Parts of the potato exposed to sunlight as they grow turn green because of chlorophyll. Chlorophyll can contain a chemical called solanine, the same toxin produced by deadly nightshade. However, a person would have to eat around ten packets of entirely green potato snacks in order to feel any ill effects.

LESSON 2. Swallowing the pips will kill you.

Apple seeds, when chewed, produce a tiny amount of hydrogen cyanide. For a child, it would take five apples' worth of pips, all carefully chewed and swallowed, before any ill effects would be felt. Orange pips are harmless and actually pretty good for you – but chewing them produces an exceedingly bitter taste.

LESSON 3. Blue Smarties make you hyperactive.

In the UK, Smarties are small chocolates covered in a hard, colorful outer shell. Blue Smarties disappeared from packs in early 2006, being replaced with white ones. Manufacturer Nestlé decided to remove all artificial coloring from the sweets, but could not find a suitable blue. Blue Smarties returned to packs in 2008, spirulina now acting as the natural coloring agent. Blue Smarties were previously colored with a synthetic dye called Brilliant Blue FCF (also known as E133) which, although not proven to cause hyperactivity, does have the capacity for inducing allergic reactions in some people, especially asthmatics.

LESSON 4. Swallow gum and it will sit in your stomach forever.

Gum is not made to be swallowed: it is made to be chewed, and to not break down in the process of chewing. Therefore, it can present a choking hazard if the chewer attempts to swallow it. Gum is also nigh-on impossible to digest, but this does not mean that it will just sit in your stomach indefinitely. Much like sweetcorn, gum (in most cases) will make an all-but-intact reappearance next time the consumer visits the toilet.

Playground folklore and childlore[1] consists of stories told and retold generation after generation – just like all folklore. However, as the above lessons illustrate, there is almost always a kernel of truth in even the simplest and silliest-sounding tale.

1   See 'Whispers' (pg. 112).

High atop Mount Huaguo in China, a curious stone once stood.

From that stone came forth an egg...

...and out of that egg was born a monkey.

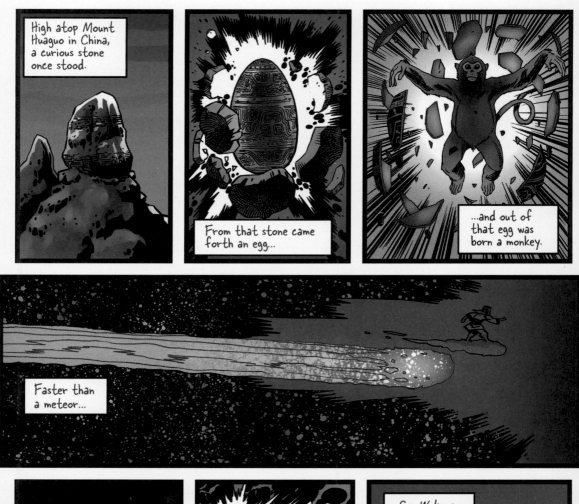

Faster than a meteor...

...strong enough to lift a mountain...

...wielder of magical staff Ruyi Jingu Bang.

Sun Wukong.

The Monkey King.

IN THE BEGINNING, THERE WAS PRIMAL CHAOS. Through the eons, the four worlds formed anew. A certain stone, old as creation, was shone upon by the sun and the moon. Slowly but surely, nurtured by the essences of Heaven and the moisture of the earth, this stone became fertile. An egg. This first egg was called "Thought" and as the Buddha said: "With our thoughts, we make the world." Lightning struck the rock, and from it an irrepressible stone monkey was born.

This little introduction will be familiar to viewers of the English-dubbed action-fantasy TV series *Monkey*, which first aired in Japan between 1978 and 1979. Known to many English language viewers as *Monkey Magic*, thanks to its ridiculously catchy theme tune of the same name, the show's Japanese title was *Saiyūki* ("Account of the Journey to the West").

The novel *Xī Yóu Jì* ("Journey to the West") upon which the TV series was based, was first published anonymously in China around 1592 and is widely regarded as one of the four great classical novels of Chinese literature. *Journey to the West* draws upon ancient themes and sources, including Chinese folk religion, Chinese mythology, and Confucianist, Taoist, and Buddhist philosophy. Disparate legends of the Monkey King – the hero of *Journey to the West* – pre-date the novel by many hundreds (or possibly even thousands) of years, but the novel came to be regarded as the definitive telling of his life and deeds.

Dà Táng Sān Cáng Qǔ Jīng Shī Huà ("The Story of How Tripitaka of the Great Tang Procures the Scriptures") is the title of a seventeen-chapter novelette written three hundred years before *Journey to the West*. Likely created to serve as a prompt for oral storytelling, the text is widely believed to have inspired the later novel. In this 13th-century novelette, our simian hero is given the name Hóu Xíng Zhě ("Monkey Pilgrim"), but his origins and adventures are easily recognizable as those of the Monkey King.

Ironically, the figure who may have been the earliest inspiration for the Monkey King journeyed east, rather than west. Hanumān, the Indian monkey god, has roots which stretch back at least four thousand years. He is mentioned as the "divine monkey" in the Vedic *Rigveda*, written between 1500 and 1200 BCE. It is believed by many that stories and images of Hanumān traveled east from India to China along with Buddhist pilgrims, and that tales of the Monkey King drew upon these influences.

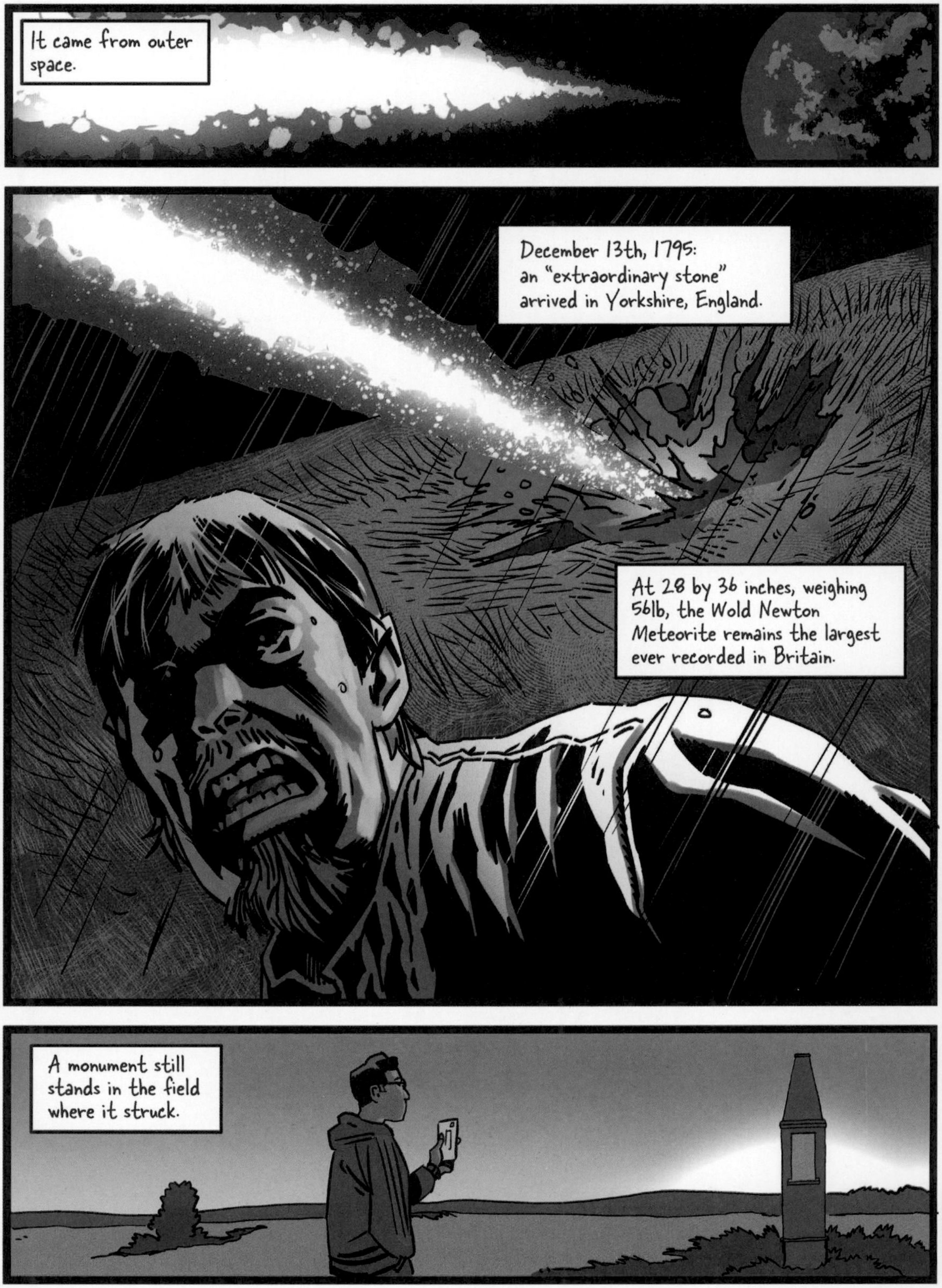
It came from outer space.
December 13th, 1795: an "extraordinary stone" arrived in Yorkshire, England.
At 28 by 36 inches, weighing 56lb, the Wold Newton Meteorite remains the largest ever recorded in Britain.
A monument still stands in the field where it struck.

In a field in England – in the East Riding of Yorkshire, to be more precise – amid the grass and nettles, there stands a lone, curious, 24-foot (7.3 meter) red brick obelisk. Constructed more than 200 years ago, a plaque set into one face reads:

> Here On this Spot, Dec. 13ᵗʰ, 1795 Fell from the Atmoſphere AN EXTRAORDINARY STONE In Breadth 28 inches In Length 36 inches and Whoſe Weight was 56 pounds.

The "EXTRAORDINARY STONE" arrived during a thunderstorm and landed two fields from Wold Cottage, which was at the time home to a magistrate named Major Edward Topham. It was Major Topham who would go on to have the obelisk constructed in 1799. The stone created a hole 3.2 feet (1 meter) in diameter, embedding itself firmly into a layer of chalk bedrock Zbeneath the soil.

Topham's shepherd was within 450 feet (137 meters) of the point of impact. Nearer still was laborer John Shipley, who signed a deposition published alongside a reprinted letter by Major Topham in the *Gentleman's Magazine* for July 1797, stating that:

> He was within eight or nine yards of the stone when it fell, saw it distinct seven or eight yards from the ground, and then strike into the earth, which flew up all about him, and which alarmed him very much.

The Wold Newton Meteorite (named after the village of Wold Newton, on whose outskirts it landed) was the largest ever observed to fall in Britain, and is the second largest recorded in Europe. However, the great scientist and occultist Sir Isaac Newton – not yet seventy years in his grave when the stone landed – had stated that there were no such things as meteorites. Having formulated the Law of Universal Gravitation, Newton's ideas were, naturally, taken very seriously. Consequently, when the Wold Newton Meteorite was put on display in 1797, many took pleasure in deriding it as a fake, or as volcanic debris. The then-president of the Royal Society of London, Sir Joseph Banks, was interested, however.

Working with the chemist Edward Howard, Banks compared samples from the Wold Newton meteorite with others, and found what he considered remarkable similarities. When his results were published, this marked the beginning of a new era of scientific interest in meteorites. Where many scientists, following Sir Isaac Newton's thinking, had refused to credit the existence of meteorites, now they were faced with proof. The Wold Newton Meteorite, now believed to be 4.6 billion years old, remains on display at the Natural History Museum in London today.

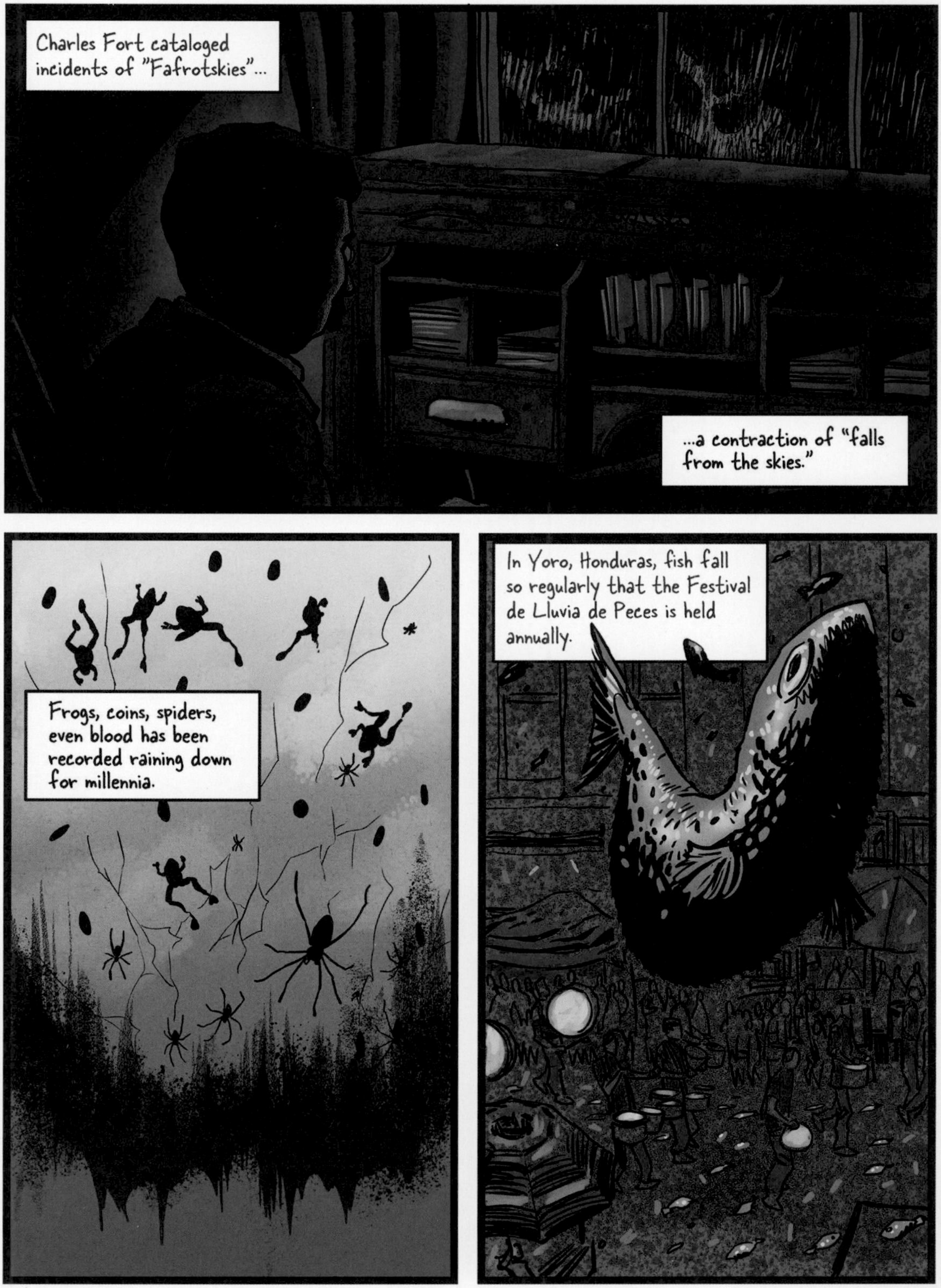
Charles Fort cataloged incidents of "Fafrotskies"...
...a contraction of "falls from the skies."
Frogs, coins, spiders, even blood has been recorded raining down for millennia.
In Yoro, Honduras, fish fall so regularly that the Festival de Lluvia de Peces is held annually.

FAFROTSKIES

Sometimes referred to as "fafrotskies" – a contraction of "falls from the skies" – accounts of mysterious objects dropping from the heavens have been around since records began. In ancient times, such events were often believed to be bad omens. Nowadays, they tend to be written off as harmless anomalies; falls of sea creatures are dismissed as having been thrown into the upper atmosphere by waterspouts; sheets of ice are explained as lavatorial waste ejected from aeroplanes at high altitudes.

A rain of live toads landed on a Mexican town in June 1997, but fish seem to be by far the most common creatures to fall from the skies. In August 2000, a shower of dead, but fresh, fish fell onto the English port of Great Yarmouth after a thunderstorm. La Lluvia de Peces (the "Rain of Fish") is said to occur at least once, sometimes twice, per year in the small town of Yoro, Honduras. First documented in the 1800s, the fish rain takes place with such regularity that, since 1998, it has become an annual festival. The date of the Festival de Lluvia de Peces is variable, coinciding with the first major rainfall in May or June, which invariably sees the town's streets covered with fish.

While showers of fish might be common, even somewhat predictable, red rains of "blood" have also been recorded for millennia, from Homer's Illiad to the 9th-century Anglo-Saxon Chronicle to the gore showers which supposedly splattered down upon Germany in an omen of the coming Black Death in the 1300s. Perhaps strangest of all in recent history, however, was the red rain which fell in India in 2001.

The article "When aliens rained over India" appeared in New Scientist Magazine on March the 2nd, 2006. The piece discussed mysterious falls of red rain which occurred in the Indian state of Kerala in 2001. After examining residue left by the precipitation, a physicist named Godfrey Louis concluded that the red particles which colored the rain could, in fact, be alien microbes carried to Earth by a comet (a sonic boom was heard before the downpour, which could have been caused by a meteorite). The scientific community were, naturally, skeptical of Louis's theories, but subsequent analysis of the particles forced critics to admit that they "looked biological." Eventually, it was concluded that the Indian red rain was probably caused by terrestrial algae spores. These tiny spores, it was hypothesized, were drawn up into the clouds by water evaporating from a pond, lake, or sea that contained the algae. The algae then effectively dyed the rain red. Despite what seemed like an entirely plausible scientific explanation, however, Godfrey Louis remained unconvinced.

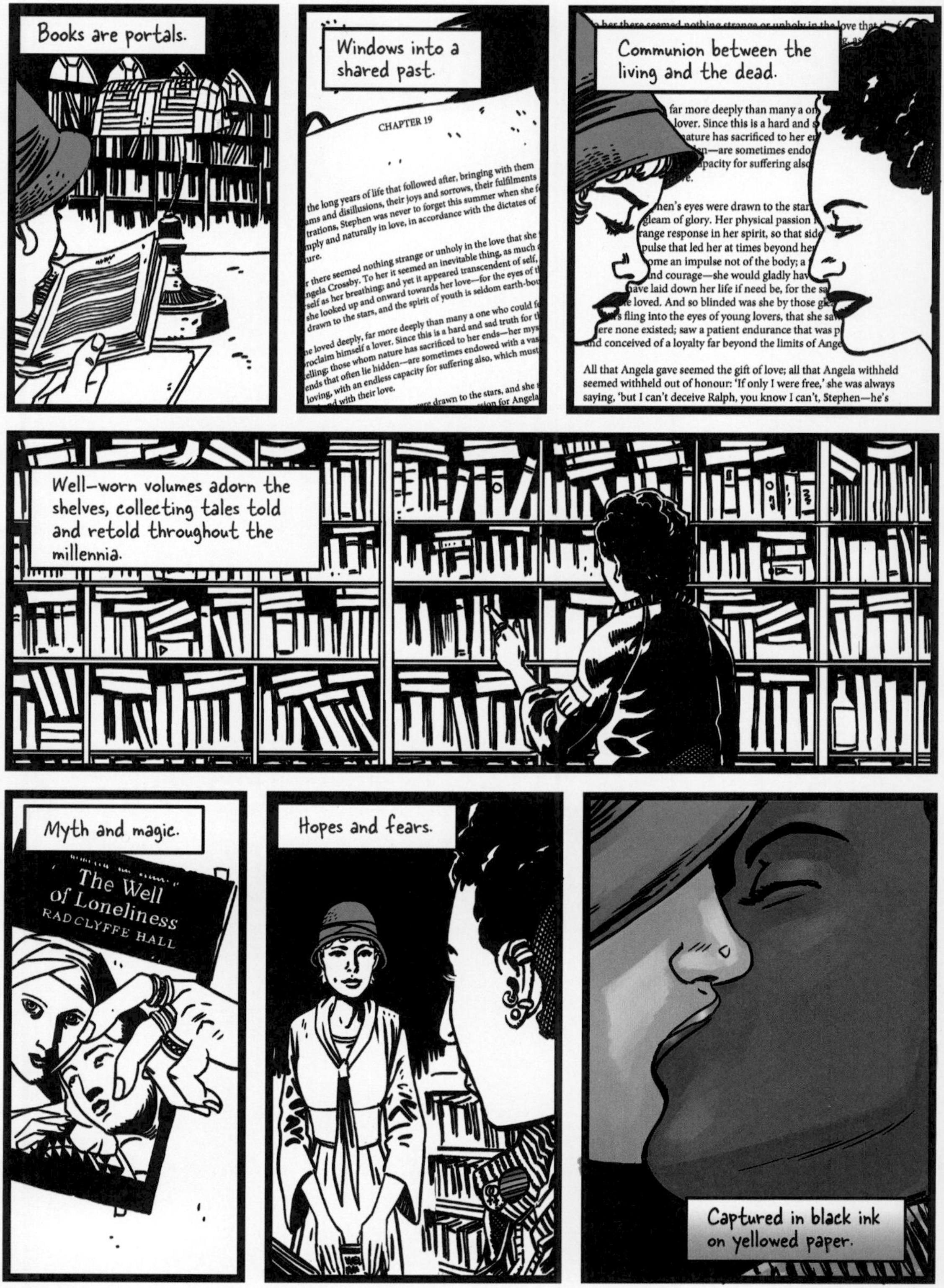
Books are portals.
Windows into a shared past.
CHAPTER 19
Communion between the living and the dead.
All that Angela gave seemed the gift of love; all that Angela withheld seemed withheld out of honour: 'If only I were free,' she was always saying, 'but I can't deceive Ralph, you know I can't, Stephen—he's
Well-worn volumes adorn the shelves, collecting tales told and retold throughout the millennia.
Myth and magic.
The Well of Loneliness
RADCLYFFE HALL
Hopes and fears.
Captured in black ink on yellowed paper.

G R I M O I R E

WRITTEN LANGUAGE IS ONE OF HUMANITY'S MOST INCREDIBLE and magical creations. It gives us the ability to set down events, stories, beliefs; to create plans, orders, and instructions which could be followed hundreds, even thousands, of years later; to record the voices and personalities of other beings, real and unreal, and transmit them into the mind of the reader. This is magic, pure and simple, but a magic we have become so used to, we cease to see it as such.

The English author and occultist Alan Moore has offered a wonderfully concise definition of art as magic(k):

> " Magick, in its earliest forms, is often referred to as "the art." I believe that this is completely literal. I believe that magick is art, and art whether that be writing, painting, sculpture, or any other form, is literally magick. Art is, like magick, the science of manipulating symbols, words, or images to achieve changes in consciousness. The very language of magick seems to be talking as much about writing or art as it is supernatural events. A "grimoire," for example, the book of spells, is simply a fancy way of saying "grammar." Indeed, to cast a "spell" is simply to spell; to manipulate words to change people's consciousness. I believe this is why an artist or writer is the closest thing in the contemporary world that you are likely to see to a shaman. "

People who love folklore, myths, and legends also tend to love books on the same. We all have our little collections, our prized volumes, and our go-to sources when we want to look things up. Many of us also have those books which we first stumbled across in school libraries, or on the shelves of an older relative which first kindled our fascination with strange things.

What are books of folklore, then, if not books of magic? They re-record tales of old, often tales which would have been lost otherwise. They allow us to catalog, categorize, compare, and contrast these tales, but above all, they preserve. There is magic in all art, in all books, but it could be argued that there is nothing quite so like a genuine, real-life magic book than a well-written book of folklore.

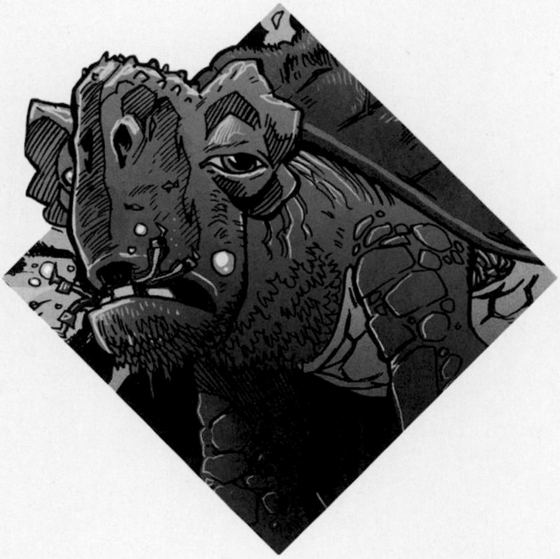
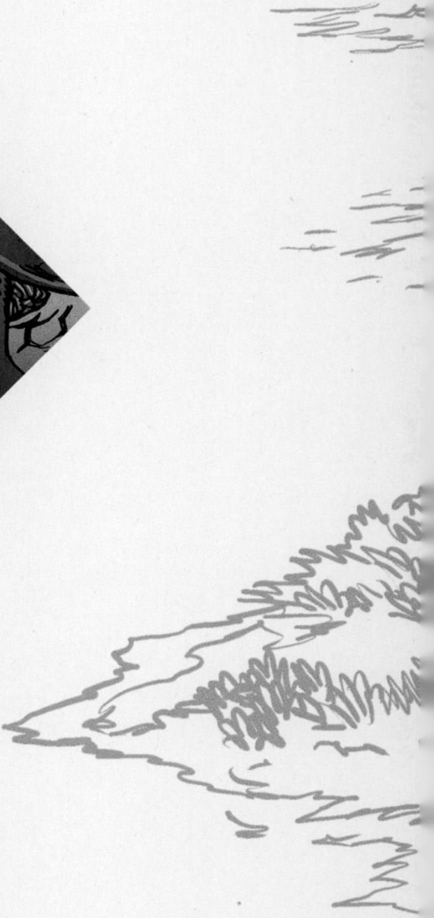

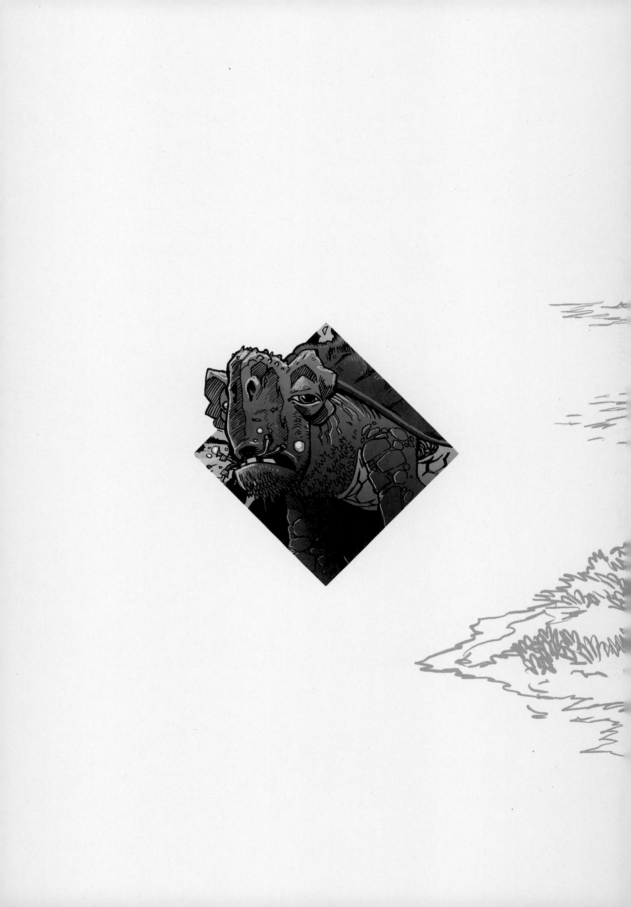

VOL.7

PLACES OF WONDER

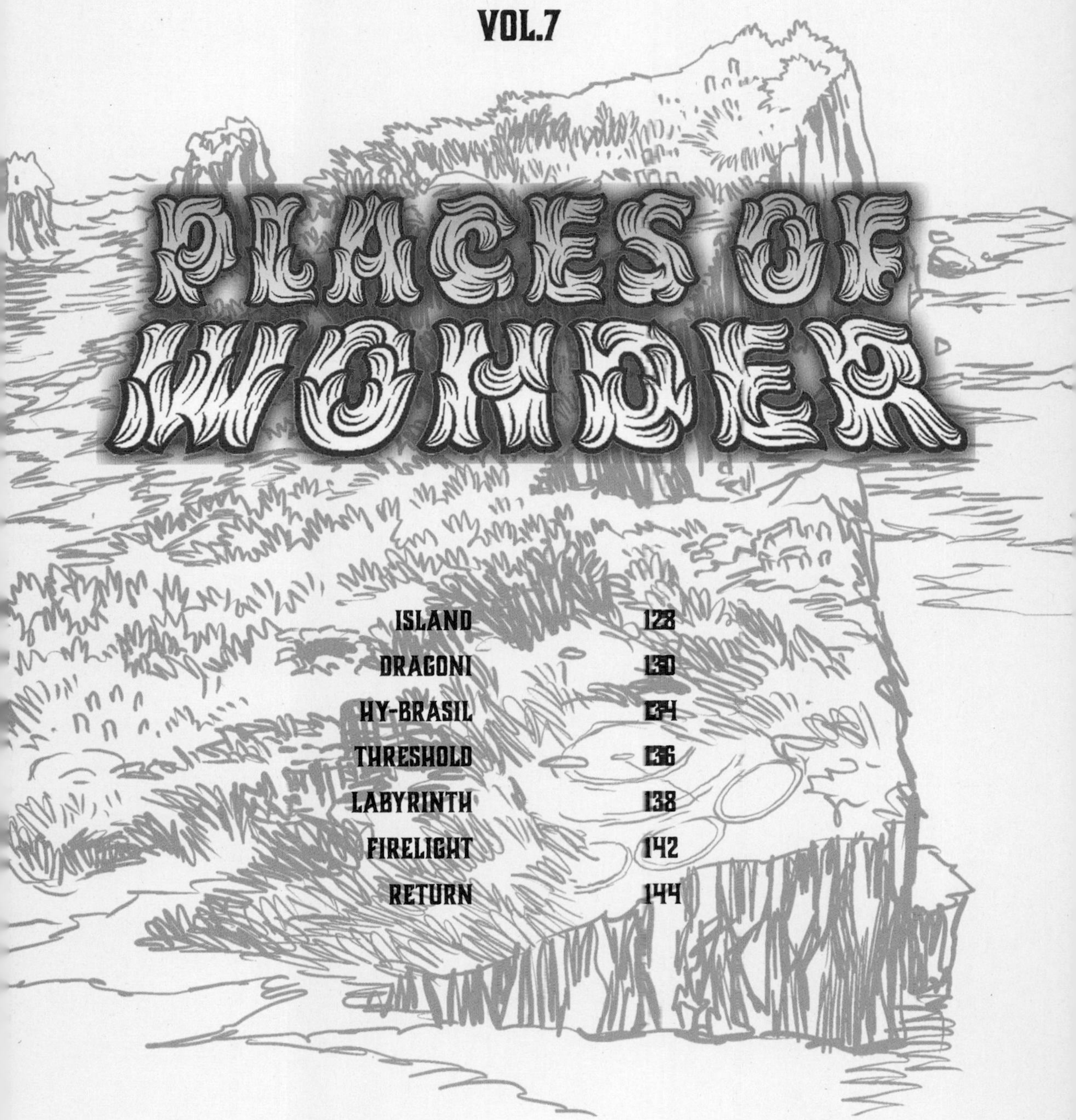

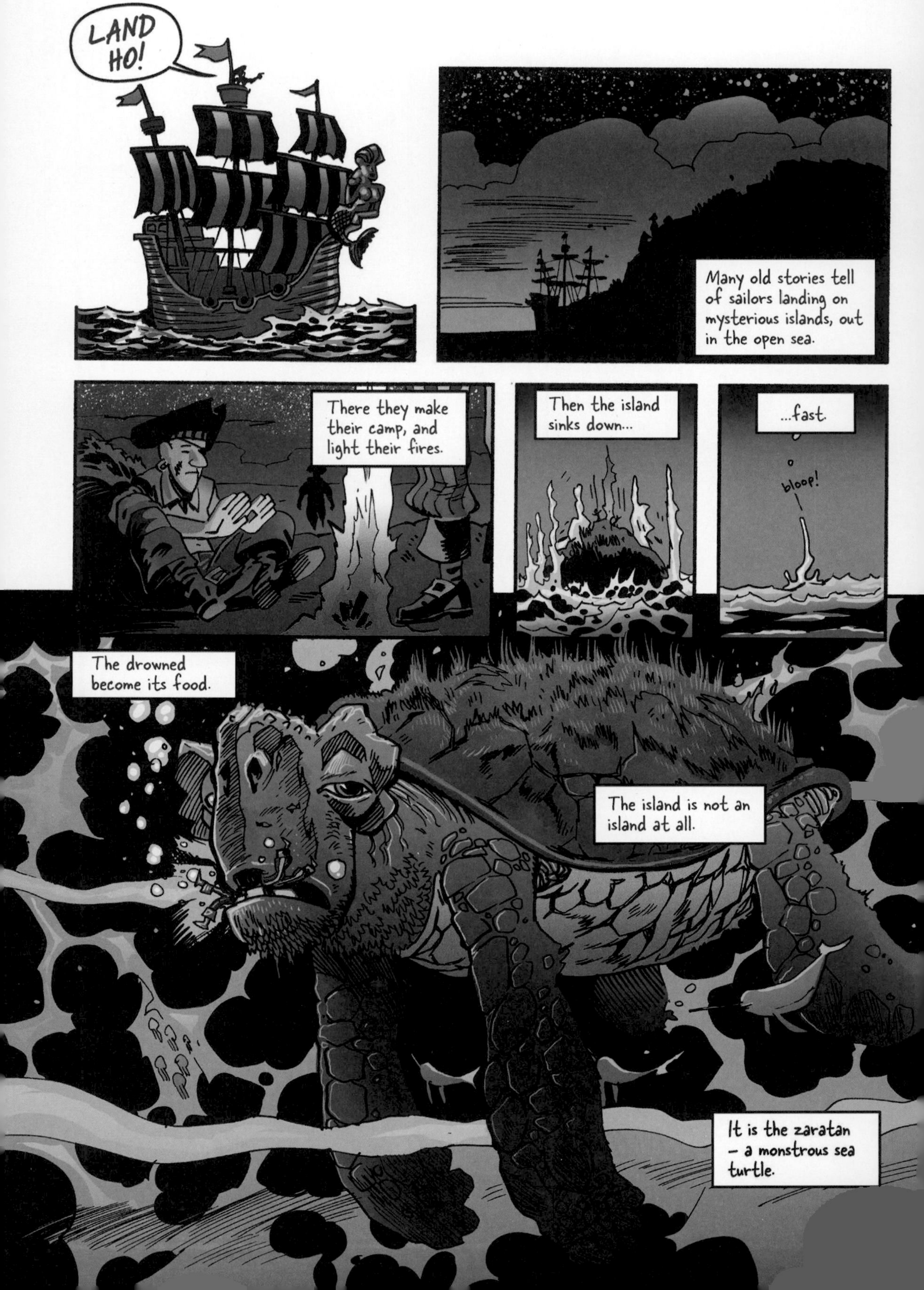
LAND HO!
Many old stories tell of sailors landing on mysterious islands, out in the open sea.
There they make their camp, and light their fires.
Then the island sinks down...
...fast.
bloop!
The drowned become its food.
The island is not an island at all.
It is the zaratan – a monstrous sea turtle.

ISLAND

The sleeping monster – so huge it appears at first to be part of the landscape, or to be the landscape itself – has become a familiar trope, especially in fantasy and science fiction. Tales of such camouflaged behemoths have been around for thousands of years, however.

> "There is a monster in the sea which in Greek is called *aspidochelone*, in Latin "asp-turtle"; it is a great whale that has what appears to be beaches on its hide, like those from the sea-shore. This creature raises its back above the waves of the sea, so that sailors believe that it is just an island [...] they beach their ship alongside it and, disembarking, they plant stakes and tie up the ships. Then, in order to cook a meal after this work, they make fires on the sand as if on land. But when the monster feels the heat of these fires, it immediately submerges into the water, and pulls the ship into the depths of the sea."

This description of a monstrous sea-turtle disguised as an island is contained in the *Physiologus* – a didactic Christian text written (or compiled) in Greek by an unknown author around the 2nd century CE. J. R. R. Tolkien's poem 'Fastitocalon' – originally published in *The Adventures of Tom Bombadil* (1962) – was inspired by the same ancient tale. The poem tells of the last of Middle Earth's mighty turtle-fish. The beast's colossal size fools sailors into believing that its shell-back is an island. Landing there, the mariners set a fire. Upon feeling the heat, the monster dives beneath the waves, drowning every last one.

Though the aspidochelone appears to be more of a gigantic fish or whale than a turtle in some tales, the name "zaratan" has become more closely linked with the concept of a giant, island-backed turtle in more recent years. This may be something of a mistake, however; perhaps a conflation of two monsters with similar hunting strategies.

The *Kitāb al-Ḥayawān* ("Book of Animals") is a medieval text in which another vast creature – its hard shell-back covered with fauna, so as to resemble an island out at sea – fools sailors into landing upon it. The *Book of Animals* identifies this creature not as the aspidochelone, but as *saratan*, the Arabic word for "crab." Perhaps then, this method of camouflage and trickery was once employed not by just one species of monster, but by several.

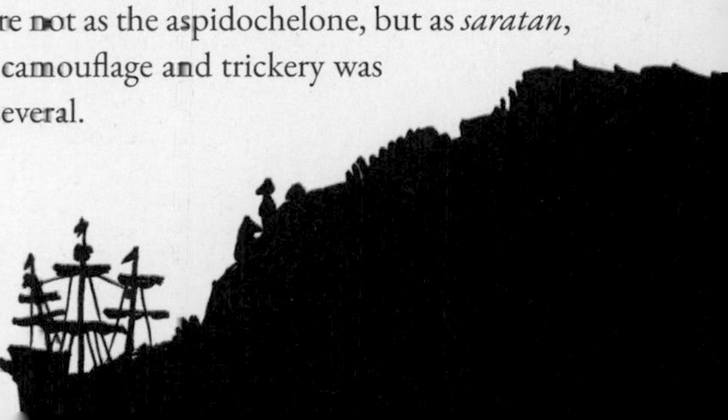

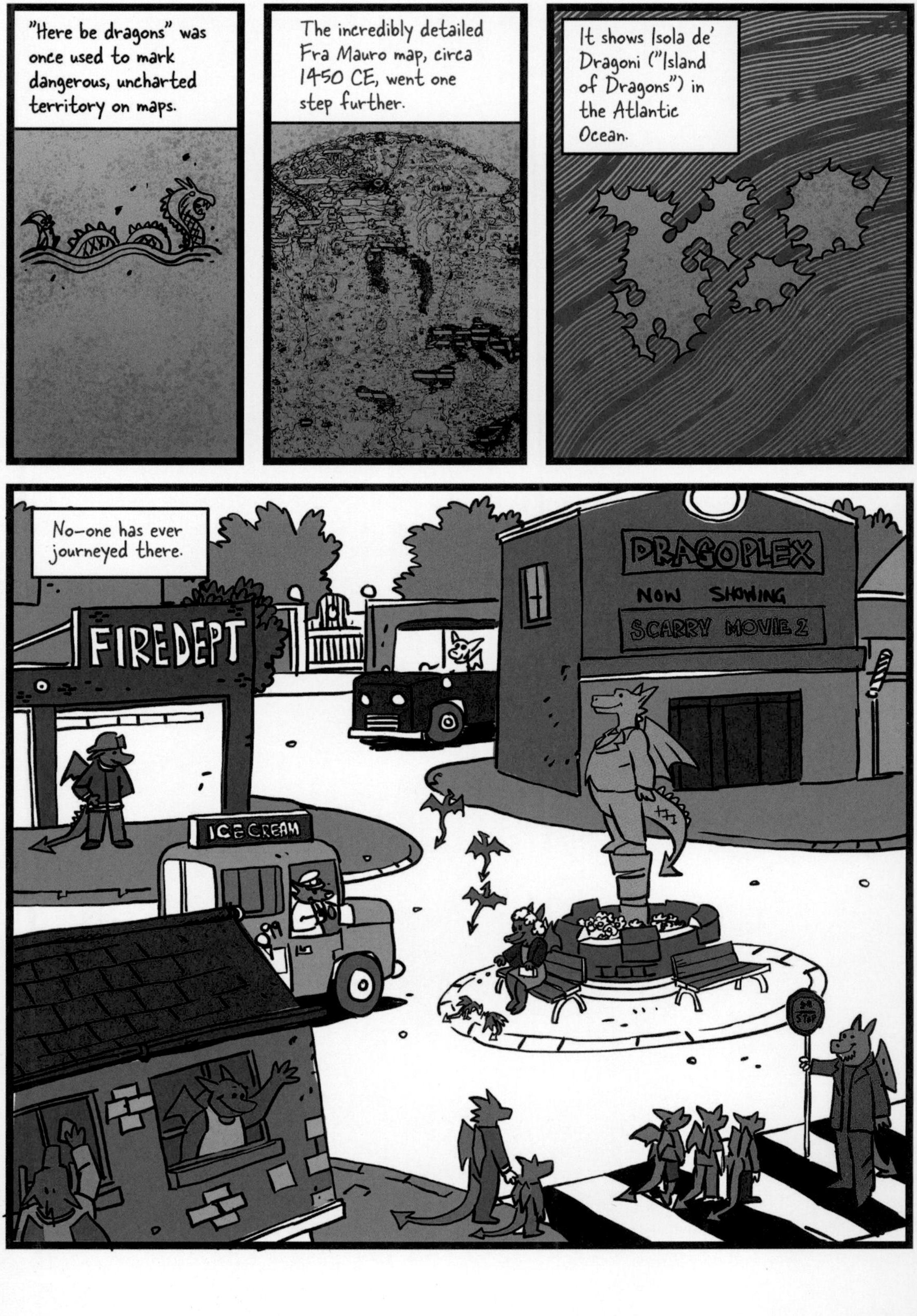
"Here be dragons" was once used to mark dangerous, uncharted territory on maps.
The incredibly detailed Fra Mauro map, circa 1450 CE, went one step further.
It shows Isola de' Dragoni ("Island of Dragons") in the Atlantic Ocean.
No-one has ever journeyed there.
FIREDEPT
DRAGOPLEX
NOW SHOWING
SCARRY MOVIE 2
ICE CREAM

D
R
A
G
O
N
I

HC SVNT DRACONES ("HERE BE DRAGONS") IS A LATIN PHRASE used to label uncharted or dangerous territories on several maps made between the 11th and 15th centuries. On Greek and Roman maps, the phrase HIC SVNT LEONES ("here be lions") was more commonly used for the same purpose.

> " There is a region moreover in Arabia, situated nearly over against the city of Buto, to which place I came to inquire about the winged serpents: and when I came thither I saw bones of serpents and spines in quantity, so great that it is impossible to make report of the number, and there were heaps of spines, some heaps large and others less large and others smaller still than these, and these heaps were many in number. [...]
>
> As for the serpent its form is like that of the water snake; and it has wings not feathered but most nearly resembling the wings of the bat. "

These words were written by the 5th-century-BCE Greek historian Herodotus in the first volume of his *History*. It should be noted though that Herodotus did not record seeing a single live specimen, merely reporting what he had been told, or had read, about the creatures' behavior and appearance. This included their roosting in frankincense trees and having to be specially handled so that the spice could be harvested. Herodotus also wrote of a similar behavior in the monstrous, carnivorous birds which made their nests of cinnamon sticks. In order to collect the cinnamon, brave Arabians would (according to Herodotus) have to trick the birds into carrying off huge chunks of butchered ox and ass, too large for their nests to bear. When the nests collapsed under the weight of the meat, the cinnamon would quickly be gathered up.

Perfumes and spices such as frankincense and cinnamon were, at the time of Herodotus' writing, Arabia's top exports, and it did well to convince outsiders that they faced literal monsters to obtain them, lest their customers get the idea they could simply cultivate them themselves. Pliny the Elder, writing in the 1st century, was on to their tricks, writing in his *Naturalis Historia* that the monstrous "cinnamolgus" was a mere invention designed to drive the price of the spice higher. Pliny also wrote of epic battles between elephants and dragons, however.

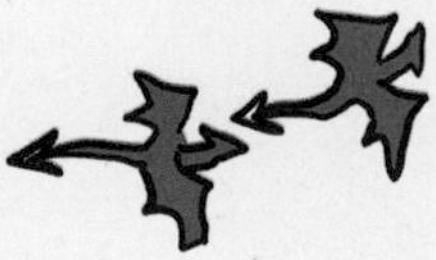

> Elephants are bred in that part of Africa which lieth beyond the deserts of the Syrtes [...] but India produceth the biggest: as also the dragons, which are continually at variance and fighting with them. [These dragons are] of such greatness, that they can easily clasp round the elephants, and tie them fast with a knot.
>
> Zelian says that these dragons conceal themselves among the branches of trees, from which they hang dependent, watching for their prey. When the elephants approach to feed on the branches, the enemy seizes them about the eyes, twines itself about the neck, and lashes them with its tail, in which manner they fall down strangled. In this conflict they die together; that which is overcome falling down, and with his weight crushing the one that is twined about him.

This appears to be a somewhat exaggerated (and you will note second hand – "Zelian says") description of an Indian python, however. Indeed, all of Pliny's mentions of dragons seem to describe other, more recognizable, creatures. It seems likely that he was using the word "dragon" as a substitute for "large predatory reptile," rather than cataloging actual dragon subspecies.

In many cases, the warning "here be dragons" marked a region on a map which may have been thought of as a point of no return. Sometimes, however, the location seems much more specific. The Fra Mauro world map, created circa 1450, is considered by many to be the greatest and most accomplished extant piece of medieval cartography. Nevertheless, the map does feature dragons, sea-serpents, and other mythical creatures. The Isola de' Dragoni ("Island of Dragons"), indicated upon the Fra Mauro map in the Atlantic Ocean, does not correspond with any known landmass.

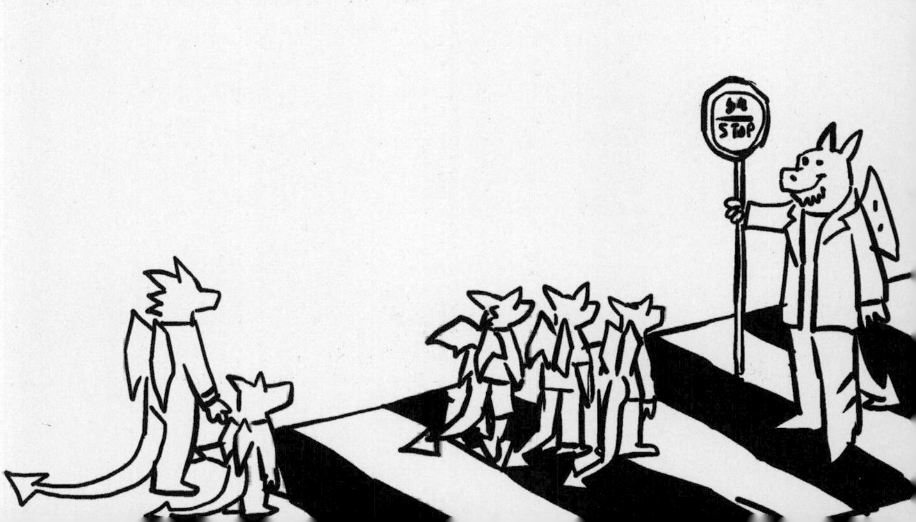
STOP

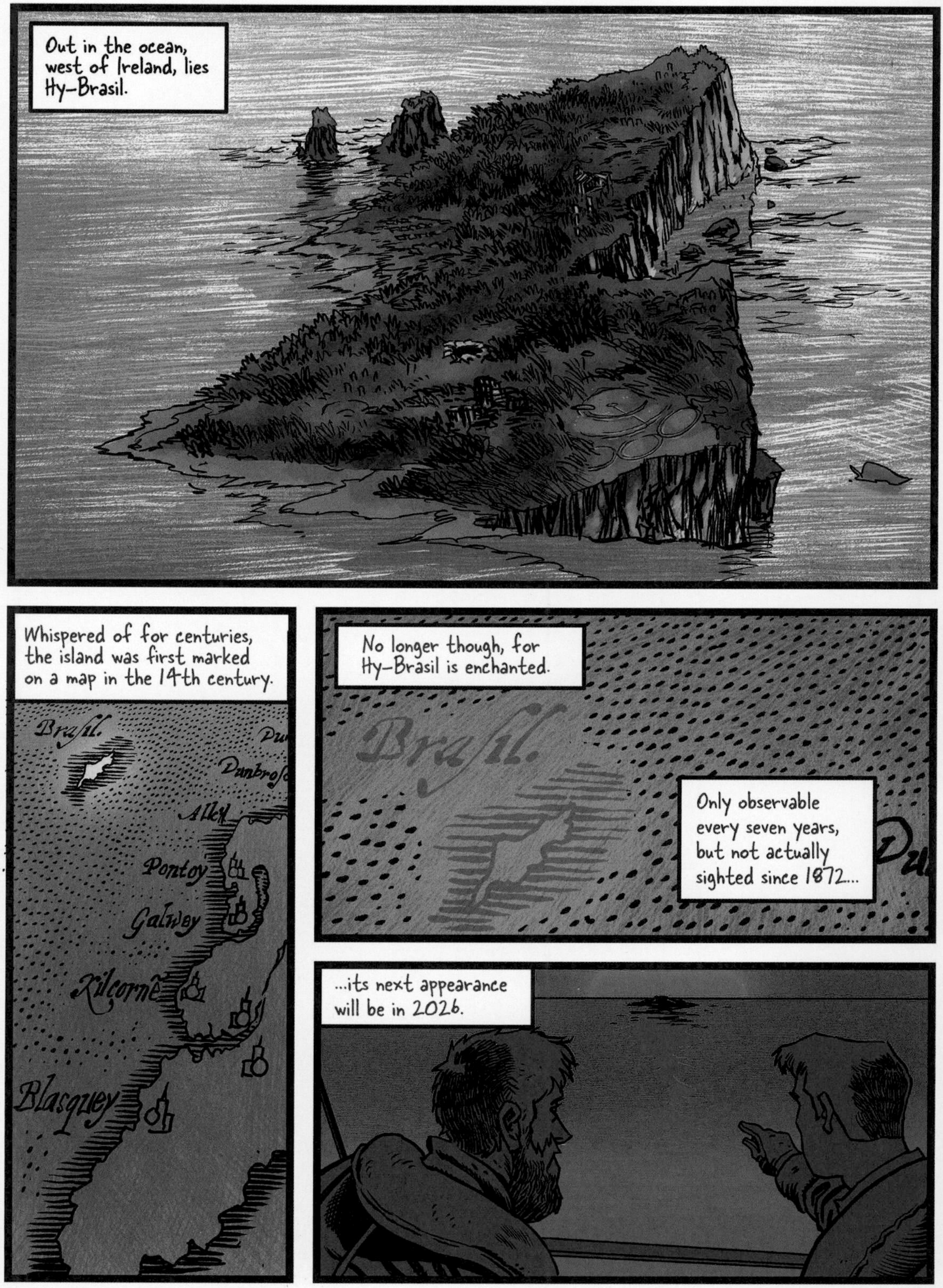
Out in the ocean, west of Ireland, lies Hy-Brasil.
Whispered of for centuries, the island was first marked on a map in the 14th century.
Pontoy
Galwey
Blasquey
No longer though, for Hy-Brasil is enchanted.
Only observable every seven years, but not actually sighted since 1872...
...its next appearance will be in 2026.

> " On the ocean that hollows the rocks where ye dwell,
> A shadowy land has appeared, as they tell;
> Men thought it a region of sunshine and rest,
> And they called it Hy-Brasil, the isle of the blest.
> From year unto year on the ocean's blue rim,
> The beautiful spectre showed lovely and dim;
> The golden clouds curtained the deep where it lay,
> And it looked like an Eden, away, far away. "

– From 'Hy-Brasil – Isle of the Blest' by Gerald Griffin, taken from *Fairy and Folk Tales of the Irish Peasantry* (1888)

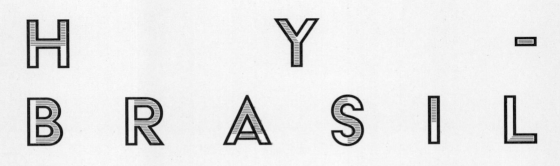

HY-BRASIL

IN 1325, AN ITALIAN-MAJORCAN CARTOGRAPHER NAMED ANGELINO DULCERT INCLUDED THE island of "Bracile" off the west coast of Ireland on his latest nautical chart, and in doing so, he created the oldest-surviving cartographic record of the island of Hy-Brasil. Already spoken of for centuries, the island's name is thought to derive from the Irish Uí Breasail, meaning "descendants of Bresail clan," who were themselves the descendants of the ancient high kings of Ireland. The island was often depicted on those early maps as a perfect circle, bisected by a large central river. The exact location of the island, and the spelling of its name, seemingly shifting from map to map.

Under the heading "Hy-Brasil," in *Tales of the Enchanted Islands of the Atlantic* by Thomas Wentworth Higginson (1898), we find the following information:

> " The people of Aran [a group of three islands off the west coast of Ireland], with characteristic enthusiasm, fancy that at certain periods, they see Hy-Brasil, elevated far to the west in their watery horizon. This has been the universal tradition of the ancient Irish, who supposed that a great part of Ireland had been swallowed by the sea, and that the sunken part often rose and was seen hanging in the horizon: such was the popular notion. The Hy-Brasil of the Irish is evidently a part of the Atlantis of Plato. "

Many sources tell of a Captain John Nisbet who, having landed on Hy-Brasil in 1674, found the island populated by strange, huge, black rabbits, and a lone man who lived in a castle. This account, however, is taken from a satirical pamphlet written and distributed by Irish author, playwright, and bookseller Richard Head.

It is possible that Old Irish tales of Hy-Brasil stem from folk-memory, passed down over generations. 120 miles (220 km) west of Ireland lies Porcupine Bank – a sea-shoal which, thousands of years ago, would have been visible above the waves.

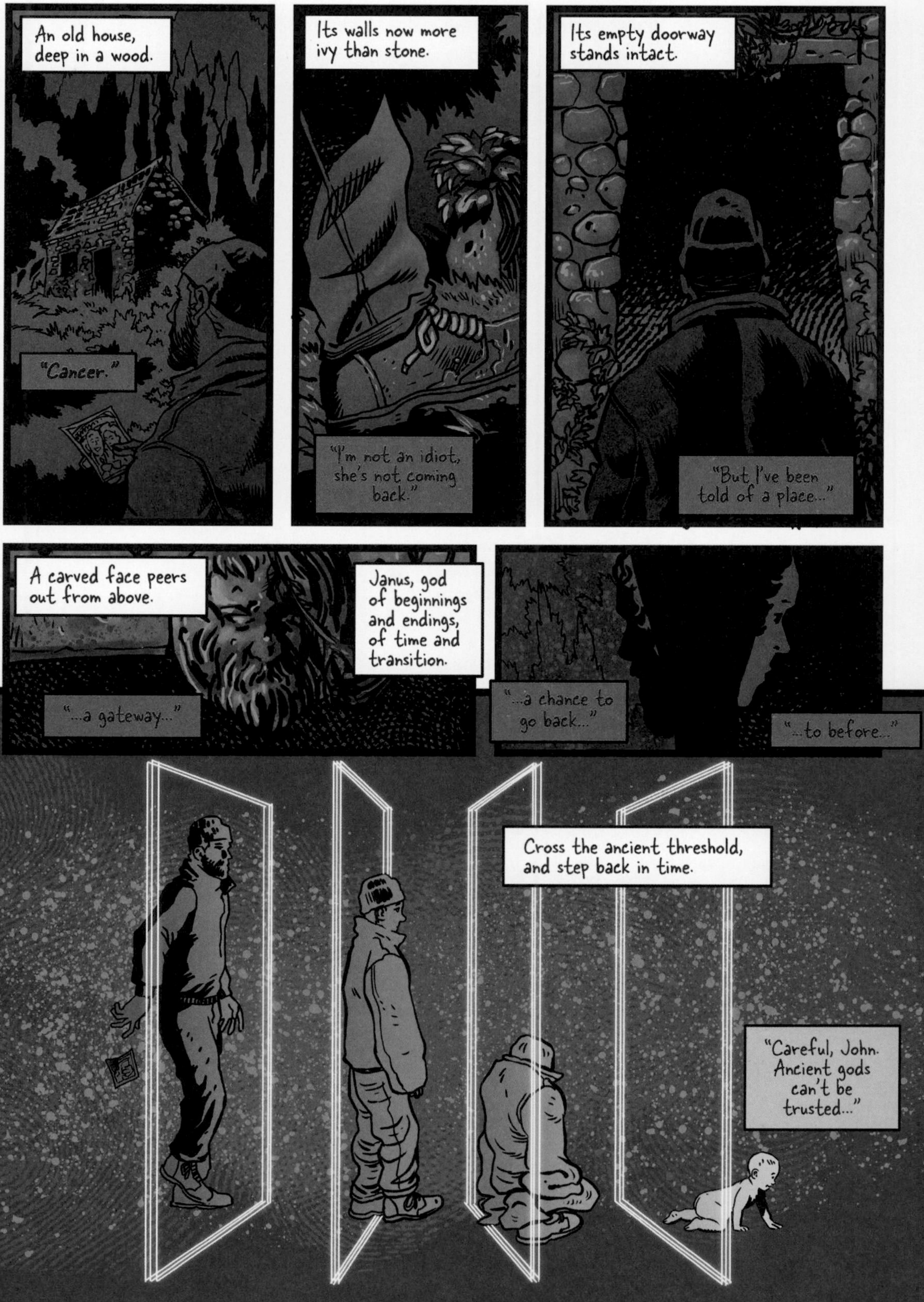
An old house, deep in a wood.
"Cancer."
Its walls now more ivy than stone.
"I'm not an idiot, she's not coming back."
Its empty doorway stands intact.
"But I've been told of a place..."
A carved face peers out from above.
Janus, god of beginnings and endings, of time and transition.
"...a gateway..."
"...a chance to go back..."
"...to before..."
Cross the ancient threshold, and step back in time.
"Careful, John. Ancient gods can't be trusted..."

THRESHOLD

The Latin word *līmen* means "threshold," and it is from this term that the words "liminal" and the more familiar "subliminal" derive. In purely physical terms, liminal spaces are the places "between": doorways, hallways, alleyways, train stations, off-ramps. They are neither destinations nor points of origin, but the connectors between A and B. Simultaneously nowhere and somewhere. Dusk and dawn, and the summer and winter solstices[1] are likewise liminal: points at which the balance tips from light into darkness and vice versa. In this context, teenhood might be viewed as the liminal transition between childhood and adulthood. Literal rites of passage such as bar/bat mitzvah, graduation, etc., all represent a tipping point at which the initiate crosses a threshold separating one period of their life from the next. In many mythologies, deities have presided over these thresholds, standing guard over the point of transition between one stage, or state, and the next.

The Hindu Ganesha is a god of beginnings and a guardian of thresholds, both literal and metaphorical. Lord Ganesha has thirty-two distinct forms in which he appears in Hindu devotional art and literature. The Dwimukhi Ganapati – the Ganapati with two faces – is interpreted by Hindu scholars as Ganesha looking to the inner and outer truths of themselves and of the universe. The Dwimukhi Ganapati is simultaneously conscious of the material and finite, and the immaterial and infinite.

Elsewhere, Janus was the ancient Roman god of gates, doorways, and passages, of beginnings and endings, and of time and transitions, as attested by the writings of Ovid (34 BCE – 17 CE) and many others. Janus was often depicted with two faces upon a single head: one facing the past and the other facing the future.

Effigies of liminal deities like Ganesha and Janus preside over many thresholds ancient and modern, their faces carved above doorways, gateways, and the mouths of caves. These gods become signposts that mark both the literal and metaphorical divide between this and the Other Realm, between past and present, the magic and the mundane, the known and the unknown.

"Mascaron" is the architectural term for an ornamental head or face situated on or above a doorway. The word comes from the same Latin root as "masquerade," and therefore "mask." Though they evolved into a Neoclassical decorative element, these faces – which are often grotesque, intimidating, or otherworldly – once served the same function as the Allhallowstide[2] lanterns set on windowsills and on doorsteps. Their purpose: to drive away malign spirits, and to dissuade unwelcome visitors from crossing the threshold.

1 See 'Celestial (pg. 94).

2 See 'Hallowe'en' (pg. 100).

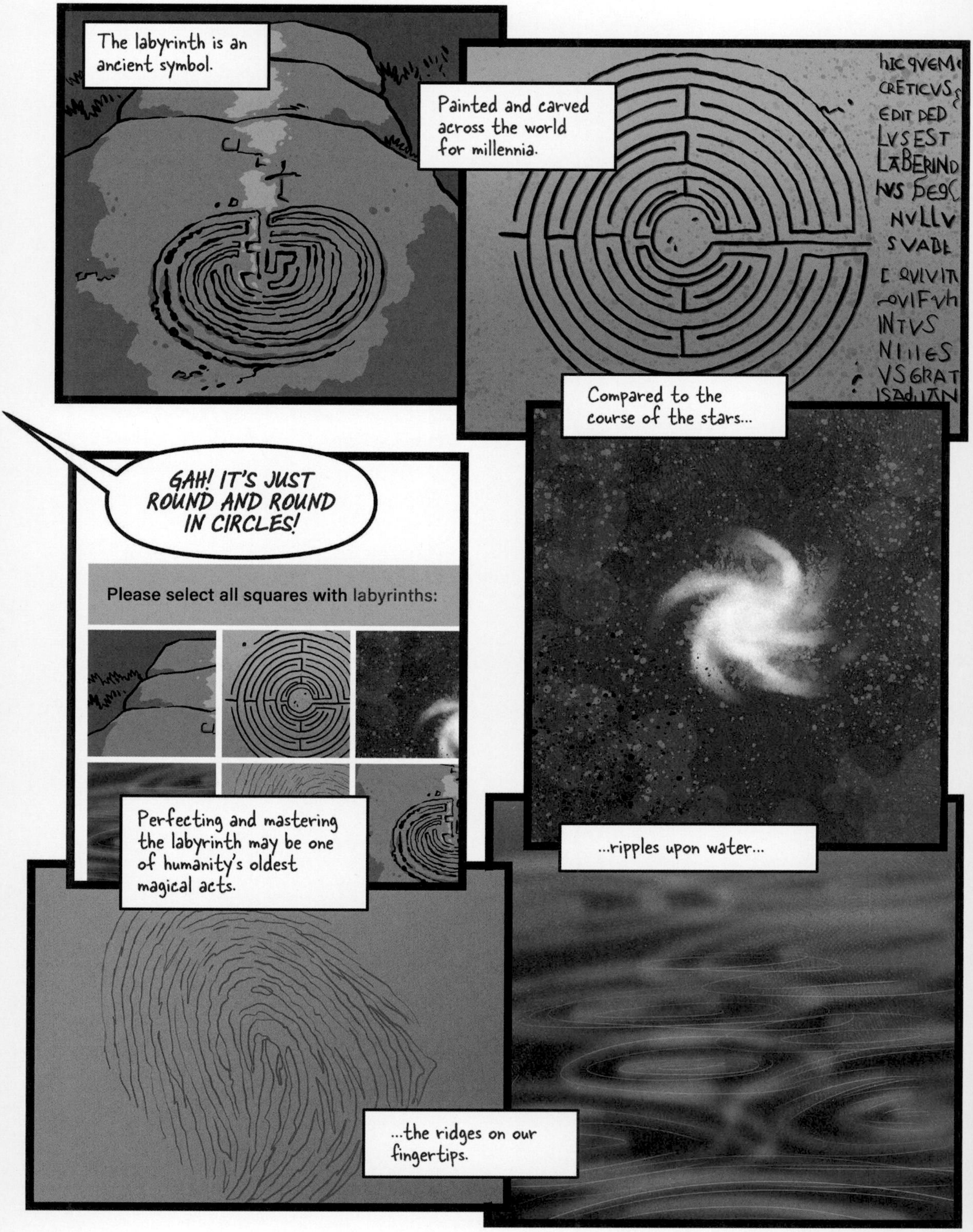

The labyrinth is an ancient symbol.
Painted and carved across the world for millennia.
Compared to the course of the stars...
GAH! IT'S JUST ROUND AND ROUND IN CIRCLES!
Please select all squares with labyrinths:
Perfecting and mastering the labyrinth may be one of humanity's oldest magical acts.
...ripples upon water...
...the ridges on our fingertips.

LABYRINTH

THE WORDS "LABYRINTH" AND "MAZE" ARE OFTEN, INCORRECTLY, USED INTERCHANGEABLY. Mazes have multiple paths, some of which may lead to dead-ends. Labyrinths, on the other hand, are formed of a single, winding yet continuous, path or route. A maze is a puzzle to be solved, whereas a labyrinth is a journey, or perhaps a map.

One image of a labyrinth, painted on the ceiling of a cave in Sicily, is believed by some historians to be 5,000 years old. One carved into the wall of a tomb in Sardinia is perhaps 4,500 years old, and another Italian painting in Val Camonica may be 4,000. Ancient petroglyphs (rock carvings) of labyrinths are rare yet widespread, with examples not just across Europe but as far away as Peru and Goa. Two very clear examples can be found engraved onto a shale outcrop in Rocky Valley, Cornwall. When we see these images, most of us tend to think of them as mere decoration, yet there is evidence that they may have been pictorial representations of long-gone, physical, walkable labyrinths.

In the Solovetsky Islands, located in the Onega Bay of the White Sea, Russia, 35 Neolithic labyrinths (known locally as *vavilons*, meaning "Babylons") can be found. These stone labyrinths were constructed between 2,500 and 5,000 years ago by arranging boulders into spiraling patterns; a walkable path formed between the curving rows of rocks.

In England, the term "Troy-town" is linked with a particularly rare and endangered species of labyrinth. A turf labyrinth is pretty much what it sounds like: a complex, winding pathway deliberately cut into an area of trimmed grass. Turf labyrinths are, by their very nature, high maintenance; if they are not tended regularly, they will become overgrown and, in a very few years, disappear completely. Today, only eight historic turf labyrinths survive in England, two of which still bear the name of Troy:

the City of Troy in Dalby, North Yorkshire, and Troy at Troy Farm in Somerton, Oxfordshire. Saffron Walden is home to the largest surviving English turf labyrinth, which was cut in 1699; according to local lore, this was a copy of an even older turf labyrinth nearby. The earliest explicit written reference to any of England's turf labyrinths seems to be when Gelyan Bower in Louth, Lincolnshire, was mentioned in a record dating from 1554.

The earliest known example of an explicitly Christian labyrinth is a 4th-century pavement labyrinth at the Basilica of St Reparatus, at Orleansville, Algeria. One of the most famous and influential church labyrinths was completed at the Gothic Catholic Chartres Cathedral, France, in 1221. Some say church labyrinths are designed to be walked as an aid to prayer, some to aid contemplation, some as a form of penance, and some have suggested they were once intended as a form of compact pilgrimage. In fact, despite their still being in use and indeed newly installed in many Christian churches, the "true" meaning and purpose of even these labyrinths seems, if not lost, then at least subject to much speculation and interpretation. This, of course, makes sense when one considers the very clear evidence (as presented above) that labyrinths predate Christianity by thousands and thousands of years.

Was the labyrinth an invention of our hunter-gatherer ancestors, or was it a discovery? Its pattern has been compared to the brain, the bowels, to the womb, to the stars in the heavens. Labyrinths, or proto-labyrinths, occur all around us in the natural world; in the rings of a felled tree, in the ripples that rain sends spreading upon a body of water, in the ridges on the tips of each of our fingers. Perfecting that design, tweaking the natural order ever so slightly to achieve something even more clean and clear – a path that could be followed all the way into, and out of, the heart of the thing – is nothing short of a magical act. The mastery of that pattern seems to have been a pivotal moment for humankind. If you could trace the pattern with your finger, you could walk a larger version – traveling in circuits designed by your own hand – and that would be a powerful thing, even if you weren't exactly sure why.

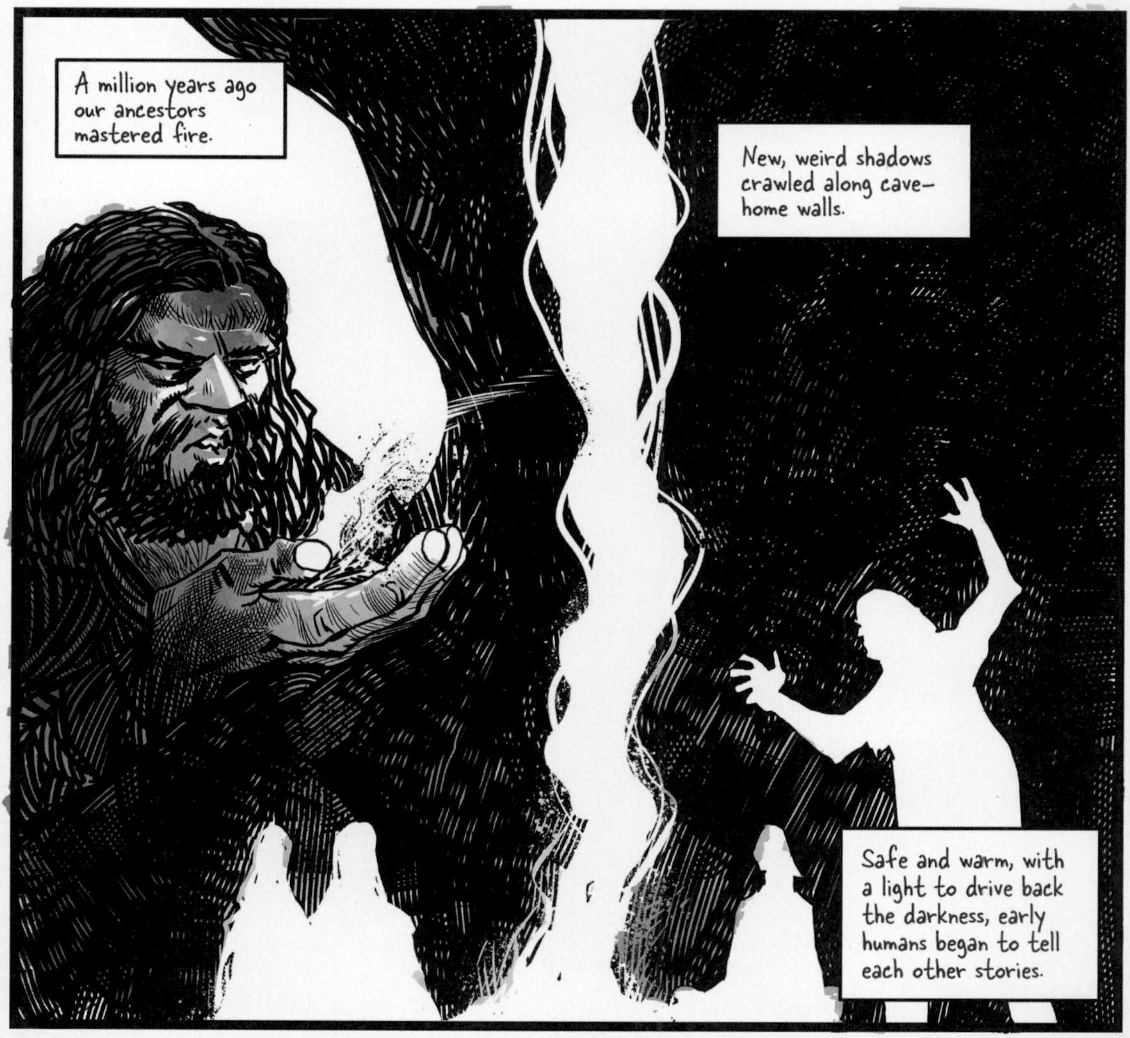
A million years ago our ancestors mastered fire.
New, weird shadows crawled along cave-home walls.
Safe and warm, with a light to drive back the darkness, early humans began to tell each other stories.

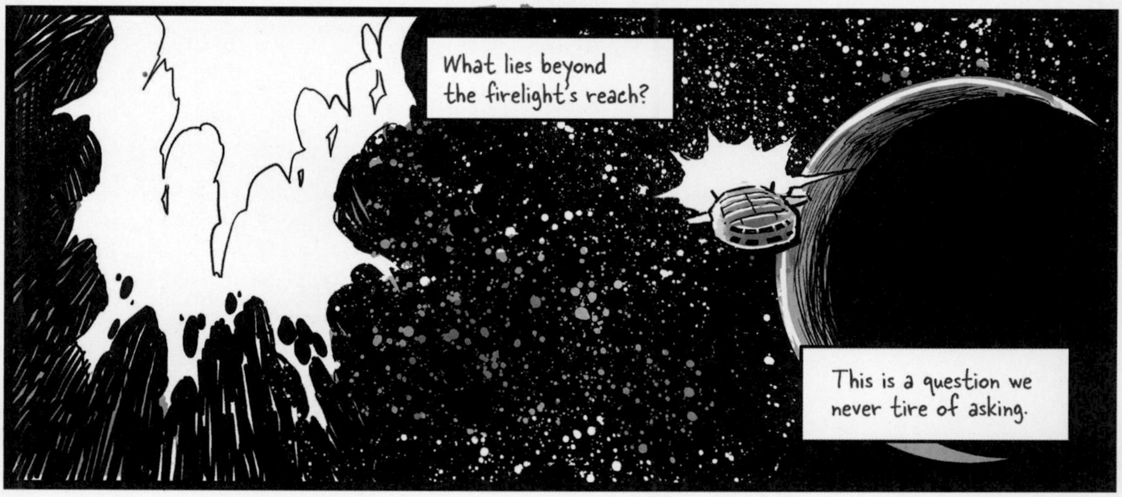
What lies beyond the firelight's reach?
This is a question we never tire of asking.

F
I
R
E
L
I
G
H
T

THE EARLIEST EXTANT HOMO SAPIEN CAVE-ART ON EARTH WAS discovered in 2017 in South Sulawesi, Indonesia. Painted using dark red ochre, the life-sized image of a Sulawesi warty pig is believed to be 44,000 years old. Hand stencils on the walls of the Cave of Maltravieso in Cáceres, Extremadura, Spain, have been reliably dated to 64,000 years ago. Shells containing red and yellow pigments discovered in the Cave of Los Aviones, near Cartagena, Spain, in 2010 are believed to have been left there a staggering 115,000 years ago. Neither of these Spanish discoveries are human in origin, however, the shells and the hands having instead belonged to our cousin-ancestors, Neanderthals.

Wonderwerk Cave ("The Cave of Miracles"), in the Northern Cape province of South Africa, is believed to have been a site occupied not by Homo sapiens or Homo neanderthalensis, but by our much older, joint-ancestor, Homo habilis. Evidence of fires within the cave date back one million years, though whether these fires were deliberately set remains contested by some. Previous to this discovery, the earliest provable use of fire by hominids occurred 700,000 years after that, and the majority of archaeologists are still more comfortable with that date, despite the apparent evidence in the Wonderwerk Cave. Evidence for these fires comes from Jebel Irhoud – an archaeological site south-east of the city of Safi, Morocco – where charred spear-tips found alongside animal bones are now widely regarded as proof of in-cave cookery circa 300,000 BCE.

The relationship between fire and prehistoric art has long been an area of interesting speculation. Deep within caves, the only possible light source which would have enabled painting or carving onto the stone walls was firelight. Firelight was also the only possible light by which other hominids would have ever seen the completed art. In April 2022, researchers at the universities of York and Durham published their findings after examining a collection of stones engraved by the Magdalenian people 20,000 years ago. Patterns of heat damage around the edges of the stones proved that they had been repeatedly and deliberately placed in close proximity to fires. This, it has been argued, may be evidence for the flickering of the fire being used as a crude means of animating the graven images. As our ancestors huddled together around their fires, they may have been watching flickering images of beasts and hunts moving across their cave walls.

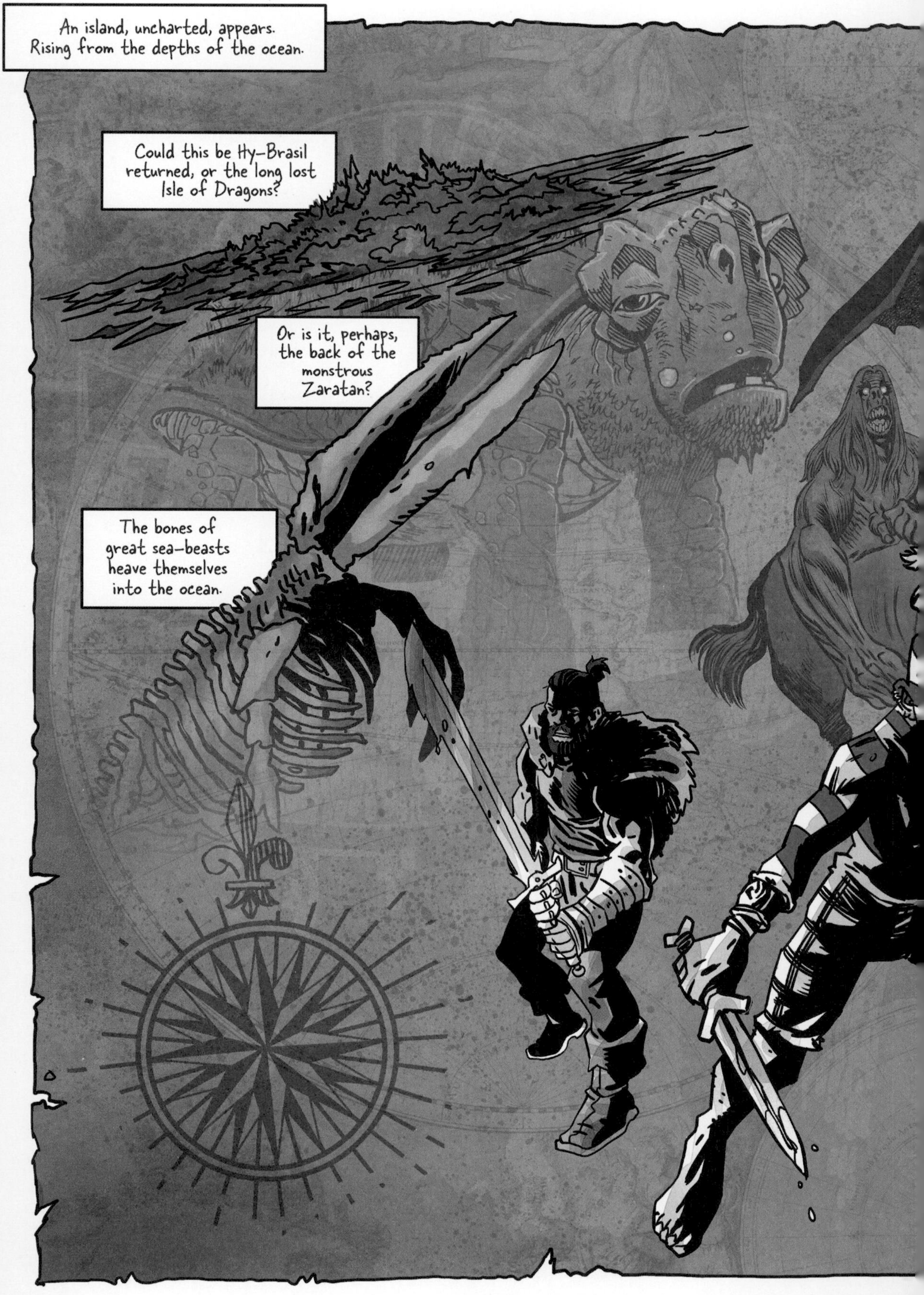
An island, uncharted, appears. Rising from the depths of the ocean.
Could this be Hy-Brasil returned, or the long lost Isle of Dragons?
Or is it, perhaps, the back of the monstrous Zaratan?
The bones of great sea-beasts heave themselves into the ocean.

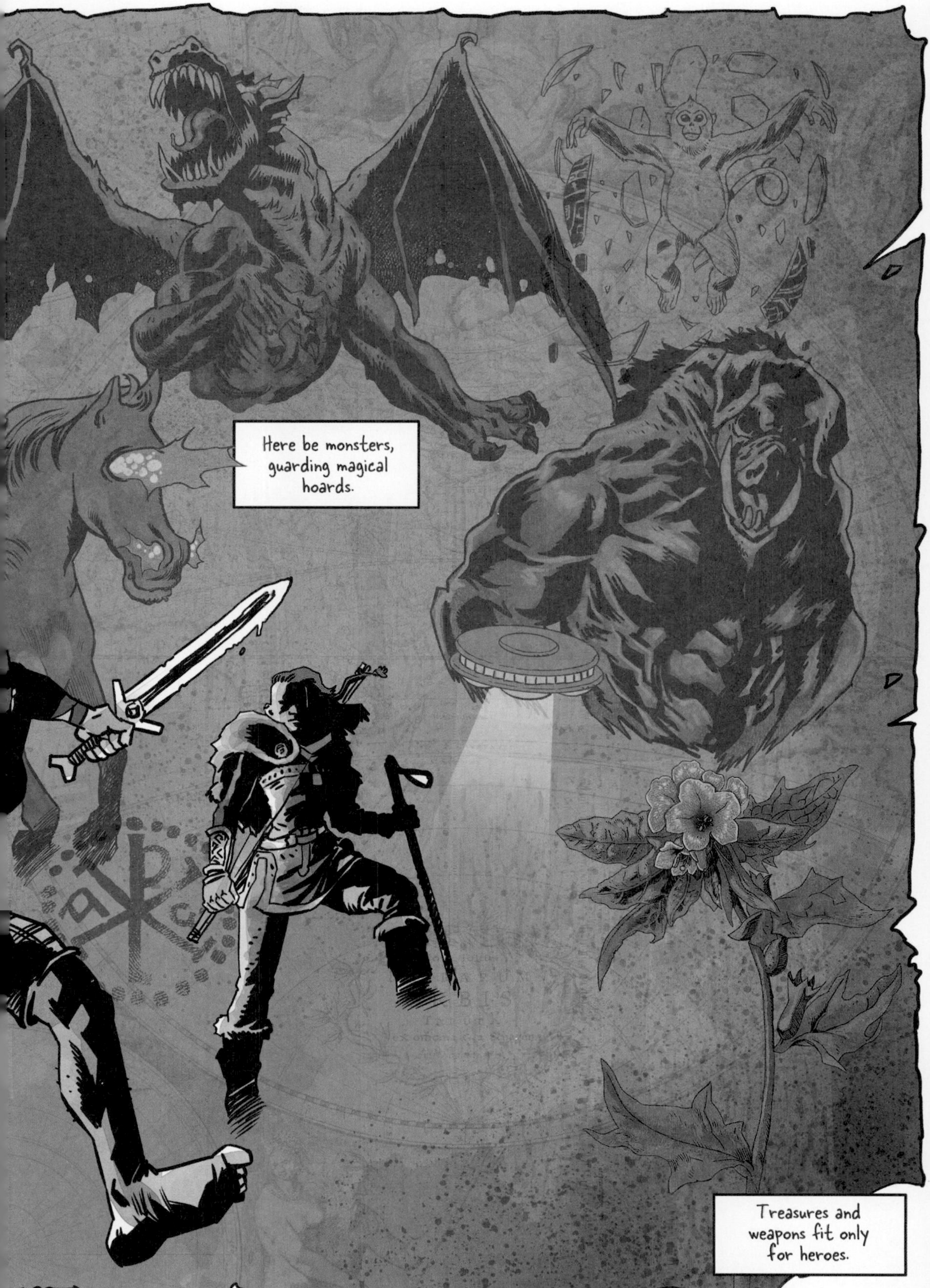
Here be monsters, guarding magical hoards.
Treasures and weapons fit only for heroes.

R E T

Heroes never truly die, but sometimes they retire, adjourning to hidden realms of perpetual rest and reward. This idea has been recorded across the myths, legends, and folklore of many, many cultures throughout history.

In ancient Greek mythology, heroes who chose to be reincarnated three times, and were judged as pure and true enough to gain entrance to the Elysian Fields three times, lived out the aeons in the winterless Blessed Isles.

In the traditions of ancient Hawai'i, the living gods Kane and Kanaloa inhabit an earthly paradise in a floating cloudland. This floating landmass is often said to be located above one of twelve islands off Hawai'i known as the "Lost Islands," or "the Islands Hidden by the Gods."

The Isle of Avalon was the location where King Arthur's sword Excalibur was forged. According to Geoffrey of Monmouth, writing in the 12th century:

> The fields there have no need of the ploughs of the farmers and all cultivation is lacking except what nature provides. Of its own accord it produces grain and grapes, and apple trees grow in its woods from the close-clipped grass. The ground of its own accord produces everything instead of merely grass, and people live there a hundred years or more. There nine sisters rule by a pleasing set of laws those who come to them from our country.

The Yolngu of north-eastern Arnhem Land in the Northern Territory of Australia have spoken for countless generations of Baralku – the island of the dead. Barnumbirr, the creator-spirit, originated there and lives there still, rising into the sky to become visible to all as the astral body we call Venus.

In Russian medieval texts, Буян (Buyan) is a mysterious island, appearing only at certain times. The brothers North, West, and East Wind live on its shores, as do the solar goddesses the Zorya sisters.

In these mystical isles also lie treasures beyond the grasp of mere mortals, guarded by monsters worse than any nightmare ever dreamed.

In Buyan, the soul of Koschei the Deathless lies hidden, meaning that he can never be killed in the mortal realm. The magical stone Алатырь (Alatyr) – with its mystic powers of healing – is guarded there by the metal-beaked and clawed Gagana bird, and by the dreadful serpent Garafena.

U R N

In Chinese mythology, *fucanglong* ("treasure dragons") guard seams of gold and diamonds buried deep beneath the earth, while their European cousins curl their wyrm-bodies[1] around ancient treasure hoards. The hero Beowulf was slain by one of these fire-breathing beasts, all for the theft of a single golden cup.

Dragurs – supernaturally strong, undead Norse warriors – guard the riches hidden deep within their burial mounds. The many-headed serpent Naga of Indian mythology dwell in a subterranean realm filled with jewels and resplendent palaces, which they defend ferociously.

Enchanted armor gathers dust, and great, fat spiders weave their webs between the age-dulled blades of swords which long ago spilled the blood of trolls. Battling through dangers untold and hardships unnumbered, the gods, goddesses, heroes, and heroines have earned their place in the sun. And yet...

... they grow restless in their retirement. They crave the old days and the old ways, when evil men paid for their evil deeds with their blood. When monsters were slain, and justice prevailed. They sleep a sleep filled with dreams of battle and magic. They await the call to adventures new.

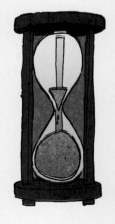

1   See 'Lindwurm' (pg. 30).

HOLDEN & REPPION

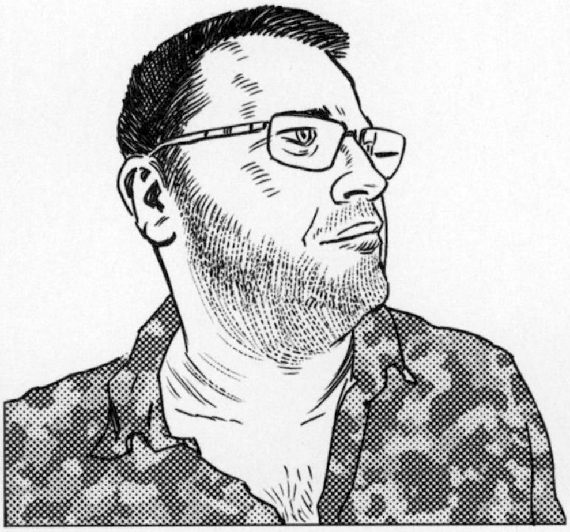

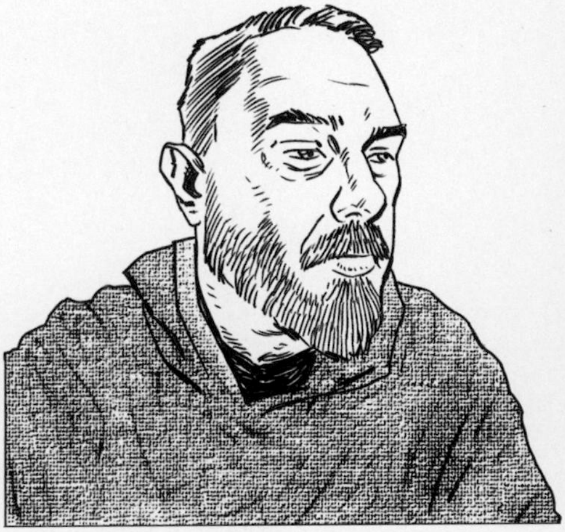

ARTIST: PJ HOLDEN

PJ Holden is a Belfast-based comic artist, illustrator, and occasional writer. PJ was born in Belfast in 1969 and grew up wondering whether he should work in IT or comics: two things he loved. He chose IT, and proceeded to have a career in computers from the age of 14, until finally giving it up for paper and pen at the age of 38, having spent the previous decade doing both.

PJ's first professional illustration work was for *Fantagraphics* in 1995, and his second professional work was drawing Judge Dredd (for the official comics and magazines), a childhood dream, in 2000. Luckily, there's never been a gap between professional drawing assignments just as long as that ever since.

In comics, PJ is best known for his work on Judge Dredd, as well as multiple war stories with Garth Ennis, and co-creating the character of Noam Chimpsky, with Kenneth Niemand, for 2000AD. PJ is also the artist on Derek Landy's first Skulduggery Pleasant graphic novel *Bad Magic*.

PJ lives with his wife and two kids, and now works entirely digitally, bringing his love of computers and drawing full circle.

www.pauljholden.com

WRITER: JOHN REPPION

John Reppion is a comic writer, author, fortean essayist, and weird fiction writer, born in Liverpool in 1978.

His first professionally published work appeared in the *Fortean Times* #187 in 2004, in which he told the tale of a giant's grave that he used to visit with his grandfather as a child. He has since written many articles on weird history, folklore, superstition, and magic for the likes of *The History Press*, *Fortean Times*, *Daily Grail Publishing*, and *Hellebore Zine*.

John has been co-writing comics with his wife, Leah Moore, since 2004. The pair have worked together on projects as diverse as adapting works of classic literature into graphic novels, to creating "walk-through" comics exhibits for museums.

www.moorereppion.com

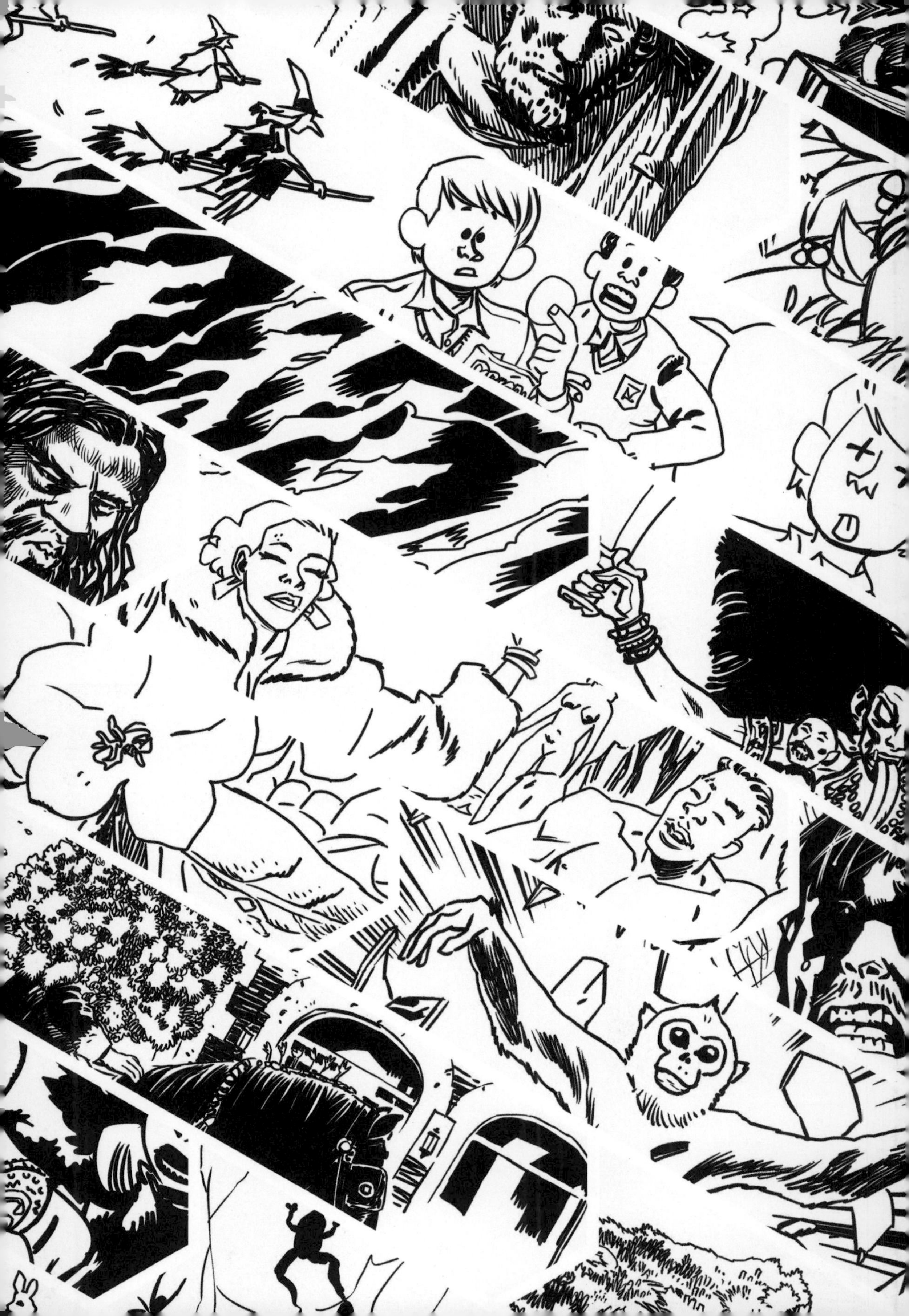